D0493137

Innocence

Two Novellas

About the author

Frank White was born in August 1927. He was brought up in Newton Heath, Manchester. He served in the Royal Navy in the Second World War. He had two novels published in the 1960s (including *A Morse Code Set*, published in this volume) and wrote plays for stage and radio, as well as a short book on the First World War. More than fifty years after his first book was published, he wrote *There Was a Time*, published to critical acclaim in 2017. Frank lived at Marshchapel, Lincolnshire, with his wife, June. Sadly, Frank died in December 2019, but he was very pleased to know his book was to be published in 2020.

By the same author

The British in the First World War

NOVELS

A Feast of Cannibals

There Was a Time

DRAMA PRODUCTIONS, STAGE AND RADIO

Bussey

A Fatal Affair

Wild Orchids

Brother's Keeper

A Hundred Years On

Bridge Over the River

Tarra Lengy

Spoil Heap

Revolution

Innocence

Two Novellas

Frank White

**HODDER &
STOUGHTON**

Innocence first published in Great Britain in 2020 by Hodder & Stoughton
A Morse Code Set was first published in Great Britain
in 1964 by Hodder & Stoughton
An Hachette UK company

1

Hardback ISBN 9781529327861
eBook ISBN 9781529327885

Typeset in Sabon MT by
Palimpsest Book Production Limited, Falkirk, Stirlingshire

Printed and bound in Great Britain by Clays Ltd, Elcograf S.p.A.

Hodder & Stoughton policy is to use papers that are natural,
renewable and recyclable products and made from wood grown in
sustainab'- ⸻ ⸻ ⸻ ⸻ expected
to con ⸻ origin.

Table of Contents

Innocence

For their invaluable contributions to this work I offer my sincere thanks to my wife, June, and to Nick Sayers, my publisher at Hodder & Stoughton

I

An assault by some sort of virus sent me to bed for a week. Under that blank white ceiling, feeling an ache now here now there, I found myself plagued by powerful memories of my early life, sometimes welcome, sometimes not, and this went on for days after I had recovered. It disturbed my routine, caught me unawares, stopped me in my tracks, and I decided that there was only one way to lay these ghosts. For the first time in years I drove the two hundred miles to my old home village, there in the hills, moors and meadows of the West Riding of Yorkshire.

I arrived at the village shortly after noon – time for something to eat – and I drove directly into the car park of the White Hart, the local pub. Just as I was making my way to the dining room, however, I thought of Margaret Connolly. She was one who had come to mind so frequently while I lay sweating in my sickbed. So I went to the bar and bought a sandwich and a drink, just as, in the past, I'd bought the same for myself and the same for Margaret. As we had always done, she and I, I went to sit in the small lounge under the stairs. Already in there were two youngish men smartly dressed in suits but behaving like excited boys, shouting, laughing and hooting. They absorbed the entire room and it was not until they had roared their way out that I was able to think.

It was summer now and the grate in the fireplace was empty, but there I saw Margaret on her eighteenth birthday, sitting on a stool by the hearth, leaning forward towards a blazing fire, warming her hands and knees. Her fair hair was swept back and tied with a ribbon, she was smiling and she was happy. Every few moments she gazed at me with her lovely pale blue eyes and my old affection for her, that old tenderness, took hold of me again. I had watched her eat her sandwich, watched her sip her orange juice. I had watched her face, animated, laughing, as she had told me one of her tales and I had watched it again as, with shadows in her eyes, she told me about something that had upset her – probably about animals because that was a touching preoccupation of hers.

I had a delightful few minutes with Margaret until three young women came into the lounge, noisily, arguing. I finished my sandwich and my half pint of lager and, leaving my car parked where it was, I set off along the lane towards my old home.

After a mile and a half or so I came to the cottage of my old, long-dead friend Hoppalong, there on the right, standing beyond his two old yew trees. I remembered it as being quite tiny – front door, window to the right of it and two windows above. It was tiny no longer. There were extensions to right and left, and all was now under an obviously new Yorkshire stone roof. There were bold red curtains at every window and standing in front of the open door was a red and white pram in which, presumably, a child lay asleep.

A few yards further on began the high wall of Cromford House, at least forty yards of it. At one point I felt impelled to pause, to look at the randomly laid millstone grit stones, and actually to touch some of them because it was here, as a lad, with other local lads, that I had so often climbed to the top and over to get into the orchards.

The wrought-iron gate to Cromford House was closed. Rising out of the rhododendrons just beyond were two poles surmounted by a large brown sign bearing words in gold paint: St. Winifred's School for girls. This seemed oddly appropriate. Miss Lovatt, sitting there in her big soft chair, listening while I read to her, had always to my mind seemed distinctly girlish, despite her age. Indeed it was a female house. In all my visits I never saw a man about the place, except of course Hoppalong John. So yes, a school for girls seemed right.

The house itself showed no sign of change, though the giant sequoia rising from the lawn seemed to have grown at least ten feet. As I gazed away, in my mind's eye I saw Hoppalong limping energetically towards me, waving an arm and smiling. The person who had replaced him as gardener here was obviously nothing like as assiduous. The lawn, over which Hoppalong was limping, badly needed cutting.

I didn't linger there long. A man hovering close to the precincts of a school is nowadays seen as some kind of menace, so I walked on towards my old home.

There it stood, some distance away on the opposite side of the lane, solid, four-square, four bedrooms, late Victorian and plain-faced save for modest decorations, flourishes, at eaves and around the doorway.

Formerly there had been a substantial, well-built greenhouse in the side garden but I was dismayed to find that it had gone. It had been replaced by a double garage, one of whose doors was wide open as if left like that by someone desperate to escape.

There had once been green-painted sash windows. Now there were the white plastic frames of double-glazing, which had completely changed the character of the place.

This house had been in our family for three generations. When my mother died aged seventy-eight in 2010 it was sold to a couple with children.

Our nearest neighbour, two hundred yards further along the lane, had been Swallow's farmhouse. The land between had been rich meadow about which a herd of cows, heads down, tearing at the grass, had slowly roamed. When, as a boy, I had stood at the kitchen sink washing up after breakfast and looked out of the window I would see half a dozen of those Fresians just beyond the barbed wire, staring at me sadly as if wanting something I couldn't give. All I could do was smile as if I understood.

Their meadow had now disappeared under a small estate of new detached houses, each of them very pleased with itself, shining with pride under the sun.

The Swallows' farmhouse, old Yorkshire stone like most of the properties hereabouts, was exactly as I remembered it, L-shaped, retiring, a bit weary. Here, with her parents had lived the friend of my childhood, Emma Sarah whose smiles and lively chatter brightened my young life. We were born in the same year – 1954 – I in the August, she in the September. I sometimes called her Bunny because when she spoke, when she rocked her shoulders and flapped her hands to get the words out, her little nose twitched in the most amusing way. She had a great gift of irrepressible fun. As young children we romped about, tried to fish in the river, made kites and flew them, dashed to one or other of our homes for water or something to eat, and in general had a great time.

I walked on to the other side of the house. It was in the field there that in our early years Emma Sarah and I spent most of our time together. It was now sown with wheat, thirty inches high. Feeling sentimental, I reached over and nipped off two heads. I put them in my pocket as a memento and began to walk back to the village.

2

Emma Sarah's mother was Mary Swallow, a laughing, happy, intelligent woman with a great gift for affection. She greeted me with warm smiles, welcomed me into her house and delighted in my friendship with her daughter. She was constructed like a Rembrandt model, shapely but substantial, buoyant and blonde (dyed no doubt). The notable thing about her was her energy. She was never still, busy at her sewing machine, dashing about feeding their flock of chickens, milking their cows, sitting their two farm hands down to a meal and pacing about arguing good humouredly with her husband. 'Oh come on you silly man,' she'd say laughing, 'what're you talking about?'

She had a peculiar way of using her feet. They flapped like paddles and she often laughed at that. 'D'you think my father was Donald Duck?' I was very fond of Mary and the feelings were mutual. It was important to me to please her. She very much liked house plants and the place was full of them, many of them from me. When I could get my hands on some exotic seeds I planted them in two or three pots and presented them to her. Well aware of my liking for chocolate eclairs she always had one or two waiting for me. Yes, Mary Swallow was an admirable woman. But the most obvious thing about her was her profound devotion for her daughter. To keep Emma Sarah happy was almost her reason for living.

Mary was a frequent visitor to our house where she and my mother sat talking for hours, drinking tea and knitting furiously. I remember that they worked together creating two large knitted patchwork bed covers while Emma Sarah lay asleep on our sofa.

Mary's husband, was Hector Swallow. He farmed about a hundred pastoral acres along the bank of the river, good grazing land, quite flat. In addition to his many cattle, Hector kept about a hundred pigs and a flock of screeching chickens. His stock must have been profitable because the Swallows were clearly well off. Hector drove about in a fine Jaguar car and when not stalking about his fields he dressed well in tweeds and shiny shoes. He was a tall, heavy, noisy man and there was a potent kind of energy about him which, if you stood within a yard of him, wrapped you about and set your nerves tingling. His agile face, with its darting eyes and leather cheeks could sometimes mesmerise you. He had a way of staring intently at you, grinning, showing his big teeth, and sucking out your complete attention. I was never completely at ease with Hector Swallow.

One notable thing about him was his inclination to burst into song. He had a powerful baritone voice that he could give vent to at the drop of a hat. At haymaking time I usually went down to help and I have a clear recollection of him, his long hair fluttering in the wind, and his bronze face as, suddenly putting aside his pitchfork, he stood with arms akimbo and sang into the dusty afternoon . . .

'I am the Bandolero, the gallant Bandolero,
I rule the mountains and I claim
What contraband may come my way . . .'

Emma Sarah danced with amusement. Her mother, tousled
and sweating, demolishing a stook, said, 'Oh pipe down,
Hector,' while Fred, one of Hector's labourers, used to this
sort of thing, went on pitching hay.

'I am the Bandolero, here in my gay sombrero.
I have a kingdom beneath my sway . . .'

He stood, arms akimbo, legs apart, bellowing across the
fields as if some vast audience was listening enraptured to
every note.

I helped out on the farm in other ways. One evening
after school when I was about sixteen I was swilling out
his yard for him. We were hard up at home at the time –
my father had left – and I had gone down to earn a few
coppers. I had been there perhaps fifteen minutes when
Hector came to stand at his back door, in his shirt sleeves.

'How you doin', lad?'

'OK, Mr Swallow.'

Once again, throwing out his chest, he gave forth . . .

'In that quaint old Cornish town . . .
When suddenly hastening down the lane
A figure I knew I saw quite plain.
With outstretched arms I took her along,
Carried her to the merry throng . . .'

'Did you like that?' he asked.

'Yes, Mr Swallow. You can let it rip.'

'Right, well when you've done you can have an extra pound.'

By the time I'd finished work it was dark. A half-moon was up and already the wet flagstones of the yard were beginning to shine with incipient ice. I went into the house, into the long lobby, a solid black wedge of darkness, and called out. 'Mr Swallow!'

At the far end of the lobby a strip of light showed under the parlour door, and there was the sound of voices coming from the television in there. 'In here!' he shouted.

He was standing leaning forward in front of the roaring fire, warming his backside. He'd finished for the day and had changed out of his grubby working clothes into thick melton trousers and a knobbly knitted sweater. His face shone – he must just have taken a shave.

Nothing was said for a moment. Mary sat knitting – perhaps another sweater – and Emma Sarah was perched on a leather buffet, with a thumb in her mouth, smiling at me round it. Under the dangling ceiling-light, flashes of reflection came from the glass ornaments on the mantel-piece. The cat sauntered towards me and rubbed its back against my ankle.

Straightening, Hector stared at me. 'Two pounds there on the sideboard,' he said.

'Thanks,' I said and turned to go.

'You look frozen,' he said.

'No, I'm all right. Just my hands.'

'Well come and warm 'em.' He stood aside while I did so.

I was wearing just my school blazer with its fancy badge and those sloppy flannels we all wore in those days, and it was the blazer that drew Hector's attention.

'Clever devil, aren't you, Tony lad?'

I barely heard it. I was wondering how they could afford all the coal that was blazing away on the fire. At home we eked things out these days, lump by lump.

'What the hell d'you do at that grammar school?' Hector went on. 'I was working like hell, here with my father, at your age.'

Mary spoke. 'Ignore him, Tony.' Resting her knitting against the arm of the chair, she measured it with a tape measure. 'How's your mother?'

'She's OK.'

Mary murmured. 'Mmnnn . . . I'll bet she isn't.' She looked up at me. 'I don't see much of her these days. Tell her to come and have a natter. Will you do that?'

'Yes.'

'You and your dad were thick as thieves, weren't you?' she went on, trying to capture my gaze.

But I avoided it and didn't answer. She was delving into a subject I had no heart to talk about. I stepped away from the fire. 'Thanks for the money Mr Swallow. I'll get going,' and I set off across the room.

Emma Sarah, who, already that afternoon, had spent twenty minutes with me, sitting in our kitchen at home, watching me work, with her plump arms resting on the table top, jumped up from her buffet as if to bar my way, saying something I couldn't make out.

'Sit down!' Hector said sharply.

She did so.

'She pesters the life out of you,' Hector said to me. For his own reasons he had never been happy about my friendship with his daughter. 'Why the hell d'you let her?' But he didn't give me time to answer. He turned to his wife. 'What've I told you, woman?'

Mary simply laughed. 'Oh shut up you silly man.'

He glowered at her, opened and closed his mouth once or twice, and then, looking at me, staring at me for a moment, decided not to go on. He picked up the poker and prodded at the fire. 'Look, lad, if you want to help Fred to fix the wire down the church field at weekend,' he said, 'you can earn another bob or two.'

'Thanks, Mr Swallow.'

He waggled the poker at me. 'But don't let my daughter hang about. You got that?'

'Yes.'

'And as for your father . . . ! He certainly let you down, didn't he? Well never mind, lad, never you mind.' He was obviously trying to show some sympathy. He went on. 'He let us all down. I thought he was a pal o' mine. Your father was a sod!'

I could have hit him.

As I opened the door and went out I could feel his insufferable smile burning into my back. From the lobby I heard his voice, serious and insistent, no doubt reverting to the subject he'd felt it wiser to interrupt a moment ago – his daughter and me. Then I heard Mary laugh again, and all the time those voices on the television droned away.

3

Yes, by that time my father had left and I walked home that evening still stinging that Hector had seen fit to make a point of it. I walked along the moonlit road, past the contorted winter skeletons of Swallows Wood, with the fields stretching down to the river on my right and the rising heap of Bower Hill on my left. Around the dim light from a window of Cromford House, in the distance at the foot of the hill, a frosty halo trembled. A train went by along the line, out of sight but clearly heard, throbbing like a rapid heartbeat into the heavy silence of the evening, and the cry of a sheep on the hill responded to it.

I was a creature of this valley, knew every square inch of it for miles around, and gave no more thought to my place in these landscapes than one of Hector's cows, ruminating in one of his fields, might have given. At the side of the road here, as I went by, under the hedge, was a patch of horseradish, free to raid; at the top of the hill was my personal rocky hollow, known only to me and to my dear friend Emma Sarah; there across the fields was the river, shallow and wadeable where, if you sat long enough, you could catch a tench or a bream; there, just this side of the village, stood the church, with its steeple probing at the stars, and, behind it, the graveyard where my mother's parents lay under a patch of gravel and a white stone flowerpot; and there, at the side of the lane, a black cube with another little halo of light in its side, with grey smoke rising from its chimney into the moonlight, sat home.

I discovered my mother, Mother, leaning back in her chair with an open book lying face down on her lap, gazing at nothing, locked inside herself. She had been in this state ever since my father had left.

He was Peter. After obtaining a degree in history from Manchester university he spent some time teaching history in Leeds. It was there that he met Mother. She was a waitress in a restaurant he often visited. They married in 1953 when he was twenty-three and she twenty-two. In the sixties Peter began to write – first a book on George IV and then a novel. It was published and so successful that he was able to give up his teaching and earn a living as a writer. Another novel followed with equal success, and for some years he was in demand as a lecturer and literary figure. Several times, I went with my mother to watch him stand at lecterns, with his head haloed in light, reading to intent audiences in his light, compelling voice. He had thin blonde hair falling over his forehead and as he read, or answered questions, he shifted his weight from foot to foot, gripped with feeling and moved to express it. I sat at the age of about ten, proud but almost disbelieving that it was my father, when he gave an interview on television.

When he was not writing, my father could often be self-preoccupied. I suppose he was usually thinking about his work. He would remain sitting at the table long after meals were finished, when my mother and I had already left the room. I worked with him in the greenhouse while he chatted and smiled at me, but then he would sit on the trough, light a cigarette and withdraw into himself, far away beyond me. I would speak to him but as if into space. Then, after half an hour or so, he'd suddenly come to. 'Where were we, Tony?' And it was very often the same during the evening. Realising that he was no longer listening, Mother would suddenly cease to speak, glance at me and put a finger to her lips, 'Shush.'

But for all that, he was then utterly devoted to my mother – and she to him. There would be spontaneous embraces, kisses and affectionate laughter. I remember trailing behind them as, holding hands, they walked slowly along the promenade at Scarborough, and I remember their bare white feet as they tripped down the beach to paddle together. I have images of them coming home together of an evening, smiling and happy with each other, of them sitting, heads close, arms around each other's waist, on the bench against the house wall. And in the living room, on the dresser, and still in fact in my mother's bedroom, many black and white images of their loving warmth were framed in photographs.

From my bedroom, through the wall, I could hear his two finger tapping on his typewriter, and sometimes it very much annoyed me. While he was at it I knew he had gone a long way away from us, just as he went away in his interminable reveries. Yet when he was free he was happy to spend time with me. He was a very useful resource when homework posed problems. He taught me all I know about growing tomatoes. He was keen on orienteering. He had a collection of ordnance survey maps and a brass, prismatic marching compass. On a weekend morning we'd leave the house, occasionally with Mother, always with sandwiches and bottles of mineral water in his old haversack, and, following a precise bearing, make our way to some previously chosen spot on the map. He marched like a soldier. 'Left, right, left right,' holding his head up, striding out across field and stream, through flocks of sheep, over fences. We found some interesting places at the end of our marches – a stone circle, a ruined church, a hilltop from where we could see Leeds, and a certain remote field with a spot-height marked on the dry-stone wall. (I was to find my way to that same place three years later.)

I always wanted to take a look into his workplace – the small fourth bedroom over the front door. Many times I got as far as taking hold of the doorknob but then, forbidden always from entering, and dismayed that I'd been forbidden, wondering why, annoyed, went back down the stairs.

But success is fickle. By the late sixties my father's fortunes had gone through something of a decline. Interest in his books suddenly waned. He wrote a third book and had it rejected, and although royalties from his earlier works came every six months they were nothing like of the order they'd been before. He was still asked to give the occasional lecture and he was able to write articles for magazines, but his income had gone down drastically.

All the same we still went off for a week or fortnight's summer holiday. My parents liked the sight of water. From the early days I remember long hotel corridors and vast hotel dining rooms where waiters in black and white buzzed about like flocks of magpies, at Bournemouth and Windermere. Then it was boarding houses smelling of cooking cabbage at Scarborough. More recently I remembered, after one of my safaris, crossing a newly shorn field back to the doorway of an isolated and rather dilapidated holiday cottage somewhere in Dorset.

In the good days, Mother, who was not particularly one for buying wardrobesful of new clothes, had preferred to spend money on her home – a grand three-piece suite, good carpets, smart decorations. Now she said to me, 'Put your feet down off the chair! We've got to look after what we've got.'

It was only with half a mind that I was aware of this situation. But then, one day Mother greeted me at the door smiling and happy. My father had been given a commission to write another novel.

On a Saturday afternoon in the late summer, Father put his novel aside and came with me to watch the village eleven play Oxspring on the cricket pitch at the edge of the village.

Cricket bored me, as indeed did all sort of games, but Father had been a very keen cricketer himself when younger. Simply to be with him, I had watched matches here in the village, at Headingley, at Old Trafford and once – in very dimly remembered days – at Lord's, doing my best to stay awake and look eager.

On every fair Sunday in summer even our small village could field two teams – a first and a second. Today the first team was playing a match against Thurgoland, in the next valley. Father and I sat on one of the benches near the pavilion. 'Well played!' he called out now and then, or 'For God's sake Umpire, that was LBW . . .' and so on. As always, I quickly lost interest and spent my time idly watching other spectators who sat on other benches or, as they often did, wandered about talking to one another.

We had not been there long when Hector Swallow, Emma Sarah's father, came sauntering up, wearing an elegant lightweight linen suit in pale fawn. It reflected the bright sunlight and caught my eye while he was still some distance off. He came to stand over us, looked down at my father with that intent, compelling expression on his face, and said, 'How you doin', Peter? Who's winning?' Jerking a hand at me, he hustled me aside and sat down between us. 'How's Daisy? You've got a good 'un there. That one of mine has nagged the balls off me this morning. That Ford I told you about . . . he's dropped the price. You can have it for five hundred now . . . Well it's up to you. Why the hell're you such a bloody stick-in-the mud?'

On the field, someone got out and Hector joined the rest of the spectators in a sudden rattle of echoing applause. As I sat hip to hip with him there was again that faint uneasiness in me about him. His elbow jabbed into me as he spoke. When silent, he cast that sharp, spearlike gaze from side to side, stabbing it at the shirt-sleeved men and summer-frocked women who sat nearby or passed in front of us.

He looked at me. 'Did you hang the rake up yesterday?'
'Yes.'
'I'll be away next week. But Fred'll be there.'

He produced cigarettes and he and Father lit up. He gazed away again, this time at the scoreboard, just in time to see another four go up. 'I don't know why our lot bother,' he said. 'They field like nancies. They're going to lose again, bet your life.' He got up. 'I'm going for a beer,' he said. 'You coming?'

'Thanks, Hector, no,' said my father. 'Things're just getting interesting.'

'Are they? You could've fooled me,' and he sauntered away again, pausing now and then to buttonhole other people.

The sun dipped slowly. The teams went in at the end of the innings for their breather and their bottles of beer. Father produced our sandwiches and our flask of tea and we ate and drank in silent comradeship. Father came out in freckles in warm weather, all across his forehead and down the bridge of his nose, and I watched his eyes, so soft, so mild – not at all like Hector's roving eyes – as he chewed his sandwich and smiled at me.

'We'll see how many Fletcher can knock up today, Tony,' he said. 'He's good. We're still in with a chance. Here – have the last of the tea.'

To another round of applause the teams re-emerged and, looking forward to what might come, Father sat back on the bench and crossed his thin legs. I'd polished his brown shoes for him and they glowed. A breath of wind lifted a strand of his thin fair hair and again he glanced, smiling at me. He lit another cigarette. His smoke drifted to me like the very essence of him – my father, that constant, cherished presence in my life, taken completely for granted like the air I breathed yet now, as we sat together, arousing in me, as so very often, sensations of tremendous comfort and pride. My father . . .

Life is full of small disappointments. Just after three o'clock the sun disappeared behind the clouds and Fletcher was out for sixteen. But we stayed there watching till the bitter end, till our team lost again and with drooping shoulders their supporters drifted out of the gateway to the field and back to the village. Then we ourselves left and walked side by side along the lane under grey skies to home.

Only a week later, my mother and I came back in the late afternoon from a shopping trip to town, went into the kitchen and unpacked our bags. It had been another hot day. The bus had been steaming and my mother was breathless. She flopped on to a chair.'Make us some tea, Tony.'

While I did so, while she got her breath back, she went on in her usual indecisive way asking me what she ought to make for our meal.

'We've just bought some chops, Mother.'

'Yes, but will he fancy chops?'

And so on. Gradually the flush drained from her cheeks. The kettle boiled and I brewed the tea.

'I'll take a cup up to your father,' she said. 'Have you put his two sugars in?'

Picking up cup and saucer she went out of the kitchen and up the stairs. A moment later she came down again. She glanced into the living room and then came back to the kitchen. 'He isn't in,' she said. 'Where is he?'

'I'll see if he's in the greenhouse,' I said. But he wasn't.

'I'm going to sit down,' she said, putting Father's tea down and picking up her own. 'I'm dead beat.' And with that, she went into the living room.

A long moment passed. Then she called me. 'Tony . . . Tony . . .'

Her voice was racked, plaintive, and I went to discover why.

Father had left two notes on the mantelpiece – one for me.

Mine was very brief. 'My dear son Anthony: You will never forgive me but I will always love you and I know you will do well in life. Look after your mother. Goodbye, your unworthy father.'

He had left three hundred and sixty pounds in pound notes on the mantelpiece and, for me, his prismatic compass.

I reached out for my mother's note, but at that moment, she collapsed in a faint to the floor.

That evening after my visit to the Swallows, still annoyed that Hector should have mentioned my father and still thinking about him, I gave my mother a kiss, gave her a grin and tried to cheer her up.

'I've got a bit of money here,' I told her.

She came out of her reverie slowly, looked up at me and smiled. 'You're a good lad.' Putting down her book, she got up and came to me, touching my cheek with her fingers. 'You've brought the cold in with you,' she said.

At sixteen I was already three or four inches taller than she. It had never occurred to me to consider whether my mother was any sort of beauty. But in fact at thirty-nine she was really quite an attractive woman, short, but with a potently female, softly fleshed body and a round, high-cheekboned, smooth-skinned face. She had tiny ears. Her hair was a true chestnut colour, in which, here and there you could see red streaks, the lingering legacy, perhaps, of some Celtic forebear. She had very nice, shapely arms.

I gave her the money. She looked down at it and hovered for a moment, as if wondering what to do with it. This new vagueness, this dreamy, almost absent air, had crept over her of late. That old bustling, darting, energy had drained away and the bright light had vanished from her eyes. She hovered. Then, putting the money down on the table, she asked, 'What've you been doing?'

I told her.

'Oh. Right. What time is it?'

The clock was there on the mantelpiece. 'It's ten to six Mother.'

'I'm a bit tired,' she said. 'I was reading. Do you want something to eat?'

'No. Shall I brew some tea?'

'Oh yes. You're a good lad.' Hovering again for a moment she went back to her chair.

There'd been a time when, rushing about with duster and vacuum cleaner, she'd kept the house very clean, very tidy. Now it was not the same. I'd had to take up the duster and the vacuum cleaner myself, and I'd had to learn how to use the washing machine. Just now, as I'd entered the house by way of the kitchen, I'd seen the pots from our earlier meal still in the sink.

So I washed them, dried them and put them away neatly. She would appreciate that. I removed the gingham table cloth, which had become stained, put it for the wash and replaced it with another from the dresser drawer. I wiped down the draining board, put the loaf that had been left out into its tin in the pantry, and quickly swept the floor. She would appreciate that, also. There was a calendar on the wall and, pinned to it, my sheet of notes – I was an inveterate note maker. Single words – 'Dobber', 'Stinker' – reminded me of masters at school I was doing work for and jobs I had to do. I added, 'Wire Saturday' and 'Washing Sat. afternoon'.

I brewed some tea and took a cup in to my mother. She smiled.

She'd allowed the fire almost to burn itself out, so I went into the yard for some coal. The temperature had dropped even lower. You could almost hear frost crackling in the air. Ice had formed on the hinges of the coal shed door and it needed a bit of effort to open it. There was not much coal left, but I took a good shovelful and went back inside. She watched me put it into the grate.

'I'd better call at Mr Johnson and order some coal,' I said.

'Oh.' Her mouth opened. 'I won't be able to pay him till Friday.'

'That's all right,' I laughed. 'He's used to it.'

'Well yes . . .' she said.

'Mrs Swallow asks you to go and have a natter with her sometime,' I told her.

'Does she? You didn't tell her I would?'

'No.'

'I don't want to, Tony.'

'Well don't. What're you reading?' I asked.

'I found it in Miss Lovatt's library. But I can't get into it.'

Since there was no other money coming into the house, she spent her days working for Miss Lovatt at Cromford House, the old manor house in the village, doing whatever she was asked to do, keeping the place as smart, I suppose, as she'd once kept this house. Each morning we left together shortly after eight. In the evening I was home for just after half-past four. I did what homework I'd been given and was usually finished just as Mother arrived. Together, we'd cobble a meal with whatever she'd brought from the village shop. And then we'd sit down to eat tea together, oppressed by the empty space at the table where Father had once sat.

Even as a child I'd had a kind of tenderness for my mother, a loving sympathy for her touching vulnerability. Despite her old quickness and verve, she had always had a most quiet, unassuming and gentle personality. When she trimmed my hair with her gentle hands there was a sensation of three or four butterflies softly alighting on my scalp. She had a thin, rather husky voice, and had once had a habit of singing to herself while she worked, making a sound like a far-off, tremulous violin. My father – and I, I must add – had been her life.

She was now wearing the felt slippers with the flower embroidered on their tongues, which I'd saved up for and presented to her myself. The large grey shawl across her shoulders had belonged to her mother who, as I dimly remembered, had once sat here on this hearth in front of this fireplace.

'Shall I put the television on?' I asked.

'If you like.'

I leant over her, took her hand, stroked her hair and kissed her forehead.

'We're OK, Mother.'

'Yes,' she said.

And I switched on the television.

4

The greenhouse had been there for decades, ever since my mother's parents had lived here, and it must surely have been very well built on good foundations for it was still intact in every detail, solid, stalwart, shrugging off rain and snow and calmly indifferent to gales.

Towards the end of March, as the days lengthened, I started the year's work in there. I sowed the tomato seeds in two venerable seed boxes which had been used as long as I could remember. This was rather late in the season. Normally it would have been done three or four weeks earlier, but in those normal days there had always been plenty of coke to fire the boiler and keep the temperature in the greenhouse at sixty degrees or so Fahrenheit, but our budget couldn't run to that now. I'd had to wait for the world to warm up a bit. After I'd sown the seeds, there were a few anxious days. Our crop of tomatoes, and the little money I could earn by selling it, were important to us this year. But the seedlings at last appeared.

Nor was it possible this year to order the load of new soil to fill the greenhouse troughs, and so, on Hector Swallow's advice, I did the next best thing. I did a few jobs for him on the farm and took six good wheelbarrow loads of cow manure from his steaming heap.

On the Saturday afternoon I was working it into the old soil in the troughs when I heard something crash dangerously against the glass of the greenhouse wall. I looked in that direction and saw that someone had clumsily propped up a bike there. A moment later Gerald Connolly stood in the greenhouse doorway.

'You nearly smashed the glass, you twerp!'

'No I didn't. It stinks in here.'

I saw Gerald every weekday at school. The back of his big round head and his hefty shoulders were very familiar, for he sat directly in front of me, never still, leaning, lounging, laughing.

'Have you heard what happened in 4A yesterday?' he asked, plonking down on the wall of the trough as clumsily as he'd plonked his bike. 'Old Deadleg turned up after dinner pissed as a newt and spewed up all over the place. I think he distils his own gin in the back room of the lab. Todger says he got great blobs of spew all over his desk.' He laughed. 'They'll sack him now. Good. He gets up my wick.'

'There's nothing wrong with Deadleg.'

'Don't talk wet. He floats about in that gown like Dracula looking for blood. And he waffles. I always fall asleep in chemistry.'

'I know.'

Gerald had a low-browed, faintly primitive face which at first glance could give the impression of a bully, a thug. But when his eyes found you, that pale, always friendly gaze, it was difficult not to warm to him. And he was a bright spark, quick and clever and good company. I liked him very much.

He had a high-headed, rather remote, amused way of looking at you as if contemplating an interesting specimen on the lab bench. It could put people off. 'Connolly's a big-headed bugger!' But if he was I suppose he had some right to be. He was one of those rarities – a lad who was as good at sports as he was in the class, a shining school hero at both rugger and soccer. He was certainly older than his years in many ways. At a time when my own libido was vestigial, his was already bubbling. I'd seen him with giggling girls several times.

He was looking at me as I worked. 'I was waiting for you last night, Bony. Why didn't you turn up?'

Now and then I spent an hour or two at his home with him. He lived in a largish terraced house close to the post office in the village. His father was a railway engine driver, reasonably well paid and secure, and his mother was a woman who could never be overlooked, as hefty as her son, intelligent, dynamic, and commander-in-chief of the household. Gerald had a twin sister, Margaret, as thin as he was thick, rather plain but with those same attractive eyes, who for some reason was nervous of me and usually vanished out of sight when I turned up.

'I had something to do.'

'And what're you doing now? Is that shit? Come on, I'll help. I like messing about in shit.'

'There's another spade in the shed.'

He went for it. 'So what do I do?'

'Shovel the soil to one side, dump some shit, and put the soil back again.'

He took off his blazer and set to. 'Poo, what a pong.'

He worked for about five minutes, grunting now and

then. But the enthusiasm quickly drained from him. I could feel it doing so. He straightened, let the spade fall from his hands with a clatter, and said, 'Look, I've just thought of something.' He had. You could see the thought that had occurred to him like a shadow in his eye.

'You've got to see someone,' I said.

'Well yes . . .'

'Then go,' I said.

'Right.' He got back into his jacket. 'I'd like to help you Bony . . .'

'No you wouldn't.'

'I might come down tomorrow.'

'No you won't.' And he didn't. Perhaps he was seeing that someone again.

But for a moment, he stood gazing about the greenhouse. 'The last time I was in here your dad was standing here, smoking.'

'That was a long time ago.'

'It was the summer before last. His fags were on the wall here, and I've got to come clean. I pinched one and smoked it later.'

'You creep.'

'I got on all right with your dad. Anyway . . .' he sniffed, gave me another long look and turned away. In the doorway, he paused and gazed at me again.

'Anyway, Bony, I hope he comes back. Tarra.'

Again, the handlebar of his bike knocked heavily against the glass and away he rode, drawn like a hunting hound towards one or other of his girlfriends.

He'd disturbed me. All at once I could smell my father's cigarette smoke and see him, standing beside me with a hand resting on my shoulder. 'Go and fetch the raffia, Tony . . .'

By mid-June I was able to force some fruit and ripen off a pound or two. I sold them to some of our old customers in the village. While doing so I visited the Connollys' several times. Their home – 17 Main Street – always full of noise, voices, laughter, music – was open house to the world. Neighbours, visitors of all shapes, sizes and ages, came and went at all hours and something seemed for ever to be cooking. All the odd corners of the place buzzed with an air of good-natured energy.

As usual, I approached by the back path and went up the steps to the kitchen door.

'Come on in!'

In the kitchen I discovered Gerald's mother, known to everyone, even her children, as Aggie, in a green pinafore dress, standing at the table, rolling something, bashing, prodding. She was then forty-four.

'You had tea?'

'Yes, Aggie.'

'You don't look like it. You always look as if you'd never had a good square meal in your life. Thin as a rake.' Voluminous herself, with thick legs, huge body and tremendous chest, she had always made it clear that she desperately wanted to do something about me. 'Look, there's some casserole left. Park your carcass and I'll give you a dollop.'

'I'm all right, Aggie, honestly. This is how I am.'

She had a tea towel over her shoulder. She dabbed her forehead with it. 'You'll fade away one of these days. How's your mother?'

'She's fine.'

'Gerald's in his room messing about,' she said. 'Here, have an apple.'

'No thanks, Aggie. I'll just go up.'

As I reached the landing of the first floor, I heard the lavatory flush. A moment later, Gerald's twin sister, Margaret, came out of the bathroom, preoccupied, just smoothing down the back of her yellow frock. Catching sight of me, shocked and embarrassed, she stood rigid for a moment. Margaret must have given her mother some heartache, for in part she was almost as thin as I was myself – slender white arms and long, slender legs. Perhaps her chest redeemed things in her mother's eyes, however, because her young breasts, round, heavy, reached out into the space between us. I paused, looking at them for a moment and noticing that the buttons of her dress just there seemed a bit under pressure.

'Hello, Margaret,' I said.

I think she was blushing, but couldn't really tell because she lowered her head.

'Hello,' she said, turning swiftly, going into her room and banging the door to rather loudly.

Gerald's own small room was in the attic, lit only by a roof light. One wall was mainly rafters, and from side to side overhead extended an eight-inch square purlin from which dangled a heavy punchbag, dented and bruised by years of abuse. Under the sloping rafters lay Gerald's bed, very neatly made by his busy mother. In the middle of the room was his littered table flanked by two creaky old dining chairs. Gerald himself was sitting in a tattered wicker chair under the light, reading. At once, he got up, examined me for a while, and said, 'Chess.'

For some months, since someone had presented him with a set, there had been no escaping this. It had become the penalty I had to pay for the pleasure of coming to the house.

We sat down to it, and, spreading his heavy arms akimbo as if chess had to be approached like a wrestling match, he pondered his first move. He pondered a lot over his chess, frowning, closing his eyes – and he'd developed an annoying habit of tapping the side of his nose with a forefinger.

'For Pete's sake stop doing that, Connolly.'

Chess itself really did irritate me, bore me. Gerald's hot intensity over it, his slow deliberation, his sudden swelling up and grinning when he'd trapped me, often made me want to kick him hard in the shins under the table.

I was given first move and, at long last, very carefully, he made his. Within a fraction of a second, with little or no thought, my hand moving with the speed of a wasp, I responded. All I wanted to do was get it over.

'Just what I expected,' he said. 'Mistake, Bony. Mistake.'

'Oh get on with it!'

He got on with it, murmuring to himself, chuckling, tapping his fingers on the table-top, leering at me. 'Now see what you can do with that, my friend . . . Oh dear – you've ballsed it up for yourself again. You should watch my queen.'

I had long ago reached the point where I tried my best actually to lose as quickly as possible. But I was so poor even at that that I could on rare occasions accidentally startle him. 'What's this? What's this? Hang on, I'll have to think.'

But that didn't happen this evening. He kicked my pieces one by one off the board, and, after about fifteen minutes, gave his irritating grin. 'Checkmate.'

'Good. Put the thing away.'

'Your trouble, Bony, is that you've just not got the brain for this, you know.'

'My trouble, Connolly, is that I don't give a damn about it.'

'Ah, you see, that's it. You don't give a damn because you can't get your feeble brain round it. Look, I've told you, I've got three books about chess on that shelf. More books've been written about chess than about anything else on the face of the earth.'

'You've told me that. You read 'em. I don't want to know.'

'Take one. You'll soon see what chess is about. All I did there on you was Alekhine's end game, simple as pie. Read one of the books, man, for God's sake. It's like bashing a baby playing you. It really is.'

'Well you've bashed me, so shut up.'

Laughing, Gerald gathered the pieces and for a while we talked of things at school.

Although chess wasn't part of it, I had gained much from my friendship with Gerald over the years – above all a warm sense of comradeship. His personality, his smiling banter and his obvious fondness for me, endeared me to him. But friendship can never be one-sided, and Connolly's fondness for me must have arisen out of something he, in his turn, found in me. Certainly I did my best to keep his friendship, going along with him when sometimes I'd have preferred not to, always supporting him in his schemes, making him laugh, happily being beaten at chess, and watching him batter his way across the rugby field. And I had managed to infect him with one or two predilections of my own.

For some time I had been taking a keen interest in the news, avidly watching programmes on the television. In a new exercise book I'd begun to keep a diary of those events which seemed important, and on my bedroom wall I had pinned a map of the world so that I could find places named in the news and keep track of things.

Having seen it there, Gerald had followed suit and pinned a map to the wall of his own room – a much bigger, glossy one. By this evening it was covered with a rash of red spots where, like myself, he'd pinpointed things.

That June there was much in the news about the Queen. 'You know, Bony, I fancy being King. I'd better marry one of that lot. But hang on, that would make Maggie a princess or something. We'd have thousands of creeps knocking at the door trying to get at her. I couldn't cope with that.'

'I just saw her. Your sister doesn't like me very much.'

'You're wrong there, kid,' Gerald said.

This surprised me. I was about to ask what he meant when there came a loud shout from the foot of the stairs. It was his mother. 'Gerald – there's some apple pie for you and Tony on the kitchen table. I'm going out.'

Gerald laughed. 'Good old Aggie.'

'What would you do without her?' I asked.

'Have a bit of peace and quiet,' he said. 'Wherever you look, there she is. She makes bloody good apple pies. Come on, let's go and scoff some.'

We went down to the kitchen where the pie, still steaming,

stood resplendent on the table, next to a jug of cream. I decided to eat a wedge, and we ate together, standing up.

'My dad's got a pal with him tonight,' Gerald said, taking my dish and dumping both his and mine into the sink. 'Let's go and see what they're up to.'

In the living room – with its upright piano, its tapestry-covered chaise longue, its sideboard laden with photographs and a pot Alsatian dog, its dark, multi-patterned carpet – sat Gerald's father whose exotic name was Conrad. He was in his mid-forties, half the size of his wife and much quieter – a still, thoughtful man.

In the chair opposite him sat another man of similar age, not much larger than Conrad, with a pleasant-looking, big-nosed face and surprisingly small feet in polished black shoes. He was introduced to me as Sam Webber, a work-mate of Conrad's, another railway locomotive driver. They must both have eaten less than two hours earlier, but Aggie had pressed plates of sandwiches into their hands. They were chewing away.

'How you doin', Mr Webber?' Gerald asked. 'Where've you been this week?'

Sam spoke with an accent not native to this place. His vowels were different and his cadences were outlandish to us. He was obviously from the south of England. 'Monday Aberdeen, yesterday King's Cross like your dad.' He showed us the last morsel of his sandwich. 'Tell your mother these tomato sandwiches're damn good, Gerald.'

'I can't. She's gone out. But I'm glad you said that.' Gerald jerked his finger at me. 'This is the person who grew the tomatoes.'

'Did you?' Sam asked, looking up at me, obviously

interested, rather surprised. 'Are you cropping so early in the year? I thought they were Channel Island. Have you got a greenhouse?'

'Yes,' Gerald said. 'He has. A big 'un. I help him out a lot, don't I, Bony?' He grinned.

'Well I know a bit about tomatoes,' Sam said. 'I rent a greenhouse on the allotments. One of these plastic things, small but all right, and I thought I knew how to grow tomatoes. But I've never managed to crop as early as this.' Looking into my face, he asked, 'How d'you manage it? What variety are they?'

'Ailsa Craig. My father always preferred them.'

'Do you force them . . . ?' But Gerald had had enough of all this. Standing in the middle of the carpet, he said, 'Shall I give you a tune on the Joanna?'

And at last his father spoke. 'For God's sake no! Don't go anywhere near that piano. Can't you see Sam and I were talking? Here, just take these empty plates to the kitchen and let us get on with it.'

'All right, Dad. Keep your hair on. I just thought you might want to hear a bit of Choppin.'

'No. We don't want deafening. Just take the plates.'

As Gerald and I went out, Sam raised a hand, halting me. 'I grow Redskins myself, from Thompson & Morgan,' he said. 'But I'm nowhere near as far on as you seem to be. How d'you manage it? Where d'you live?'

'A mile down the road.'

'I'd like to see your greenhouse. Would that be all right? If you like I'll fetch half a dozen Redskin plants in pots. You can try 'em out. Perhaps I can have a chat about things with your father while I'm there.'

'He's not with us any more . . .'

'Oh dear – I'm sorry.' Sam had jumped to the conclusion that my father had died, and I was in no mood to enlighten him.

'It's all right,' I said. 'You'll find us on the left hand side of the lane, almost opposite the wood.'

'Weekend perhaps. Will that be all right?'

'Yes.'

'You can show me how you do it.'

'Yes.'

I followed Gerald out of the room and closed the door.

We began to climb the stairs, but then Gerald put a hand on my arm and asked, 'D'you fancy a walk? A girl I know will be playing tennis on the court at school. We can have a game ourselves before it gets dark.'

'I can't play tennis. You know that.'

'Right. Well up the blinkin' stairs . . .'

He lay stretched out on his bed and I sat in his wicker chair. At about half past eight the outer door banged to. Aggie had come home. From the room below, Margaret's room, came the uncertain trembles of a violin, starting, stopping, and then wavering on into 'Liebestraum'.

'That's Yehudi Menuin,' Gerald said. 'Go and strangle her for me.'

When I finally left for home it was dark. The street was deserted. A small, hairy dog trailed at my heels for a while and then turned sharply back towards the place he'd come from. In the wood, the resident owl was hooting. As I walked up the path to the house I could hear cows close by in Hector's field chewing cud with a sound like slow, stealthy footsteps. Mother had already gone to bed. I made some tea, drank it, and went to bed myself.

That Saturday afternoon, I heard Sam arriving before I actually saw him. He came on a motorbike which revved down as it drew near the house, coughed once or twice, and grew silent. I was already in the greenhouse. Stepping out, I was in time to watch him prop his bike on its stand, smooth down his hair, take out a handkerchief and blow his nose. He turned and saw me. 'Hello,' he smiled. 'Am I all right? Not the wrong time, is it?'

'No. It's fine.'

He surprised me by reaching out to shake my hand.

I led the way around the side of the house.

'I've often passed this place,' he said. 'It's in a good spot.'

As he turned the corner and came within sight of the greenhouse, he paused, obviously impressed. 'Lord, it's twice as big as mine,' he said. 'One of the old sort, isn't it? Those brick walls.'

'I think my grandfather built it.'

'It's a beauty. That brick shed on the end as well.'

'Yes. Come in . . .'

I stood back for him to enter. Doing so, he touched the high potting bench. 'This is handy.' He saw the hank of raffia, the scales, the pile of paper bags. 'Short of nothing,' he said. He touched the well-fingered notebook and wondered at it.

'I keep a record of everything,' I told him.

'Do you? My God, you're keen.' Then he spotted the boiler. 'You've got heating.'

'Yes. The pipes go right to the end of the greenhouse.'

'It's a proper job. I've got no heating myself.'

I opened the inner door and led him through into the hot air of the greenhouse itself.

'What's the temperature in here?' he asked.

'The thermometer's just behind you.'

'You got vents? Yes, I see you have. When d'you open them?'

'The plants don't start wilting till it gets to almost eighty degrees.'

He gazed about at the plants. 'Yes,' he said. 'Somebody here knows what he's doing.' He touched my arm so that I'd look into his face. 'I'm sorry . . . I told you I'd bring some Redskins but it's just as well I couldn't. It would have meant a long walk with the wheelbarrow and I was working last night and a bit tired and not up to it. I'll bring 'em again. But they'll look puny against this lot.' Fingering a truss, he said, 'Further on than mine, all right – but still green most of them.'

'I just ripen some off,' I said. 'We sell them to neighbours and people we know.'

'Do you use liquid manure?'

We sat down on the trough wall and went on talking tomatoes. Presently, he took out his handkerchief and dabbed his forehead. 'Can I smoke?'

'Yes.'

And he lit up. Once again, as the smoke wafted into the air in here, my father was brought back to me, powerfully, and I missed something Sam said to me.

'Pardon?'

'I said if you touch tomatoes with nicotine on your fingers it gives them some sort of disease.'

'Yes, I know.'

'You seem to know all there is to know about it. How old are you?'

He spoke rather quietly, moving his hands in slow oscillations, and had a very ready smile. He seemed slightly different from when I'd seen him in Connolly's parlour, and I realised that he'd had his hair cut. He was wearing a grey suit, a blue woven silk tie, and those polished black shoes.

'Where can I put my cigarette end?' he asked.

'Just leave it on the wall.'

Doing so, he gave me a long look, smiled, and said, 'You're a pal of Gerald.'

'Yes. We're at school together.'

'He's a bit of a lad, isn't he?'

'Gerald's all right.'

'He can be very funny. You certainly know he's there.' Sam turned to me again, studying my face. 'You don't seem to be the same sort. You're quieter, aren't you?'

He was a compact man, contained, as it were. Sitting beside him you felt no pressing, pushing emanations from him, nothing to make you in the slightest bit uneasy. His blue gaze clearly showed interest in me but I felt that if I decided not to answer his questions he would simply smile again. There was a little scar above his left eye.

'I work at the same shed as Conrad, you know.'

'Yes. You drive trains.'

'Yes. For years I worked mostly on freight. Up and down from York yards to Newcastle. I'm on passenger work now, long runs. Back from King's Cross last night.'

'It must be the best job in the world.'

He laughed. 'I thought that myself when I was a lad. There's a hell of a lot of responsibility. You can never forget that. Yes, I drop in on the Connollys quite a bit. They're a cheerful lot. An hour there does me good. I live alone, you know . . .' But he shook his head and dismissed all that. 'Tell me,' he went on, 'where d'you get your manure?'

'Plenty of it at the farm next door.'

'Horse manure?'

'Cow. It's all right if it's old. I put it at the bottom of the trough.'

He was silent for a moment. Then he straightened. 'Well, thanks for letting me look round. It's been very interesting. You must come and take a decko at my set-up some time. I've got a bit of an allotment – mostly spuds these days. Arran Banner. But I'd better be off. I've got one or two things to do.'

He got to his feet. As he did so, I felt a little spasm of disappointment. I liked this man. I liked his agreeable manner, the expressions on his face, the uncondescending and friendly way he'd dealt with me. 'What about a cup of tea before you go,' I asked. 'I can have it done in a jiffy.'

'That's good of you. Yes, I could do with a drink. You get damn thirsty on a motorbike, you know. Thanks . . .'

He followed me into the house and into the kitchen. I sat him down, made tea and gave him some.

'Thanks. Got the house to yourself this afternoon, have you?' It was obviously said merely in passing, but it gave me something of a problem. I did not have the place to myself this afternoon at all. My mother was somewhere about and she was not very welcoming to visitors these days. But he was smiling at me, and I could not bring myself to tell him a lie.

'My mother's here. I'll get her.'

'No, don't bother her . . .'

But I'd said it.

I found her in the living room, knitting, self-absorbed and distant as usual. 'Sam's here,' I said. 'I told you he was coming. He's in the kitchen.'

She was, as I'd expected her to be, dismayed. 'Oh no . . . Why did you have to bring him in?'

'Come and say hello to him.'

'No, no . . .'

'Please, Mother. He'll be going soon. Don't let's be rude. Come on.'

'But look at me! I'm in a mess!'

'No you're not. Please, Mother . . .'

'Why should he want to see me!'

'Because you're here. Just say hello.'

'Oh hell!'

'Please . . .'

'I'm not ready for visitors. Just look at me.' Jumping up, flustered, she went to look at herself in the mirror over the mantelpiece, angrily patted her hair and hopelessly looked down at herself. 'Why d'you make life difficult for me!'

'I don't. Just say hello to him. Please. Come on, Mother . . .'

I took her arm and, most reluctantly, she allowed me to lead her into the kitchen.

'This is my mother,' I said.

Sam got to his feet, smiled, 'I'm Sam,' and held out his hand.

She hesitated awkwardly. He looked at her, extended his hand closer, and at last she took it, but only for a moment.

'Sit down, Mother,' I said, forcing the issue. 'I'll pour you some tea.'

She was ridiculously embarrassed, nervous, and it showed in her as a cool, resentful stiffness of her body. But, having no option, she sat down facing him.

'I'm glad to meet you, Mrs Walton.' Sam himself sat down. 'I was just looking at your greenhouse. Your lad knows his stuff.'

She said nothing. She simply looked down at the table.

'He offered me some tea,' Sam went on. 'But it's all right, I'll be off soon.'

She still said nothing.

'I was just saying what a good spot this is. Nice and quiet . . .' Obviously, he could see the look on her face and taste her silence, so he said it again. 'I'll be going in a minute. I told him not to bother you. I'm sorry.'

And that almost abject apology did manage to affect her. At last she realised the impression she'd given him and I saw that she was feeling guilty. Finding a sort of smile, she looked into his face. 'It's all right,' she said.

'I work on the railway.'

'Yes. Tony told me.'

'And my mother's name is Daisy,' I said, bringing her tea to her.

'It's a nice name,' Sam said. 'I live in Yeadon – just past the Green Dragon.'

'Oh yes?'

'I met your son at the Connollys' the other night.

'He told me.'

'He's a good lad.'

'Yes, he is.'

'Looks after you, does he?'

'He can be a pest.'

'I never had any children myself. But there we are . . . There's a nice feeling in this house, Mrs Walton.'

'Is there?'

'Yes, there is. That means there's good people in it. I pass it quite often.'

'Do you? It was my parents' house. We've lived here for ages . . .'

The conversation went on and gradually Mother relaxed. The stiffness left her, that coolness went from her eyes, and on to her face came that open, interested expression which can only appear when you begin to feel completely comfortable with someone. He had impressed her just as he had impressed me. They laughed, leant their elbows on the table, looked each other in the eye.

Brightly, my mother asked, 'Would you like more tea, Sam?'

'Yes, thanks, Mrs Walton. I could manage another.'

She got up, poured him more tea, carried it quickly to the table, sat down again. My mind had wandered. I was gazing out of the window and thinking of other things. But the topic must have drifted a good bit, because Mother suddenly left the table. She went out for a moment, and came quickly back with the knitting she'd been doing, placing it on the table in front of him.

Sam looked down at it. 'That's very good. My mother was a knitter.' He turned it over. 'Very neat. Do you do a lot of it?'

'I do some sewing these days as well,' she said. 'In fact I made this dress myself . . .'

I had become thoroughly bored with it all. I walked towards the door. Neither of them noticed. So I carried on, returned to the greenhouse, and resumed what I'd been doing earlier.

Time passed. He'd told me that he wanted to be away, that he had things to do. But half an hour went by and then almost another half-hour.

But at last he poked his head into the greenhouse. 'I'm off now,' he said.

I followed him. I watched him crank his motorbike and straddle it.

'Thanks for coming,' I said.

'It's been a pleasure. I'll come again. I'll bring the Redskins. Cheerio, then!' And, doing a noisy U-turn on the lane, he rattled away, with his hair fluttering, towards the village.

When I went back into the house, Mother was standing by the fireplace, hovering once more, thinking, miles away.

'He's a nice man,' I said.

'Yes.'

'He drives locomotives. What a job.'

'Yes.'

'You did a heck of a lot of talking.'

'Did we?'

'Yes, you did. I'll go and wash the teacups.'

'Thanks, Tony.'

5

Later that Spring Mary took Emma Sarah for a week's holiday in Blackpool. I was at the house when they came home. Hector had asked me to paint his front door – a startling green. Their taxi drew up at the gate and, seeing me, Emma Sarah came running excitedly. 'I've been to Blackpool!'

'Yes, I know.'

'I've come home!'

'So I see.'

'I had a swim, Tony, I got my cossy wet . . .'

But I saw that the taxi was driving away and that Mary was lugging a suitcase in either hand so I went to carry them for her.

'What's he had you doing now?' Mary asked, looking at the new paint on the door. 'What a daft colour!'

As I put the suitcases into the hall Emma Sarah came dragging at my sleeve. 'I've got something for you . . . Mam, Mam, the bag, the bag!'

Mary had a large bag dangling from her shoulder and Emma Sarah went fidgeting at it.

'Hang on, Emma! Hang on!' From the bag Mary produced a stick of rock wrapped in plastic. Emma Sarah grabbed it and presented it to me with a flourish. 'It's for you, Tony!' Turning again to her mother she demanded, 'The sock, the sock!'

'Here,' Mary said, handing me a pair of black socks held together by a paper band which said, 'For the elegant *gentleman*.'

'She must be keen to keep your feet warm, Tony.' Resting a hand on her daughter's shoulder, she said, 'In you go, Emma. Let's get home.'

Ten minutes later, Emma Sarah reappeared. 'Can I have a bit of rock, Tony?'

She came three more times. When at last I finished the job and walked home there was about two inches of it left in my pocket.

From time to time I took my father's compass and his maps and, partly in remembrance of him but in fact to commune with him, I went on one or other of the long walks we'd enjoyed together. He was by my side at every step. I saw what we'd seen together, breathed the air we'd breathed, and very frequently I heard his voice: 'We'll skirt this field . . . We'll take another bearing from here . . .'

One warm Sunday I made for the little church at Rythorpe, about five miles away across country, to which we'd navigated our way over two years before. It was gone one o'clock when, with my father's satchel, bottle of pop, cheese sandwich, compass and map, I climbed the hill opposite the house. It was a bright, warm day, shadowed only intermittently by drifting white clouds as big as your hand. Navigating by the landmarks my father had formerly selected – a lone ash, an outcrop of rock, I went on through heather and bilberry across the top moor. From somewhere on my left came the trilling of a high skylark.

On across fields where sheep grazed, and on into a stubble field where rabbits, startled by my sudden appearance, displaying their white alarms, scattered away under the dry-stone walls. I skirted a beech wood, where my father had spotted some badger sets, and so began the long walk down into the far valley. After about two hours, I came at last to the high garden wall of a large house. I followed it round to the corner where, on a little hump in the ground, we'd sat to eat our sandwiches, and there I sat down again.

From that place, as, surrounded by flowering weeds, I ate and drank, I could look away and see below me the houses of Rythorpe village and the little grey church, presiding like a concerned guardian over the weary and leaning, the proud and upright, the somnolent and shining gravestones that surrounded it. Save for a woman who sat in a deckchair, asleep it seemed, in her back garden, there was not a sign of life. Polished windows reflected the sunlight. From this elevation it was like gazing down at a lovingly constructed model – a neat jumble of cottages and a mosaic of gardens, geometrically enclosed by wooden fences, green with lawns and colourful with blooms.

But then the hot silence was suddenly broken by the sound of the church bells. Within minutes, people began to emerge, into the lane and on to the road. It was time for their evensong.

I ought to have expected that, but I hadn't. I was frustrated. On our previous visit, my father had led the way into the church and we'd spent half an hour in there while he read inscriptions on the plaques on the wall, examined the font, peered at the carving on the pulpit, touched the old stone walls – and I'd wanted to go inside again this afternoon to relive that half-hour. Now, dismayed, I felt that I couldn't.

Just as I finished my last mouthful of sandwich, the sound of the church organ reached me, a faint whispering against the hum of the afternoon. The service had begun. I made my way down to the road, through the lychgate of the church and so into the porch.

Pausing there for only a moment while the congregation sang 'Oh worship the king', I pushed open the inner door and entered the nave. The congregation was very small, occupying only two rows of pews, since the congregation had their backs to me, no-one noticed me. I went into the nearest pew and stood there alone. When they sat down, I sat down.

The service went on – through the canticles, the responses and the credo. It was something I was reluctant to admit to my friends, but in those days I was a firm believer. I often went to Matins at our local village church, alone and fervent. I said my prayers every night. I said little about that then and I'll say little about it now. But this afternoon I was involved with only a part of my mind. I was looking at the things my father had looked at, had touched, had lingered over in this church, and seeing him again in white shirt and grey trousers standing in the shadows by the vestry door, beckoning to me to show me the ancient oak chest which stood there. I remembered listening to his slow, echoing footfalls on this tiled floor and hearing his quiet cough as he stood at the lectern reading the open Bible.

The vicar climbed into his pulpit and sermoned for ten minutes. By the time he climbed down again I was ready to leave. Hesitating for a second by the lychgate to let my father go now, as I'd always been obliged to let him go after my frequent thoughts of him, I set off for home.

The afternoon, sinking slowly down into that dreamy blankness of Sunday evening, was still bright and I was nowhere near ready for another meal, so I decided to go to my hollow for a while. I had been coming to this place for some time – a small, deep depression in the ground close to the low wall of a field, at the edge of a clump of gnarled hawthorns and rimmed by thistles and nettles. Once ensconced you were invisible to the world.

But when I got there I found Emma Sarah lying stretched out on the grass. Having quite recently followed me to this spot one afternoon, she was the only person other than myself who had any idea of its existence. But now, here she was. She lay fast asleep, dressed in a thin blue frock. Mary always kept her turned out well, in crisply ironed blouses or frocks, home-knitted jumpers, pleated skirts and black patent leather ankle-strap shoes which heliographed shiny messages back to the sun. Her dark hair was always neatly trimmed but the fringe across her forehead often irritated her and she had a habit of slapping it with her hand as if it were some hairy insect crawling about there.

That smile of hers was beautiful – bright, trusting, radiating warmth. It gave the girl to you like one of her open-hearted gifts. By now she was easily five feet four tall, by no means thin, and a definite presence. Over the months I'd seen her blouses, her jumpers, swelling week by week, first lopsidedly – left side still flat, right side burgeoning – but now splendidly symmetrical and thrusting.

She was wearing sandals today and her bare toes poked upwards out of them. Her face, her plump legs and arms, were tanned after weeks of sunshine. As always, my heart went to her. All I ever wanted Emma Sarah to see in me was a smile. And all I wanted to see in her was that vague, puzzled happiness which could so easily take possession of her.

'Hello, Emma Sarah!'

Waking with a start, she lay there mouth open, alarmed, staring up. My back was to the sun, my face was in shadow and for a moment she was unable to recognise me.

'It's Tony,' I said.

At once, she gave me her wonderful smile, sat up, and reached for my hand. I gave it to her and, tugging at it, she drew me down to the grass at her side.

'I can tell your fortune,' she said, clinging on to my hand, turning it palm upwards.

'Can you, Emma Sarah? How can you do that?'

'My mam showed me . . . See . . .' With her first finger she drew random patterns on my palm. 'The sun will shine for ever for you . . .'

'Will it? Is that what your mother says?'

'You are a beautiful person and you deserve the world.'

Yes, obviously, she was remembering what her mother had said to her. She drew her finger around my palm in circles for a while longer, trying to recall what else she'd been told. But then, failing, frowning, annoyed with herself, she said, 'Oh – everything, everything . . . !'

'Thanks, Emma Sarah. Can I have my hand back?'

'I've got some new shoes,' she said, waggling her feet.

'Yes. Very smart. But the point is, Emma Sarah, how long have you been here waiting for me? Let me see your watch.'

It was almost six o'clock. 'How long have you been here?' Although I asked the question again I knew she wouldn't have any idea. 'It's a treat to see you, Emma Sarah,' I said, 'but I think you'd better skidaddle. If you've been here as long as you seem to have been your dad'll be wondering where you are.'

'No he won't.'

'Yes he will and he'll tell me off.'

'I want to talk to you,' she said, twisting her mouth.

'I know. And I want to talk to you. But it's six o'clock. They'll be looking for you. We'll see what happens tomorrow.'

With that little shaking of the shoulders, that pouting of the lips, she got to her feet. 'All right, Tony.' Standing there for a moment, she smiled down at me. 'The sun will shine for ever for you . . .'

About half an hour later, I set off again and came within sight of home. As I did so, I heard the sound of a motor-bike and saw Sam riding, not very quickly, away along the lane towards the village.

Mother was busy in the kitchen making the meal. She greeted me with a cheerful smile. 'You must be famished. You look a bit bedraggled.'

'I've walked about ten miles. What's for tea?'

'You'll see when it's ready. Go and get washed.' Gazing at me for a moment, she stepped to me, put both hands to my face and kissed my cheek. 'You're my lovely lad.'

I had put the map and my father's compass down on the table and they caught her eye as she turned away.

Looking down at them for a moment, she reached out, picked up the compass and held it in her hand. 'Why did he do it, Tony?'

She'd asked it a hundred times and had still found no answer. With her head bowed her hair partly hid her face, and I fully expected more tears. But not so. When she turned to me again her eyes were dry and in them was a look I'd begun to see there of late – a cool, rather far-off look, not very pleasant. 'It broke my heart,' she said, equally coolly.

'I know that, Mother.'

'I loved him with all my heart.'

'I know.'

'Never a word, never a hint.'

'Yes.'

'He was a swine, Tony.'

She'd said it before and it had always wounded me. My expression showed it and she went on, 'It broke your heart, too, didn't it? And you still love him. And I understand that. But he was a swine, Tony, a selfish . . .' she searched for words, and then screwed up her face in a degree of anger you rarely saw in her. 'He was a selfish, awful bloody bastard.'

'Don't say that . . .'

'I will say it. I gave him years of my life, I gave him everything, and he left me like throwing off an old shirt, without a thought, like a bastard – left me to fend for myself, just like that. Well he can rot! I hope the bastard's dead – dead!'

'Don't say that . . .'

'He can piss off, Tony. Piss off, piss off!' Hovering,

shaking for a second, she raised her arm and flung the compass with all her strength across the room. 'Piss off! Piss off!'

Out of breath, stiff, clenching her fists, she raged – but then she suddenly sagged, sighed, brushed hair from across her forehead. 'Go and get washed, Tony.'

But I didn't move.

She pottered about the table with her back to me.

'I've had enough, Tony,' she said. 'I've had enough. I can't weep any more. Go on – get washed and then come down for your tea.'

I picked up the compass. It had made a small dent in the plaster of the wall, and there was a small dent in the brass of the compass itself. When, in my room, I looked at the compass again, opened its flap and saw that its glass was cracked, it seemed to me as if in that wild gesture she had indeed cracked, broken, smashed everything to do with the man who for so long had been the light of her life. But I was glad to realise that, despite the damage, the compass was still devotedly showing north.

I washed and sat down on the edge of my bed. Although Mother had never revealed those feelings so blatantly, so furiously to me before – had shown me only gloomy abstraction, a dreamy self-absorption, a sad hopelessness – they must obviously have been working in her for some time, and I wasn't quite sure how to confront her again. But the more I gave thought to it, the more easy I became. I'd always been well aware that sooner or later she would have to come to something like this, to dismiss Father from her thoughts, or else go into deeper decline and misery, and I began to feel quite happy for her.

She shouted after me. 'Where are you!'

'Coming!'

The table was laid, the tea had been brewed, and she was fully herself again now. In the light from the kitchen window, dressed in a frock she'd made for herself, and, I now noticed, made up with lipstick and so on, she looked, I thought, very nice indeed. She gave me another cheerful smile.

'I got one of Mrs Havers' steak and kidney pies,' she said. 'You like them, don't you?'

'Yes,' I said. 'Why don't you ask her how she makes them? We could do 'em ourselves then.'

'Why deprive the lady of her income? Don't let it go cold. Eat your chips. Where did you say you've been this afternoon?'

'Rythorpe.'

'That's a long way.'

'I told you, I did ten miles.'

'You must be tired.' She dabbed her lips with her napkin. 'Oh yes, Mr Swallow called for you while you were out.'

'What did he say?'

'Wanted you to do something for him.'

'I did something for him this morning. I gave you the money.'

'Yes,' she said, with a chip impaled on her fork, 'and that's another thing. I'm fed up of being broke. I'm going to find another job.'

'There aren't any jobs round here, Mother.'

'I've ordered the *Evening News*. I'll find a job in Leeds, maybe. There's the bus, it's only half an hour. And it's high time I found something decent. I'm not an idiot. I don't see why I should be a servant for ever, do you?'

'No, I don't. Get cracking, Mother.'

'And anyway, I'm not happy at Cromford House.'

'Why?'

'Miss Lovatt's brought a friend in, a woman she met in Torquay when she spent a month there earlier this year. Years younger. And I don't like it.'

'Why not? You mean you don't like this other woman?'

'No – it's not that . . . It's just . . . Oh never mind.' She shook her head. 'But that reminds me, they're throwing a party for some reason next weekend. I told her you'd help out for an hour. Is that all right?'

'Course it is.'

'Just for an hour or two.'

'It's all right, Mother.'

'There're some chips if you want them.'

'Right.' I emptied the remaining chips on to my plate.

'God knows why you stay so thin,' she said, watching me. 'You eat like a giant. And Tom Marshall came for some tomatoes.'

'Well I'd bagged up a few pounds in the shed.'

'Yes. I found them.'

We ate silently for a while. She was enjoying the pie.

'I might go for a stroll myself when we've finished tea,' she said, cutting up a morsel of kidney.

'Why not?' I said. 'It's still warm. It won't be dark for a bit.'

We finished the meal.

'I enjoyed that,' she said.

'I could see you did.'

Getting up, she cleared the table and then stood at the draining board with a tea towel in her hand while I washed the pots – a chore I'd taken on myself for a long time now.

'I saw Sam Webber on the lane on his motorbike as I came home,' I said.

'Yes, you just missed him.'

'He'd been here, then.'

'Yes. I'd asked him to call.'

'Had you? Why?'

'I'd promised to knit him a pullover.'

'I didn't know that,' I said.

'Well you don't know everything.'

'You knitted him a pullover. That was quick.'

'Yes, I did. Have you an objection to that?'

'Did he bring the Redskins for me?'

'No. He'll bring them some other time. He's a nice man.'

'I told you that.'

'He's an engine driver.'

'I told you that, also, Mother.'

'Why don't you just wash the pots, Tony?'

6

On the morning of the party I left for Cromford House shortly after half past eight.

'What am I supposed to be doing for her?' I asked.

'She didn't say. Does it matter?' Mother asked.

'No.'

'It'll be sorting things out in the garden, I think. She wants you away before the party starts – so you should be back for dinner. I'll leave something for you.'

'Are you going out?'

'Yes.'

'Where to?' I asked. To have Mother actually going out alone was another new development.

'Why don't you mind your own business.'

'All right. I'll mind it, Mother.'

'If you really want to know it's a woman I used to work with, years ago. I meet her now and again in the shops. I'm going to see her. We might go out somewhere. It's time I got out a bit.'

'Well don't leave me sardines for dinner. They made me sick yesterday.'

And with that I began my mile-and-a-half walk to Cromford House. We were still enjoying one of those rare, apparently neverending, spells of glorious weather. Already early mists had evaporated and I could feel the heat of the sun like a blanket across my shoulders. Cromford House was the old manor house, very private, discreetly withdrawn among its forest of trees, hidden away behind a high stone wall. The only sight of it I'd had until now had been when, with other lads from the village, I'd climbed the wall to raid their large orchard which, always in early autumn, was festooned, weeping, dripping with apples and pears. We were rarely interfered with and could actually bring carrier bags and baskets to reap our harvest. But on odd occasions, as if to offer a token resistance, the gardener would put in an appearance. 'Hey-up – here's old Hoppalong.' He was a man in his early fifties, short and wiry. He'd served in the Second World War and had lost the lower half of his left leg. He hopped along on some sort of stump. His chances of getting one of us by the scruff of the neck were just about nil, but as soon as he was spotted we rapidly dispersed, back over the wall, because, after all, he was an old soldier.

Unusually, the great wrought-iron gate was open. I passed through it and walked on along the wide, curving gravel drive between banks of rhododendron, under the arching branches of beeches, until the house came into view. It was an impressive sight – dark grey millstone grit, partly ashlar at quirns and window surrounds but mostly random, two storeys high, under a heavy stone-slab roof, rambling, quiet and self-preoccupied. At either end of the house, gables of deep bay windows, the lower ones glazed almost to the ground, pushed out into the forecourt, and four chimney stacks rose up like pricked ears.

In front of the house was a large, circular lawn in the

centre of which stood a gigantic redwood, two or three yards in diameter, immensely high. Two crows flew round and round its peak as if unable to break away. The shortest way to the central doorway of the house was across the lawn, but it had been newly mown to a surface like a billiard table. You could smell it. Sensing that I might be under observation and that the lawn was sacrosanct, I walked on around the arc of the drive.

The great oak door, between two stone urns overflowing with nasturtiums, was wide open but there was one of those old doorbell buttons like half a tennis ball let into the wall and I gave it a good push.

Nothing happened. So I did it again and Miss Lovatt suddenly appeared.

'You must be Anthony. Mrs Walton's son.'

'Yes.'

She weighed me up and seemed quite pleased with what she saw. 'Well thank you for coming. I'm most grateful.'

At that time, I suppose, Miss Lovatt was in her early sixties, tall for a woman, just about as bony as I was myself, shapeless, but wearing a long, silky, multi-coloured dress which I thought was quite beautiful. She had silver-grey hair and although her long, bony face was distinctly horsey there was an attractive, smiling, soft and gentle look in her eye which reminded me of my mother. I felt immediately comfortable with Miss Lovatt. I noticed that she was discreetly but colourfully made up. Her fingernails were quite red.

'Come in, Anthony,' she said, and she led me into a long lobby which passed from front to back of the house. Both walls were clad in dark brown panelling, against which hung many paintings in heavy gilt frames. There were several wall tables bearing vases and whatnot, and we passed five or six heavy doors. I was wondering what kind of wealth a person must have to live in such a grand house. But then I remembered that Miss Lovatt's father had been the owner of a woollen mill in Huddersfield – that and, I'd been told, other factories. When we came to the door at the farthest end of the lobby, I saw that it stood wide open, and I glanced inside to see a woman in a black dress standing gazing out of the window in there. We turned right, through a large kitchen, and came at last to the rear entrance. There, at the top of the steps which led down into the garden, Miss Lovatt paused. Coming to stand beside her, I looked out with her across the grounds.

Before us was another very large lawn, again newly mown, surrounded by banks of sycamores, limes and ancient yews. At the far side a blue and white striped marquee had been erected and close to it lay piles of things I couldn't make out.

'John just needs a little help with the tables and things,' Miss Lovatt said. 'Is that all right?'

I didn't know what she meant exactly, but I nodded. 'Yes.'

'Good.' Miss Lovatt touched my hot hand with cool fingers. 'That's kind. You're very like your mother, you know.'

'Am I? That's news to me.'

'Well you are. Now look, Anthony, if you feel you want a drink or something, you'll find milk and tea in the kitchen. And if you want something to eat there's plenty in the pantry.' She looked away. 'I can't just see John. But he'll be back soon. I'll come and see how you're going on later.'

I wandered across the lawn to the marquee, entered it, wandered about in its cool air for a moment, and then went to look at those piled-up things outside. One heap turned out to be three folded trestle tables. The other was a dozen or so folded chairs with canvas backs and seats. Opening one of them, I sat in it and gazed at the house, at the trees, and down at my trousers into which Mother had ironed sharp creases. A few more minutes passed and then Hoppalong came hopping around the side of the house. I'd learnt his name now: John.

He was wearing a grey shirt rolled up at the sleeves and floppy grey trousers – a little, fleshless, dynamo of a man. I saw that his stump had some kind of imitation boot on the end of it, articulated, flapping oddly. 'Hello, lad,' he said. 'What's your name? Thanks for coming, but I didn't really need help, you know. It's the lady – she's like that. Too kind for her own good. All we have to do is set things up. I'll show you how.

'Come on . . .'

He proved to be an agreeable man, concerned for me. 'Can you manage that? Careful – you'll trap your fingers . . .' And he was by no means silent. 'They're lucky with the weather, aren't they? How's your mother? She works like hell in this place. Miss Lovatt thinks the world of her . . . That table not quite straight, son . . . She tells me she's thinking of leaving. They'll miss her – but I don't blame her. Things've changed round here. It's not the same. But I'll soldier on. No option. What else is there for a twerp with a gammy leg . . .'

64

We were just arranging the third table against the wall of the marquee, and I managed to get a word in at last. 'You were in the war, weren't you?' I said. 'Did you get blown up?' I asked, glancing at his false boot.

'No. Trod on a mine. I was lucky. They only chopped me off at the knee.' He straightened. We'd been working without pause for half an hour and he was a bit puffed. His face was quite red. 'Too bloody hot,' he said. 'You fancy a drink of water?'

'No thanks, I'm all right.'

'Well just hang about a bit. I'll be back,' and, flapping his left boot, he hopped across the expanse of lawn, through the sunlight, and up the steps into the house.

I sat down again, but only for a moment. As I'd walked along the lobby with Miss Lovatt I'd been visited with a mild curiosity as to what might be inside those rooms behind those closed doors, and there, looking at me, were the big windows of the house ready to be peered into. Since no-one seemed to be about at the moment to see me do so, I slid across the grass.

The window I chose, to the right of the kitchen, revealed a room that was almost empty. A blue carpet on the floor, a large polished table with a silver ornament of some kind sitting on it, two more paintings on the wall, and that was it. So I sidled along to the next window. It was surrounded by dusty ivy and the room beyond was much more interesting. Bookshelves lined three walls. On the carpet, one with its back to the window and the other under a standard lamp opposite, were two vast leather armchairs. In one corner was a three-foot-high marble statue of a man in a flowing cape – Tennyson actually. But it was the books that held my attention – dozens and dozens of them, some with matching brown bindings but others of all colours, height and thickness. I put my nose almost to the glass to see if I could read any titles, and was just trying to make one out when I heard Miss Lovatt's voice behind me.

'D'you like books?'

Caught like Peeping Tom I squirmed a bit, but she gave me no reason to so do. She was smiling. 'Would you like to look at them?'

'Yes, thanks. I would.'

'Well come with me,' she said, gesturing towards the steps.

She led the way through the kitchen where John sat drinking tea, and I followed her into that treasure trove.

'I don't read a great deal now myself, I must say,' she smiled. 'It's my eyesight.' Turning in a full circle and beaming like a lighthouse at the shelves, she went on. 'My father bought most of these books from Sandways when they were knocking it down. He didn't read very much either as a matter of fact.' She gave a little laugh. 'So if you can make use of them I wish you would.'

'Thanks, Miss Lovatt.'

'Borrow what you like. Come any time. But please, do return what you borrow, won't you?'

'Yes, yes, I will.'

She glanced out of the window. 'But I see John's out there again, Anthony,' she said. 'Perhaps you'd better come back later.'

We moved towards the doorway of the room but didn't get very far. The woman I'd seen earlier, dressed in a densely black dress, suddenly confronted us. Totally ignoring me, she stood with her hands on her hips and her legs spread, frowning at Miss Lovatt.

'Jane Summers has just been on the phone,' she said.

'Has she?'

'It seems you invited her.'

'Well yes, I did,' Miss Lovatt said uneasily.

'You didn't tell me that.'

'Didn't I, Clara?'

'It was very silly of you. She's the last one we needed here this afternoon.'

Clara was no older than thirty-five, much shorter than Miss Lovatt, dark-haired and quite fleshy. The fingers of both of her hands shone yellow with gold rings. Her dress was cut low and a large gold pendant jumped about there as she spoke. 'Why on earth did you do it?'

'But Jane and I have been friends for years . . .'

'Well more fool you. I tried to put her off, but it's like trying to put off a mad wasp.'

'But I've known her so long . . .'

'Oh, Dora – you are so silly. The woman will ruin everything.'

'I don't think so.'

'I tell you she will. She's a predatory bitch . . .'

Clearly embarrassed by this, since I was standing at her side, Miss Lovatt put a hand on my shoulder. 'Excuse me, Clara . . . This is Mrs Walton's son. He's helping John.'

Clara gave me a quick, unseeing glance.

'Go along, Anthony . . .' Miss Lovatt said, very much wanting me out of the way. 'You can come and look at the books later.'

And so I went. I had no sooner left the room than Clara

was at it again. 'Well we'll have to do something about her. You can't possibly have her here overnight . . .'

John had already opened the chairs. 'We'll just spread 'em round a bit,' he said. 'Will they want them in a circle? Or shall we just leave them to sort 'em out themselves . . . ?'

We finally arranged them in a circle. Giving the scene a long look, John now seemed satisfied and we sat down together.

'By hell, it's getting hotter,' he said, taking out a hand-kerchief and draping it over his head. He waved an arm from east to west. 'What a carry-on. What's come over her? You know, I've worked here for donkey's years and nothing like this has ever happened before. What's got into the old girl?' He found a pipe, looked at it, prodded the tobacco already in there, and lit it. 'I didn't know she was like that. It's that Clara, you know. She's behind it, you bet your life. And she's a right one she is. Miss Lovatt wouldn't have thought of all this. It's that Clara . . . Poor old Dora . . . It's that damned Clara . . . She's got her where she wants her.'

'Like what?' I asked.

'Never mind son.' He blew a cloud of smoke towards me. 'All these trips she had, that must've been it.'

'What trips?'

'Never mind. She was a lovely girl when she was younger. Could've had any bloke she fancied. But there we are. Dora's got a heart of gold. What was she saying to you?'

'She's letting me borrow her books.'

'Well there you see – heart of gold. That one's going to make mincemeat out of her. What a rotten shame.'

At that moment, three women appeared on top of the

steps, Miss Lovatt and two others, both dressed as colour-fully as Miss Lovatt herself and both wearing big hats. They viewed the scene for a moment, laughed at something said, and went back inside.

'Where the hell's Tim?' John said suddenly.

'Tim?'

'Tim Beverley – the grocer from the village. He's supposed to be bringing some grub for them. That's what the tables're for in the marquee. Where is he?'

A thought then struck me. 'D'you think while we're waiting I could nip inside and get a book?'

'Why not. Go and do it.'

I ran to the house, along the lobby, and into the library. While I browsed the bookshelves, I heard women's voices, piping, laughing, as they passed the room door towards the rear garden.

There was so much on offer in that library that I was literally spoilt for choice. Most of the old brown bindings seemed to be works on theology or ancient science, but amongst the rest were complete collections of Dickens and Walter Scott, encyclopaedias, dictionaries, and atlases – enough reading to last a normal man's lifetime. I finally selected *The Vicar of Wakefield* and a volume of Lamb's essays, beautifully bound in green leather and illustrated with excellent drawings. Just as I was about to leave, I heard the sound of a motor engine and, looking out, I saw Tim Beverley's little Bedford van actually driving indiffer-ently, loftily, across the virginal lawn.

During my brief time in the library, the garden had suddenly become populated. Seven or eight people, all women, were milling about there like butterflies, chattering, smiling, waving their arms at each other. One or two glanced at me as I went back to the marquee. One or two even smiled.

Tim, big, bald-headed, loud Tim, was offloading a large wooden tray from his van. He walked with it to the entrance to the marquee, stood growling at John for a moment, then took the tray back to the van.

I drew close and he looked at me. 'What're you doing here?'

'The lad's helping out, what d'you think?' John said.

'Yes, well he can put the tablecloths out. I forgot about them. Here . . .'

I held out my arms and over them he draped sheets of folded, starched white linen. 'Spread 'em on the tables. Quick, I'm half an hour late. That bloody baker with his bloody sausage rolls . . .'

John, hopping from side to side, helped me to spread the cloths. 'Get 'em straight, lad. This way a bit . . . Smooth it out . . .' And when that was done I helped to unload three or four trays of food – including sausage rolls – serviettes, plates and cutlery.

It was hot work. When all was laid out, we three stood sweating together, taking a breather in the shade of the marquee entrance. Tim lit a cigarette, John sucked on his empty pipe. By now, several of the chairs John and I had set out were occupied by ladies, most of them also smoking. Miss Lovatt was circulating, passing from one woman to another, reaching out for their hands and putting gentle kisses on to glowing cheeks. There was an air of great camaraderie, of joyful friendliness. These women were clearly out for a pleasant afternoon.

There was a frown on Tim's face as he contemplated it all. 'What d'you think of this lot?' he asked John.

'I don't think anything,' John replied. 'It's a garden party.'

'Well I've done the catering at garden parties before, but not like this one. All women? You know what they look like to me, don't you?'

'It doesn't matter what they look like to you, does it?' John said.

'Just sort the food out.'

'They're a lot of . . .'

'Keep your thoughts to yourself, Tim. Mind your own damn business. The ladies're having a garden party.'

'They're a lot of dildo wallahs.'

'Shut your mouth, Tim. What the hell's it got to do with you? Just sort the food out . . .'

But the argument came quickly to an end because we were all now drawn to the sight of Clara who was approaching at speed, swinging stiff arms, with a purposeful rather menacing look on her face.

'Are you finished?' she asked, passing between us like a battering ram, stamping into the marquee and marching about between the tables. 'Where're the drinks – the drinks?'

'We've not got 'em out yet,' Tim said, not pleased with her.

'Well do so. Glasses?'

'Of course,' said Tim.

'Whisky? Gin? Vodka – and what about ice?'

'Half the North Pole,' said Tim.

'Well get on with it,' Clara said, turning sharply away. 'The ladies will want refreshment.'

'Yes, and she wants a bloody good going over,' Tim said, gesturing at Clara's back as she walked away.

The two men moved towards the van for the bottles of drink and I moved with them. But John took hold of my arm. 'We can manage without you now, lad. You just bugger off home.'

'You sure, John? I don't mind . . .'

'Yes, lad.' He smiled. 'You've done all right. Thanks. Buzz off out of here.'

Instead of going through the house I walked across the lawn and around the side of the house to the front. There were four cars parked in the drive now, and one was just arriving, a Vauxhall. Out of it stepped what seemed at first sight to be a man, short-haired, in a loose black coat, baggy black trousers, collar and tie. But no. On further inspection it was definitely a woman.

As she walked towards the doorway, Miss Lovatt came out, once again holding out her arms in greeting and ready to kiss. But then she saw me. Pausing for a second, she raised her arm and waved me goodbye. 'Thank you!' she called. Then she went on to meet her guest.

On the Monday, Mother handed me a twenty pound note. 'From Miss Lovatt for your help.'

'So much!' I was amazed.

It was about a fortnight before I went to swap my books for others, but while I was browsing the library I took the opportunity to consult Miss Lovatt's encyclopaedia and dictionaries in search of dildo.

It was more or less as I'd thought.

7

By the end of August, Mother found herself a new job in Leeds. At the same time she seemed to have found a new, vital version of herself. A new self-confidence had altered the way she held her head, the way she spoke, and she seemed to have been infused with a new kind of energy. Interested to see her at her new place of work I got the bus to Leeds one Saturday morning and went to seek her out.

I found her in a large ladies' clothing shop on the Headrow, then the main high-class shopping street of the town. I stepped across the threshold into a crowd of motionless, silent, haughty-faced female bodies, adorned in carefully draped dresses and coats, posing with ridiculous extensions of the arms, odd placings of feet. There was a strong leavening of perfume in the air and an overwhelming sense of femininity, which was daunting.

A polished, gliding woman, colourfully made-up and seeming to move on rails, emerged from between the mannequins and came to stand before me. She came with lowered brows and was clearly not happy to see that a gangling young male had taken the liberty of penetrating into these premises. 'Yes?' she asked, sharply. 'What is it?'

'I'd like to see my mother, please.'

'Oh. Is she shopping here?'

'She works here.'

'Oh. I see.'

'Mrs Walton.'

'Oh – Mrs Walton.' She still disapproved of me, but, hesitating only a moment longer, she said, 'This way . . .'

With other women, assistants and shoppers, giving me wondering looks, we went through a glittering silver-meshed screen into another silent, motionless crowd of bodies, now semi-naked, dressed only in shining pink knickers, shining pink brassieres, shining pink corsets, and frilly things like sword belts with dangling suspenders.

Dodging and weaving between these shapes, we came to Mother at last. She was standing at a table folding something.

'Your son's here, Mrs Walton.'

She was surprised and not very pleased. 'Tony – what're you doing here!'

'I came to have a look at you.'

'Well you shouldn't've done.' Mother looked at the other woman and said, apologetically, 'Thanks, Jean. He won't be here long.'

'Yes, well we are a bit busy,' said Jean, turning away.

'Well!' Mother now smiled at me. 'So you found me, you pest.' She gave me a quick kiss. 'You can come into my cubby hole for a minute. But I'm here to work, not chat to visitors.'

The cubby hole smelt even stronger of perfume. In it, there, on its thick pink carpet, were two hard-backed chairs and a bench littered with more shiny pink things. Dangling from the wall, obscuring a calendar, was an outlandish interloper, not pink at all but pure white – a brassiere with bulging cups, exactly like one of David's slings waiting for his encounter with Goliath. As I sat down my hand brushed against something soft and silky. I snatched it away as if it had been stung.

'I've got half a cup of coffee left here – going cold,' Mother said, offering it to me. 'You can finish it off and get going. You weren't up when I left this morning.'

'No. I was a bit tired.'

'Why? What were you doing yesterday?'

'Maths and a dollop of other homework.'

'Have you had any breakfast?'

'Some porridge.'

'When I ask you if you want porridge you turn your nose up.'

'I thought I'd fight it. This is a very posh kind of place, Mother.'

'It's lovely. Everyone's so civilised here, so nice. I love it.'

'You look as if you do.'

In fact she looked lovely herself, I thought, radiant with that new personality of hers, with her neat body and her bright face, and wearing a red frock which had come from this very shop.

'This coffee's a bit grim. Don't you have tea here?'

'You're going to drink coffee at home.'

'Am I?'

'Yes.'

'Oh. Do any of these people want to buy tomatoes?'

'No.'

'Oh. Anyway, Mother, I know where you are now, don't I?'

'Yes. So come on, go home. There're ladies out there waiting to be served.'

I was happy to see her so perky and full of life these days, and I sensed that there could well be a kind of delight for a woman to find herself working in that shop, surrounded by fancy dresses and lovely people, as she'd described them.

But I was well aware that the shop had not been the only thing to wreak the changes in her. There was that new friendship of hers – that mysterious woman she said she'd once worked with. Who was she? I had no idea. I'd never been given the chance to see her. When setting out to meet her, often on a Sunday, sometimes on a Wednesday afternoon when her shop had half-day closing, Mother went to see her on the bus, but why did the woman never take the bus in the opposite direction and come here? Why was I not allowed to meet her?

And there were other things. Mother seemed so very concerned about her appearance when setting out to meet the woman. She stood before me, dressed to the nines, 'How do I look?' 'How's my hair? Do I look a bit pale? Do my feet look big in these shoes? You sure this dress really does suit me?'

She always looked immaculate but we still had to go through the ritual. Unlike me, she took a bath most evenings, but she would always take one just before she was due to go out.

And all these things were not lost on me. I had long since come to the firm belief that there was, in fact, no woman. What was lighting her life now was a man, a man, obviously – and I knew who he was.

Sam had called several times – never to bring the Redskins – but always to sit and talk to Mother. A day or two before I'd visited Mother's shop he'd turned up with a plate rack he'd made for her himself. He must have been an excellent part-time carpenter because it was expertly jointed and beautifully stained. He brought a big hammer and a bit, punctured two holes in the kitchen wall, plugged them with bits of wood, and mounted the rack only after much messing about with a spirit level. Thereafter, as always, I was ignored. I went up to my room to record the daily news in my book.

She must have been well aware that I actually liked Sam. So why couldn't she just tell me the truth? Did she think I'd see it as a betrayal of my father and throw a tantrum? At my age? Did she think, knowing of my inclination towards a belief in God, that I would think of it as some kind of sin? Didn't she know that I was happy for her and that her own happiness these days had come as a blessing to me?

'D'you like my new perm?' And her dressing table in her bedroom was creaking under bottles, tubes, tubs of all kinds of make-up such as you'd never seen there before. She really was looking most attractive these days, and I was proud of her.

The summer was drawing towards its end. The tomato crop was by now more or less exhausted and only the last poor specimens remained on the trusses. I collected about a pound and a half and decided to take them down to one of my best customers, Mary Swallow. I liked her and I would also be able to say hello to Emma Sarah. I put the tomatoes into the wicker basket which had been fitted to the handlebars of my bike for this logistical purpose, and I was just pedalling down the lane, almost at my destination, when I heard the hiss and puff of another cyclist behind me.

'Hang on . . . !' It was Gerald. 'Stop!' he said. 'Pull up . . .'

He was sweating. 'You look hot,' I said.

'I've been chasing after you. I shouted you.'

'I didn't hear.'

'No, you're deaf.' He looked into the basket. 'On your rounds, are you? – Well look, how about coming up after tea . . . ?'

He paused. Something had attracted his eye. He was looking towards the farm. Gazing in that direction myself I saw that Emma Sarah's antenna must have been active that morning, for there she was, standing a few yards away at the farmhouse gate, waving at me.

I waved back.

'What do they call that kid?' Gerald asked.

'Her name's Emma.'

'Emma, that's right. Daft as a brush.'

'Come off it, Connolly. The kid can't help it.'

He gave me one of his long examinations. 'Sorry, Bony. Forgive me for breathing.'

'What were you saying?'

'Come up after tea. It might be interesting. You know my sister plays the fiddle – or murders it rather – well two of her mates do the same. They're going to crucify everybody at a school concert and they're having a practice at home tonight. The oldies're going to the pictures in town out of the way. It could be hell.'

'Well why put me through it?'

'These mates of hers are on the nifty side, Bony. At least, one of 'em is.'

'Oh – that's it.'

'No . . . I thought you'd find it a bit of fun.'

'Oh all right. But no chess.'

'No chess. I'm fed up with it.'

'Good. All right. What time?'

'They're turning up at six. Don't be late.'

He pedalled off back towards the village and I went on to join Emma Sarah at the farm gate. As I came close, she did two little jumps. Together, we entered the house at the back door and turned into the kitchen where there was a powerful smell of roasting beef. Mary, her mother, standing on a low stool, was just washing the window. From one of the beams in the ceiling hung a large ham and, alongside it, two strings of onions.

'I've brought you some tomatoes, Mrs Swallow.'

'Oh thanks, Tony. Hang on.' She did two or three more strokes with her chamois and got down. 'I'll find some money . . .'

'No – I don't want anything.'

'Don't you?'

'No. They're the last few left. They're ok but I think I'd just use them for cooking. See . . .' I opened one of the bags. 'Two or three've split. I must've over fed 'em. I don't want paying.'

'Well thanks, Tony. I'll tell you what, we'll do a swop. You can have a dozen eggs.' Mary turned to look at her daughter, who was standing close. 'Emma's been doing some drawing, haven't you, love?'

Emma nodded with enthusiasm.

'Well fetch it,' Mary said. 'Show Tony.'

Darting away with her skirt fluttering, Emma Sarah disappeared and returned with a sheet of paper, which she carried very carefully and spread out on the table. Emma Sarah drew very slowly, very gently, concentrating hard – not with pencil or pen but with those wax crayons which tended to snap in everyone else's hands. The lines she made were thin, pale, yet quite steady. Proudly, she stood back for me to see her work.

There were three coloured sketches – a cat, drawn the way I'd shown her, and two figures, both with large heads, wide beaming smiles, and plenty of hair. On one was a red triangle dress from which two spindly legs descended. But I'd shown her how to draw feet in perspective and she'd remembered it well.

'Excellent, Emma. That's great,' I said.

She beamed like one of her drawings.

Mary came to the table. Pointing a finger at the drawing with the red triangle dress, she said, 'Tell him who that is.'

'It's you, Mam,' Emma Sarah said.

'And who's that with the feet?'

'It's Tony.'

In fact it was almost half-past six when I arrived at Gerald's that evening. He was in the kitchen just finishing eating what might have been a pork pie. The rehearsal had already started. You could hear the wailing of violins coming from the living room.

'You're late. They're already at it.'

'It sounds like it.'

'Well come on . . .'

Innocence

All three girls were standing up, fiddling away, with that enrapt, soulful look you often see on musicians' faces. Gerald's sister, Margaret, slim and supple, was wearing a thin linen skirt, blue, and a blue jumper which in no way attempted to obscure her well-developed breasts. She had let her fair hair grow long. It trembled on her shoulders. Her lips were moving. She was counting time and there was something about her that made me feel a warm sympathy for her. She was a very nice girl, I thought.

Of the other two girls, one was short and plump, dark-haired, rather lugubrious looking. This turned out to be Liz. The other was Julia, tall, blonde, blue-eyed, quite a beauty, erect and distinctly proud of herself.

As Gerald and I entered the room the music stopped, all three lowered their violins, and there came a concerted groan.

'Did someone send for you, Gerald?' Julia asked.

Gerald ignored that. 'Sorry to interrupt, girls, but Bony here heard your super music and wanted to come and listen. With your permission we'll just sit down.'

'But you haven't got our permission,' Julia said, standing high and waving her violin bow at him. 'Vanish.'

'Yes, Gerald,' Margaret said. 'Go away.'

'Yes,' Liz said. 'Buzz off.'

Gerald made a performance of recoiling as if deeply wounded. 'We've not got the plague, you know.'

'Yes you have,' said Julia.

'Now come on, girls. Look at Bony. You've offended him.'

The girls could actually see me grinning. But I thought it only fair to back Gerald up and I straightened my face at once.

'What's his name?' little Liz asked.

'His mother hated him so she called him Anthony . . . He's a great music lover, he really is. What is it you're playing?'

'It's Brahms if you must know.'

'Well there you are, you see. He knew it was Brahms. He said, "That's Brahms," didn't you, Bony? He thinks Brahms is great. He's always on about old Brahms.'

'Are you?' Julia asked, looking closely at me. 'Is he telling the truth?'

I could only say yes.

'Well that's nice,' Julia said.

'Look, girls,' Gerald pressed on. 'Let him listen.'

Julia smiled at me now, with her blue eyes showing interest. 'Hungarian Dance number two. You probably know it.'

'Good,' I said.

The girls looked at one another. Then they looked at me. I smiled. Then they looked at one another again and, with little nods, apparently agreed to relent.

'Well just keep quiet, please,' Julia said.

Margaret spoke, turning to her brother. 'Don't say a word, Gerald. You hear? If you're going to sit down, sit. All right, girls, just ignore him.'

When talking at Gerald and when dealing with her pals, Margaret was quite positive, assertive – a definite personality. But when at one point she furtively turned to me and saw that I was looking back at her, she gave me her usual feeble little smile. She was as uneasy with me as ever.

'I could make a quartet of it on the piano,' Gerald said.

'Will you please shut up!' said Julia.

All three of them attended the girls' high school in town. Julia and Liz were wearing the school blazer, bright green with yellow piping, with badges emblazoned with some kind of symbol which I couldn't make out. As it happened, they played remarkably well. Julia was obviously in command. It was she who, poking her bow into the air, interrupted things now and then to point out nuances and to remark on wrong notes. She was clearly fond of her two friends. Indeed, they all seemed fond of one another. As they played, so very seriously, their gazes met, they smiled. It was very pleasant to watch it.

Gerald lounged on the sofa and quickly became bored. He shifted his feet, scratched his head. But it was manifest where his interest actually lay. His gaze was fixed almost constantly on Julia, who was very aware of it and obviously not pleased. She would not let herself look back at him.

They played on for about a quarter of an hour and then paused for tea. The girls bustled away into the kitchen and Gerald, keeping close to Julia, went with them. I preferred to remain where I was, by the window, while the pot Alsatian dog on the dresser glowered harmlessly at me. I could hear Gerald's rumbling voice and the shrill cries of female irritation which kept drowning it.

At last, with their cups of tea, they returned to the living room. Margaret carried two – one of them for me. 'Here, Tony,' she said, in that restrained voice she used when speaking to me. Since all the other seats had been taken, she had no option but to sit quite close to me on a stiff dining chair. At once she seemed to feel a cold emanation from me, for she shifted slightly in her seat.

Gerald, sitting on a stool at Julia's feet, was doing his

best to attract her attention. 'I was going to tell you about Annie Evans, Julia . . .'

But Julia was still pointedly not looking at him. She insisted on ignoring him and talking to Liz.

Margaret, two feet from me, sipped her tea, stared now at the picture of Mont Blanc on the wall opposite, now at the carpet, and said nothing. That peculiar, distant attitude she'd always shown towards me had puzzled me for months. I'd once thought that perhaps she was a shy kind of girl, but having seen her behaviour this evening I could no longer think that. But she was there, next to me, and I felt obliged to say something.

'You can play very well, Margaret,' I said.

She gave me only the shortest glance. 'You don't mean that.'

'Yes I do. Haven't I been watching you? You're good.'

'Really?'

'Yes.'

'Honestly.'

'Really and honestly.'

'Well thank you,' she said. Now, at last, she allowed herself to show me her face with its nice eyes and smooth cheeks. That little smile passed briefly across it. Then she turned away again.

'Are your two friends in your form at school?' I asked.

'Liz is, but Julia's one up. She's six months older than me.'

'Ah.' For the moment I couldn't think of anything else to say and so silence fell between us.

Meanwhile, Julia nattered at Gerald. 'I don't like you sitting there with your big hands jumping about,' she was saying. 'Could you go and drown yourself in the river, please?'

After a few more minutes, the silence between Margaret and me once again became awkward, so I sought for something else to break it. 'You don't like me very much, do you, Margaret.'

It seemed to give her a start. She darted another glance at me. 'Well you don't like me, so what's the difference?'

'Who said I didn't like you?'

'Well it's obvious.'

'Well if it's obvious, it's a lie,' I said.

'Oh.' She gave that thought. 'Is it?'

'Yes.'

'Oh.' Raising her head she looked me in the eye. 'I'm sorry.'

'What're you sorry for?'

'I don't really know.'

'If you don't dislike me, why do you always dash off when I turn up?' I asked.

'I don't.'

'Yes you do.'

'Well I'm sorry.'

'Are you?'

'Yes.'

'Good. Then don't do it again.'

'Well I won't.'

Suddenly her whole attitude had changed. She looked at me for a long moment, gave me a warm, friendly smile such as I'd never had from her before, and still went on looking at me. It was as if, having never let herself really see me, she now wanted to see all she could. 'I've known you a long time,' she said.

'Yes.'

'Always with my brother.'

'Yes, we've been pals for ages.'

Her gaze dropped. She grew thoughtful for a moment and sipped her tea. She stroked her hair. 'You're nothing like him, are you?'

'Aren't I?'

'No. Not a bit.'

'I don't get you.'

'I'm just saying you're different.'

'So what?'

'Well . . .' She hesitated.

'Well what, Margaret?'

'You seem so . . . so . . . Well, I don't know. You're not like any boy I know . . . I can't say it any other way.'

'Oh come on, Margaret!'

Again she was looking at me, quite without any restraint, trying to make me understand what she was saying.

But I couldn't understand and this was disturbing me – annoying me in a way, so I changed the subject. 'Actually,' I said, 'I don't know a thing about Brahms.'

'Don't you?'

'No. Not a sausage.'

She found that very amusing. She laughed, and I laughed with her, after which we went on smiling at each other. The ice had been broken between Margaret and me.

'Right girls!' Julia said, standing up. 'Back to work. Gerald, get from under my feet.'

At about nine, the rehearsal broke up. Liz and Julia went to catch the bus and Gerald escorted them.

'I'm off up to my room, Tony,' Margaret said. 'You don't mind, do you?'

'Of course not.'

'I have some work to do – blinking chemistry.'

'Well I wish you luck.'

'You'll be coming again soon, won't you?' she asked.

'I suppose so.'

'Good.' And she went up the stairs.

When Gerald came back, he grabbed my arm and led me into the kitchen. 'Fancy a sandwich?'

'No thanks. I'll have something when I get home.'

He began work on a loaf, slicing off two thick pieces. Then he went into cupboards, slid his hand along shelves. 'Sod it. I'll have to have jam. Sit down.'

Chewing, he asked, 'Well, what did you think of her?'

'Who?'

'Julia, man. Isn't she a bit of all right?'

'She is,' I said.

'I've been trying to pin her down for ages and I think I've cracked her shell tonight.'

'You could've fooled me.'

'What d'you mean?' he asked, frowning.

'She thinks you stink.'

'Don't be stupid, Bony.'

'You got up her wick, man. You could see that.'

'Well perhaps you *thought* you could see it, but you don't know a thing about girls. I tell you, Bony, I've got her under my spell.'

I laughed. 'She looked as though she was going to spit in your eye at any minute.'

'You know, Bony, you really are an uttermost dope. It's all a show. That's how the female of the species is. I've been swotting things up. I've got a great book stashed away upstairs which explains it all in very interesting detail. It's all about how they work, from inside out – periods, ovaries, fallopian tubes and whatnot – and how they tick. They work in cycles, Bony. I've seen it in my sister. They're up, they're down, they're all over the place.'

'Well whatever place Julia was in tonight she didn't want you there,' I said. 'You could see her brain working.'

'But that's it, man. Their brains don't matter. It's all these hormones and stuff. At certain times their hormones go dormant, but at others they go berserk and it's then you can get at 'em. That's how it works. That's when you can get at it.'

'Get at what?'

'Oh hell, Bony! Into their shirts, man, up their knicker legs.'

'Oh, that.' I was laughing at him.

'What's funny?'

'You've been after shirts and knicker legs as long as I've known you. Not so easy, though, is it?'

'I'm just telling you, I've got the hang of it now. You have to wait till the right moment comes, when their hormones're swarming like bees, then you strike. Julia was in the dormant stage tonight. It was one of those times when her brain really was working. But I've got to her. When the moment comes they just can't help themselves, Bony, the man says. They get all excited. Oestrous the man calls it. It's a good word that, don't you think? Oestrus. Things happen to them. They go into heat – a bit like female dogs I suppose. I'll give her a week – and then see what happens.'

'Nothing will happen,' I said. 'Just like all the other girls you've told me about.'

'Ah, well I've not told you everything, have I? I know the way round a pair of tits like the back of my hand and I can undo a brassiere as quick as a flash.'

'So you've undone Julia's brassiere as quick as a flash have you?'

'Well no. Not yet. She won't even let me get at her buttons. But it's only a matter of time, Bony.' He smiled and nodded and finished the last bit of his sandwich. 'I'm clued up now. I'll dog her footsteps till the moment comes. I'm going to make some tea. Want some?'

'No thanks, Connolly. I'd better get home.'

'Right. Look, borrow that book. You'll learn a lot. Hang about and I'll get it for you.'

'No thanks, Gerald. I don't think I'm in the mood for fallopian tubes.'

'You're such a deadleg, Bony. You really are. Right, well sod off. See you at school on Monday.'

8

Next day, Sunday, I slept late, as I often find myself doing. I opened my eyes at about noon to be dazzled by a brilliant beam of sunlight full of dancing motes. Feeling an urgent need for the lavatory, I dressed quickly and went along the landing to the bathroom, only to find the door locked. Mother was bathing again. I knocked impatiently at the door.

'I won't be a minute!' she cried.

'Well hurry up, Mother.'

I heard water running briefly. I heard the gurgling as the bath emptied itself, and then Mother opened the door. She was wrapped in a green bath towel knotted under her chin and had that ridiculous bathing cap over her hair.

'You didn't give me time to wipe the bath,' she said, all pink and hot. 'Will you do it for me?'

I went into the steam and the sweet smell of toilet soap. She had left a pair of white briefs by the side of the bath.

Over my cornflakes I glanced through the *Daily Express*, and snipped out a few cuttings for my notebook. I had planned to spend some time in the greenhouse, cutting down the wasted plants and tidying up in there, but as I drank my tea she came in to me and presented herself, wearing one of her new frocks and looking a treat.

'How's my hair? Do I look all right?'

'You look fine, Mother.'

It was then that I changed my mind as to what I might do that afternoon. If she was going off somewhere, so would I.

I went with her to the door and watched her to the bus stop. We waved.

Since this shining day might well be the last of this Indian summer, I'd decided on another safari, as my father had always called our marching excursions. At so late in the day my choice of destination was limited. Digging out the maps, I selected one that I thought I could reach in about two hours. It was there, marked by my father with a black dot within a red circle – the crossroads near a grove of trees called Foster's Wood in the middle of nowhere.

We'd been there before and I could recollect the actual crossroads, but the walk proved more taxing than I remembered. It was across the river by the packhorse bridge and on through two valleys, mostly by way of cultivated fields. Some had already been ploughed after cropping and one or two were stubble after harvest, but many were still flourishing. I was obliged to find my way around them, and this involved many pauses for fresh compass bearings. It was well after three o'clock before I reached the crossroads.

The scene was utterly deserted. All that could be seen along all four of the narrow roads was sun-filled dust, glittering specks here and there in the grey tarmac, the black shadow of overhanging branches, and low dry-stone walls almost hidden behind scrambling roadside weeds in their last throes of the season.

Foster's Wood occupied the angle of the roads between north and west and covered at least two or three acres. It was mostly mature elm and beech, closely packed, but there was a dense undergrowth of hawthorn and elder. In places, the finger of approaching autumn had touched a leaf with colour. Beyond an open five-barred gate was a track which disappeared away though a tunnel of darkness. For a moment I considered following it, but I changed my mind. Tucked in among the trees down there, barely to be made out, was a shape which might have been a car, a tractor – a vehicle of some kind. But I was ready for my snack and my drink, so I went into a field and followed the wall which skirted the edge of the wood. Over the years, parts of the wall had crumpled away. Here it was six feet high, there, in a jumble of fallen stones, it was reduced to three or four. Walking on for about a hundred yards to a place well away from the road, I sat down with my back to the wall and took a drink from my bottle of water. I opened my parcel of sandwiches.

All was deadly quiet – no song of birds, not even a buzz of insects, not even a whisper from the trees. I'd put Bovril on my sandwiches. I was hungry and I wolfed them. Then, doing the right thing, screwing up the wrapper and putting it into the haversack with the emptied pop bottle, I leant back with my knees up and listened to nothing. A few minutes went by and then something startled me. I heard a man's voice some little distance away over the wall – a kind of snapping, high-pitched complaint. A fraction of a second later I was even more startled to hear a woman's voice, very much closer, replying to it in a giggling little scream. 'Give me a minute!'

Naturally very curious, I decided to see what was happening. Careful not to let myself be observed, I moved a foot or two to my right until I found a gap between the uneven stones and peered through it into the wood. There, only a few yards away, I saw a woman, with something like a plaid car rug draped over her shoulders, crouching among the weeds facing me. The rug indeed covered her shoulders and her arms but otherwise she was quite naked and exposed as she crouched, looking down, over in the grass. The sight of her white dangling breasts, the heavy fullness of flesh, immediately thrust into me, like a spear, a most powerful sensation of breath-stopping shock mingled with a sudden excited, prurient fascination.

The male voice came again, like a quick exclamation mark, and the woman now raised her head. 'Let me finish!'

My breathing stopped. I froze. Oh God . . . it was my mother, my mother!

Shattered, racked with another kind of shock, ashamed and painfully guilty to have seen my mother exposed like that, to have had those erotic feelings I'd had at the sight of her, I fell back into the weeds. My heart went on thudding. I screwed up my eyes and clenched my fists with emotion. 'Oh Mother!' I thought. 'Oh Mother, I'm sorry – I'm sorry.'

Then I heard her voice again, laughing. 'There's nettles here.'

And now I heard the man's voice – clearly enough this time. He must have come to fetch her. 'Have you done, have you done!'

Yet another shock struck me. That wasn't Sam's voice – surely not Sam's voice.

It came again. 'I bet there's a flood here. Come on.'

I recognised it now without any doubt at all. It was Hector Swallow's loud, bold, grating tones.

There came more giggling and grating and then silence as they returned to their nest in the trees.

It was some time before I felt able to move my limbs. But at last, I got up. I walked back under the wall, back to the road, into the field at the other side, and on towards home, moving I suppose like a zombie because I was aware of nothing but the agonising sight of my mother and the heart-aching sound of their voices.

She came home quite early – at about seven o'clock, looking hot and happy. 'Hasn't it been a beautiful day!' she said. She went to her room and came down with her face washed and her hair brushed and in a different frock without her silk stockings. 'What's the matter with you?' she asked.

'Nothing.'

'Well give me a smile. That's better.' She kissed me. 'Have you had anything to eat?'

'Yes. I have.'

'What've you done today?'

'Not much.'

'And what d'you plan to do this evening?'

'Not much.'

'Well I'll let you get on with it,' she said, making for the kitchen.

9

That episode in Foster's Wood had affected me deeply. I had never liked Hector Swallow and now I detested him. The thought of seeing his face angered me and for some time I couldn't bring myself to go anywhere near the farm. I'd also been at pains to avoid his daughter, but on arriving home from school one afternoon and going round to the back door, I heard Emma Sarah calling to me. She'd been waiting for me in the greenhouse out of the cold. She stood in a thick green coat, long scarf and ear-covering bonnet, looking forlornly at me, wondering at me because I'd allowed her so fleeting glimpses of late.

In her tentative, almost apologetic way, Emma Sarah held out a hand and gave me a little parcel wrapped in brown paper. It was one of the linen bags, embroidered with a flower, which she'd made at school. I already had a collection of them. 'Thank you, Emma Sarah,' I said. 'Are you all right.'

'Yes. I'm here.'

'So I see.'

I took her into the house and let her sit at the table while I cut myself a piece of bread and made us a drink. I could think of little to say to her but she watched me intently, smiling when I looked into her face. In fact, I looked into it many times while we sat there. These past weeks had been our longest separation since the beginning of our friendship. The episode of her father with my mother had made the thought of visiting the farm, of seeing the man, of seeing anyone connected with him, intolerable. I resented even Emma Sarah. But in her presence my heart softened. She had taken off her coat, her plump arms rested on the table, and the look of pleasure at being with me that glowed in her eyes very much moved me.

I reached out and touched her hand. She opened it and clenched my fingers. 'Don't leave me,' she said.

'Don't be daft, Emma Sarah. I've not left you. But I've had a lot of things to do. I won't be able to come to your house I'm afraid . . .'

'Why – why!'

'Because I can't . . .'

'Why – why!' she asked again.

'Look, Emma Sarah, I'm still your friend. We'll see each other now and then. We've seen each other today, haven't we? But you must not, *not* come here again. If your father knew he'd go crazy.'

Her fingers tightened over mine. 'I've drawn a ship and a lovely flower and all that today.'

'Good.'

She pulled at my hand and her lips trembled. 'Don't leave me . . .' And now the tears began to flow. Her free hand fluttered, she leant across the table to appeal directly into my face. Her cheeks sank. She was distraught and, as always, I could not endure it.

'Look, I'll come down and see you and your mother.'

'When? When?' she demanded, pulling hard at my hand again.

'Soon, Emma Sarah. Soon.'

'Promise, promise.'

'I promise.'

She rolled her head with relief. She gave one of her little squeaks. 'Lovely!' Then, letting go of my hand, she brushed away the tears, and smiled. 'When, when, when?'

'I've told you. As soon as I can.'

'Lovely.' She danced about in her chair. 'When, when?'

'Soon, soon, soon.'

Suddenly, her happy smile grew rigid. She put her thumb into her mouth and an alarmed look came into her eyes. A second passed, then she jumped to her feet, put her hands to the sides of her head and exclaimed, 'I want to wee!'

'Well I can't help you with that, Emma Sarah,' I said, and, darting into the lobby, she ran up the stairs at top speed.

When she came back to the kitchen she stood in the doorway and looked at me for a long moment, as if remembering what had been said.

I took her coat to her. 'Get this on. And leg it home as fast as you went up those stairs or you'll get shouted at.'

She resisted, straightening her arms so that I couldn't get the coat on her. 'When're you coming? When're you coming?'

'As soon as I can. Let me get your blinking coat on! Lower your arms. Here, put your hat on . . . Put your scarf on . . . Now scoot!'

'When?' she asked as I bundled her out of the door. 'When're you coming?'

* * *

I had wanted very much to see Margaret Connolly again and the chance came a bit later, actually during Christmas week. I was invited to her girls' school annual concert. I went with the rest of her family – Conrad, Aggie and of course Gerald. He sat next to me.

Despite the banter, brother and sister were as fond of each other as they ought to have been. 'The thing about our Maggie, you know, Bony,' Gerald said, 'is that she puts her heart and soul into everything she does. She swots like hell, she plays netball like a demon and fiddles that fiddle for all she's worth. I think she'll be great tonight.'

First the school orchestra came on to the stage in black dresses, carrying their instruments, filing in military order to the laid-out chairs, standing till they'd all gathered and then, as if at a sharp command, sitting smartly down. One of the two girls with cellos accidentally twanged a bottom C and could be seen to wince. In came the conductor, a most weighty woman in a dress which reached to the floor. She nodded at the audience, turned to the orchestra, lifted her baton, brought it down – and the music which thereafter filled all the spaces of the hall was so confident, so accurate, so unexpectedly disciplined that the whole audience must surely have been as impressed as I was myself. 'The entrance of the Queen of Sheba,' said the programme. I was familiar with it from my avid listening to music on the wireless, but here, live, played so well by those pink-faced girls, it completely entranced me.

They played two more short pieces, just as competently, to rapturous hand-clapping, and the curtain fell. A few moments passed while the stage was cleared, and then, with that same head-high walk, again in black dresses, on came the three girls, Julia leading, Margaret following, and little Liz marching after. They stood side by side centre stage and bowed graciously to acknowledge the applause that had greeted them. Then, at the same moment, with crisp movements, like soldiers at a well-practised drill, they raised their violins. They looked at one another for a second, Julia nodded – one, two, three – and full-blooded Brahms, in perfect three-part harmony, gripped the audience by the heart.

Gerald sat with a great smile on his face. 'That's our Maggie!' he whispered, proud as Punch.

When the performance was over and the girls gave their low bows, hair falling over faces, there was more unrestrained applause.

We sat through another short break while a piano was trundled on to the stage. During it, I looked at Gerald.

'I suppose you'll be nipping round to see Julia when it's all over,' I said, baiting him.

'Julia? Don't be daft, Bony. I've left her behind. But just look round.'

I did as he asked and took in that large, smiling audience – many parents, but overwhelmingly girls, girls, girls, of all ages from twelve to eighteen. 'What about it?' I asked.

'Think of all those hormones floating about in here, Bony. Can't you sniff it?'

A very tiny black-dressed girl whose arms seemed too short to cope with all the keys, sat at the piano and played some Chopin and a bit of Schubert, stumbling here and there, but brave, fighting on, chewing her lower lip, and sighing with relief when it was all over. The sympathetic applause was as loud as ever. Finally, the orchestra played some Mozart and the national anthem. The lights in the hall went up and we all tripped out into the school yard. Julia and Liz no doubt went to join their own people and Margaret, smiling, obviously satisfied with the evening, came running directly into her mother's outstretched arms.

'It was beautiful, love. Beautiful.'

'Aye it was grand,' said Conrad, waiting for his daughter to be released by her mother and embracing her himself. 'Worth all the effort – grand, lovely. Give us a kiss . . .'

Her father's moustache must have tickled Margaret's nose. As she parted from him she scratched it. Now she turned to look at her brother. He stood rigid, aloof, as if unwilling to go anywhere near her, staring at her with an ugly sort of frown.

'Well, Gerald?' she asked. I saw that she was surprised by his manner. 'Well?'

'It was awful, terrible,' Gerald growled. 'Rotten, grim. Sickening . . .'

It struck home. Her face fell. Gerald frowned on for a tense moment and then, almost doubling with amusement, he gave a loud guffaw, stepped to her and almost crushed her ribs.

We went back to the village together on the bus. Gerald expected me to sit with him, but I didn't. Very much wanting her to know how much I'd enjoyed her perfor-mance – and indeed mighty proud of her – I sat next to Margaret. I told her what I felt.

'Thanks, Tony. We were lucky. It was one of those times when things go just right. It doesn't always happen, does it?'

'It made my hair stand on end,' I said. 'It really did.'

She laughed. 'I wish I'd seen that.'

The bus drove on through a moonless, icy night, out of Leeds and into the countryside.

On Christmas day, Sam joined Mother and me for dinner. Indeed, Sam had provided the meat – a joint of sirloin. He brought a large bottle of sherry with him, also, and a large box of crackers. Mother had bought the tree in Leeds, a small one but now, after much standing back and many second-thoughts, decorated by her, draped with tinsel, baubles and little parcels to the point of invisibility. The living room was festooned with streamers, there was a roaring fire, and Mother had done her very best to achieve an atmosphere of uttermost festivity. She, too, had brought home crackers and after the meal a good half-hour was spent snapping them apart and laughing at the jokes, all the more amusing because they were so naive. Half of the sherry was drunk and Mother's eyes began to shine.

Replete, wearing those ridiculous paper crowns from the crackers, we sat slumped for half an hour and watched the television. Then Sam went into the hall and came back with a game of Monopoly. 'We'll enjoy this,' he said in his outlandish southern accent, holding up the box for us to see.

We sat at the table, spread the Monopoly board, and set out to bankrupt each other. Mother was uncertain about the game, nervous about spending money and missed an opportunity to buy.

'That was a mistake, Daisy,' Sam said. 'Go back and buy Fenchurch Street, love.'

I protested, 'No, she's missed the chance.'

'Well she's not learnt yet. She can buy Fenchurch Street.'

'That's not fair,' I said.

'Now come on, Tony,' Sam said, quite seriously. 'Don't be like that. You can buy Fenchurch Street, Daisy.'

'Thank you, Sam,' she said, pulling a face at me, tapping Sam's hand, smiling at him.

Ever since they'd met there had been between Mother and Sam this same easy, warm rapport. Watching them now as they played – she sometimes looking at him for approval when she moved, he nodding or shaking his head – I saw again the signs which had led to my assumption that Sam was the man she'd been seeing. Sam's attentiveness was touching. His manner in addressing her was concerned. Whenever he looked at her he smiled, his eyes searched hers, and, just like a doting husband, he had that way of surrounding her with himself. He was clearly in love with her.

But this Christmas afternoon, despite her affection for him, despite her happy response to him, it also became clear, through subtle nuances, that she did not love him. There were moments, noticeable to me now, when, under the emotional weight of him, she ever so slightly stiffened, drew back a fraction of an inch from him, did not smile so easily.

I noticed furthermore that Sam himself was very obviously aware of these gentle rebuffs. His expression fluttered, he himself drew ever so slightly back. 'Very well, Daisy . . . All right . . .' Sam smoked a lot. By evening the room was full of it. We finished the Monopoly – I losing as always at games – had Christmas cake and more sherry for tea, listened again to the wireless and at half past eleven Sam said, 'Well I suppose I'd better be off.'

When he'd put on his great overcoat and flat cap and

scarf, Mother gave him a quick kiss on the cheek. I went with him to the door and watched him get on to his motor-bike. It was another icy night.

As he rode away his tail-light flickered. Perhaps there was a loose wire.

On the Friday, Mother went back to work – apparently the sales had started at the shop and, after a poor autumn, they were hoping for improved business. I had almost a fortnight's holidays to get through.

On the Saturday, I went to Cromford House to change my books, entering by the back door. Mother had been replaced here as dogsbody by Alma, a very thin, wild-haired woman in her fifties from the village. I felt quite sorry for Alma. She had a little pale face, nervous hands, and very large feet. She always wore a green overall supplied by Miss Lovatt which seemed never to be buttoned correctly, and she had an agitated, harassed air at all times of day. I'd drunk tea with her and talked to her. Her husband and daughter were both out of work and hers was the only money going into the house. She'd made that clear at once. 'But you can't let these things get you down,' she'd said, and I could see that she was trying not to. While drinking her tea she jumped up and down, moved to the pantry, darted to the door, spent moments gazing into space wondering what she ought to be doing, but kept a deter-mined, eager look on her face.

'Can I help you?' I'd asked.

'Oh no, no, no . . .'

As, on this Saturday morning, I walked along the lobby, she was dusting one of the tables. She gave me a wave.

Winter sunlight flooded into the library. I'd been asked by Miss Lovatt to catalogue her collection and had got about one third of the way through, so I knew where to look for what I wanted – *The Good Companions* by J. B. Priestley and another work of his which I'd heard about, *English Journey*.

There was no heating in the library and, though I was well accoutered for winter, I had no wish to sit about. I replaced my old books where they belonged and, putting the two I'd selected into the brown paper carrier bag I'd brought, I made to leave.

Just then, Miss Lovatt's friend Clara entered the room, smiling. I now noticed that she had very dark brown, rather small eyes. I could hardly miss them because they were gazing at me intently, into my face and then up and down my body. She had seen me many times, and this close scrutiny set me wondering. 'Hello,' I said.

She went on staring. A kind of smile had appeared, not unpleasant but rather disconcerting. She had a red ribbon in her hair and at her throat dangled that pendant which was always there. She was wearing red high heeled shoes. 'You were here last week,' she said.

'Yes.'

'You must read like an express train.'

'I suppose I do.'

She reached out and, with her fleshy, be-ringed fingers, brushed something from my overcoat sleeve. 'How old are you?'

'I'm seventeen.'

'A rampaging adolescent.'

'Pardon?'

She laughed – one of those rather superior things that don't wish to harm but which irritate all the same. She looked at the carrier bag. 'What books're you taking?'

I told her.

'Mmnnn . . . Well, let me know if either is worth reading.'

At that moment, Miss Lovatt entered. She saw me, said, 'Hello, Tony,' and went to stand touching sides with Clara, nestling to her. Furtively, she clasped Clara's hand tenderly and hid it behind them.

'How are you, Tony?' she asked in her quiet voice. Her grey hair had been cut much shorter than when I'd last seen her. Her soft eyes contemplated me. 'Did you have a happy Christmas?'

'Yes, Miss Lovatt.'

'And how's your mother?'

'She's very well.'

'Good.' But it was Clara whom Miss Lovatt actually wanted. 'I wondered where you'd got to, dear. I was showing you that fabric . . .'

'I know, I know, Dora! You do pester . . .'

It was time for me to go. Saying goodbye to them I eased myself past them and they watched me do so.

When I went back around the side of the house I saw Hoppalong John near one of the borders, piling dead leaves into a wheelbarrow. I went to him.

'Hello, John.'

He had on tattered wool mittens and a scraggy overcoat, and had allowed two or three days' growth of beard. Perhaps he found that some kind of insulation from the cold.

'You here again?' he smiled. 'Have a good do at Christmas?'

'Yes, did you?'

'Aye. Just me and the wife, but all right.'

'Listen,' I said, 'what d'you think of that Clara?'

'I've told you what I think. She's a real bugger. God knows why Miss Lovatt brought her here. She's turned the old woman into a bloody ghost. Why?'

'I'm on holiday till next Monday,' I told him. 'Can I help in any way?'

'No, lad. There's not much doing at this part of the year. I'm just passing time. You push on.'

'Right . . . Well tarra, John.'

'Tarra, Tony. And happy New Year.'

'Same to you!' Giving him a quick wave, I walked on down the drive.

At home, I stoked the fire, sat down, and read for the rest of the day.

10

The Christmas holidays had given me a chance to lie in. When I got up one morning, I found a note from Mother. Over the holiday we'd run out of bread and other things, and I was asked to walk up to the village and replenish our larder.

Many other people were in the same position, apparently – Tim's grocery shop was full of village women, with shopping baskets over their arms and purses in their hands. One or two knew me. We talked as we queued. One or two bored kids stood about, quietly waiting.

Then something was said by one of the women that immediately attracted my attention. 'What d'you think about Hector Swallow, then?'

'Terrible,' said her neighbour. 'I just heard about it from Mrs Groves. Well he did drive that blinking car fast, didn't he? It wasn't long ago that he almost ran me over.'

Interrupting, I asked, 'What happened, Mrs Savage? Has he had an accident?'

'He's dead, Tony.'

'Dead?'

'Yes. Last night. Crashed his car somewhere near Oxspring. Went over the side of the bridge or something. And the thing is, he had a woman with him. They say it was the wife of the landlord at the Black Bull in Thurgoland. Two of 'em dead just like that.'

'What was he doing with the woman?' her neighbour asked. 'As if we didn't know.'

'Well he was always that sort, wasn't he? Even when he was a lad at school. He was a sod.'

'All the same, it's rotten bad luck.'

'And what about his wife?'

'Aye . . . And that poor kid of theirs . . .'

'Aye . . . It's a mess . . . Hey-up, Tim — it's my turn now!'

I carried my two bagsful of groceries home and put them away where they belonged.

After what had indeed been a busy day at Mother's shop, she arrived at six looking rather tired. Her make-up had faded and there was a dried film of exertion on her face. But she was still in that lively, bouncing mood.

'Did you get the bacon?'

'Yes.'

'The tea?'

'I got all you wanted,' I said.

She gave me her coat to hang up and began to climb the stairs to change her clothes.

'What shall we have to eat?' I asked. 'I'll make a start.'

'No. We'll do it together. Just put the kettle on.'

She came down in an old blouse and skirt. She'd taken off her make-up and washed. 'We did well today,' she said. 'Non-stop from opening to closing. We needed it. What shall we have? Some of the bacon and an omelette . . .'

We had learnt to work together automatically, like two parts of an efficient machine.

'We had a flurry of snow in Leeds this afternoon. Did you see any of it here?'

'I've been reading.'

'You'll read your eyes out.'

We sat down to our meal and she went on talking, lightly, about something and nothing. I glanced up at her over and over again, trying to decide whether I ought to give her the news and, if I gave it to her, what her reaction might be.

We finished eating and washed the pots.

'Have you got a good fire going?' she asked.

'Yes.'

'Good. It's so damned cold. I wouldn't be surprised if we really did get snow tonight or tomorrow.' She hung up the tea towel she'd been using. 'I forgot the teapot – see to it will you, love. I'm going to get warmed up.'

Having washed the teapot, I sat down again there in the kitchen, still pondering what I ought to do. Ought I to wait until she got the news from someone else? Would that be better for her? I was in a dilemma. But at last I made up my mind. I decided that the onus was on me, that she ought to be told at once here in her own home, and that I really had no option.

I followed her into the living room. She was standing before the fire, looking at herself in the mirror over the mantelpiece, putting clips or something into her hair.

'How are we off for coal?' she asked, absently.

'We've still got plenty.'

For the moment she was in her own world. Her thoughts were distant, and she was fiddling with her hair almost unconsciously.

'I heard some bad news today,' I said.

It barely registered. 'Oh yes?' She was touching her eyebrows now, looking at them in the mirror without real interest.

'Hector Swallow's been killed,' I said.

It took a second to sink in. Then she came back to the present with a sudden start. She faced me. 'What did you say?'

'He crashed his car near Oxspring. He's dead.'

She froze, hands still to her face, her startled eyes staring at me. 'When – how . . . ?

'Last night.'

'Dead?' Already her tears were welling up.

'Yes. There were two of them. Both dead.'

'Two . . . ?'

'Yes. He had a woman with him.'

'What?' she was frowning now. 'Who? Mary?'

'No. It was the landlord's wife from the Black Bull at Thurgoland.'

I had seen Mother's knees buckle like this once before. She shuddered, staggered and seemed about to collapse. I jumped up and went to her, but she waved me away. Wobbling, groping, she slumped into her chair. Shocked to utter confusion, she twisted about from side to side. Then, sagging, she sat for a long moment staring down at the carpet.

'Mother . . .' I said, concerned for her.

She raised her head. There was no sign of tears now, only a blank, twisted expression on her face. But then she got up. It was clear that she wanted to escape my gaze, and, walking slowly to the door, she went out, into the lobby and up the stairs. I didn't see her again that evening.

At the loss of my father, Mother had gone into deep depression and when she lost her lover I'd half expected something of the same. But it was not so, and, watching her closely as I always did, sensing her feelings as I was always able to, I understood why. On discovering (as it had happened, from me) the manner of Swallow's death, and realising that she'd been merely another of his peccadilloes, what she felt was not so much a sense of betrayal and loss but an angry sense of insult. I could see it in her. For some days, she walked about the house, went off to and came back from work, with a very straight back, squared shoulders and a distinct air of injured but determined dignity. I had seen the same thing in her many times before when she'd had to endure some kind of offence. This time it was equally obvious and more prolonged. There were also spasms of shame, and I saw them, too. Over meals, or when listening to the radio, and at other odd moments, she lowered her head, screwed up her eyes, and showed some pain. But presently all that ceased.

In early March, something happened which not only restored her self-esteem but actually enhanced it – in fact, inflated it. She came home one Friday evening, looking as always rather tired, but bright-eyed, bubbling with excitement. She came barging into the living room where I happened to be drawing the curtains, saw me, almost ran to me, and gave me one of her juddering hugs. 'What d'you think, Tony! They've made me lingerie buyer!'

'That's great, Mother. What is it?'

'It's promotion – we'll have lots more money – I'm one of their managers now! And I've not been there a year yet!'

I was as delighted as she was herself. 'That's wonderful, Mother. Great! Good for you. Aren't you lucky!'

'Rubbish! Don't say that. Didn't I tell you I wasn't a fool? My boss retires next week and there were half a dozen women they could've chosen – people who've worked there for ages. It was not luck – it wasn't. They chose me because I was the best. You don't know your mother – you don't know what I can do. It wasn't luck!'

'Sorry, Mother . . .'

'Things're going to be different for us from now on . . . Give me a kiss . . .'

I kissed her.

'You should congratulate me!'

'Congratulations. Full marks!'

'You should be proud of me.'

'I am. I always have been.'

That touched her. She grew still for a moment. 'Have you?'

'Of course I have.'

'Well *I'm* proud of you, Tony.'

'Well that makes two of us,' I smiled. 'What is this new job, what's it all about?'

'It's a lot of responsibility, Tony. I buy all the new stock, you see. You have to know what women're likely to want well in advance. We do it by the season. I'll be responsible for spending thousands of pounds – thousands. We have six branches – York, Sheffield, all over the place. But I can do it, Tony!' She squeezed my hand for emphasis. 'I can do it!'

I squeezed her hand in return. 'I know you can.'

'I'll have to travel about now and again – buying, visiting the branches . . .'

'You'll see the world.'

'Yes!' she laughed. 'Do you mind?'

'Of course not. Why should I?'

'Isn't it marvellous?'

She'd run out of breath. 'Give me your coat, Mother,' I said. 'Go and get changed and we'll have tea.'

Yet another transformation came over Mother. She was working hard and thoroughly enjoying it. She went to the shop now in smart suits, grey or navy blue, had her hair done differently, and sometimes came home late.

And over the weeks her manner changed. That some-times dreamy air vanished completely into a bustling, rather brusque, often busily pre-occupied kind of energy. 'I'm sorry, Tony, love – but you'll just have to excuse me . . .' Her posture was different, more erect, somehow more self aware. The look on her face was different, too. From mildly thoughtful or mildly smiling it became alert, steady-eyed. What I saw now in Mother was the woman who had always been there, who, after shedding the constraints of conven-tional married life, of dependency on men, of emotional submission, and given the opportunity to reveal herself, had in fact done so with a vengeance. I became genuinely proud of her and even more fond. Her attitude to me hadn't changed in the least. We talked as always, laughed as always, embraced each other as often as always, and she remained as close to me, as concerned about me, as ever. Get on with it, Daisy, I thought.

Casting off the past, she gathered together all the photographs of my father and finally got rid of them, and one day asked me to help her clear out his old study – the fourth bedroom of the house, which had not been touched since he left. We first had to suck mountains of dust up the vacuum cleaner pipe, open the windows and exchange dead air for live. Then we turned the place over, she in something of a frenzy, muttering, passing dismissive gestures through the air. She decided to keep his typewriter because it could be of use to her, but insisted on throwing everything else away – even his books. 'Take this lot down to the bin, Tony' – and even the manuscript of his novel – 'Rubbish, burn it, bin it . . .'

I didn't. I took the books into my own room and put them on the shelf in there, and I parcelled up the manuscript and put it in my cupboard. I have kept it to this day.

She turned his writing table into a desk for herself, had the telephone moved on to it, bought a new carpet patterned with blue flowers, and new curtains to match. Thereafter, always for some reason putting her hair up, drawing it back from her face, she spent many hours up there, working at her papers and, even on Sundays, making telephone calls, mostly to men. I overheard, 'Ronald, what happened to the delivery you promised on Friday? We can't go on like this. Ring me tomorrow at my office without fail.'

Let 'em have it, Daisy!

A new three piece suite arrived and a new carpet and

new curtains for the living room. She decided to renew my wardrobe as well as her own. 'You're coming to town with me on Wednesday afternoon, Tony. You need two new pairs of trousers.'

She'd bought herself a smart, pale tan attaché case with bright brass lockable catches, which she took everywhere with her. I sneaked a look into it one evening. It was full of papers, brochures, sample swatches, sample garments with frills – lacey, silky, all smelling of that same perfume I'd sniffed in the shop. Travelling light, with only this attaché case and an overnight bag, she went off on her travels several times that spring, not on the bus but by way of a taxi to the station, which called for her at seven in the morning. I was always certain to receive a telephone call from her on her first night away. 'I'm at the Midland in Manchester. Is everything all right, love?' And, 'I'm at the Strand in London. How did you go on at school today? I'll be home on Thursday. There should be enough food there for you – but if not there's some money in the sideboard drawer.'

However, she could always find time for Sam, who persisted in cropping up every two or three weeks. He surely noted the changes in her but seemed as happy about them as I was myself, for her warmth towards him, her always very friendly welcome, was the same as ever. Should she have little time to spend with him on occasion, she held his hand for a moment, looked into his eyes and spoke apologetically – 'I just have things to do, Sam, this evening. But sit down. Put the telly on and I'll be with you as soon as I can.'

'That's all right, Daisy.'

'There's some sherry on the sideboard.'

'Your mother's a wonder,' Sam said to me.

I thought Sam himself was a wonder. His devotion to Mother was very moving, and it must have been considerable because after weeks and weeks their relationship had gone no further than friendship – close, understanding, happy – yet still merely friendship.

But I was swotting in my room one evening when he knocked at my door, poked his head round and beamed at me. 'Your mother said she'll come to the pictures with me!' His manner was such that he might have gone on to say, 'And what d'you think about that!'

I was delighted for him. 'Good!' I said. 'When?'

'Tonight. Now. I'm not on till Tuesday morning. We're off . . . !' Most pleased with himself, he closed the door.

A few minutes later, Mother appeared. 'Sam and I're going out, Tony.' There was distinctly a question in it, as if she wanted my permission.

I did not tell her that Sam had already made his announcement. I simply nodded, as if it mattered to me neither one way nor the other. 'Right, Mother.'

'It's all right, isn't it?'

'What d'you mean? Course it is. Look, Mother, I'm concentrating.' But I was truly pleased.

From then on they went out a number of times. Sam had expanded with joy. He bought a new suit. Living alone and being well paid, he must have built up some capital for a week or two later he arrived at the house on a cold Sunday afternoon with a brand new Mini car. It stood outside the gate shining, glistening in the thin sunshine, as proud as its new owner. We all three piled into it, Mother and he in the front, I spreading out in the back, and he drove us sedately into Swaledale. We sat in a café, had tea and cakes gazing out over the river and the sheep strewn hillside, went on through Grassington, where it started raining, and on, not caring, on into Wharfedale and, finally, home.

'That was lovely, Sam,' Mother said. 'Wasn't it, Tony?' But as we went into the house the phone was ringing and she had to rush upstairs.

'Doesn't your mother get any time to herself?' Sam asked.

That evening, Sam left early. Mother was tired and at nine she went to bed early.

A few days later, towards the end of March, I stepped from the bus after school and walked towards the house. It had been a bright, cold day with cloudless sky. The sun was sinking and you could almost feel the temperature dropping. Fifty yards away along the lane, running now that she'd seen me, was Emma Sarah, waving both arms. Despite my promise, I hadn't found a way of visiting her home since the death of her father and I was as glad to greet her as she was to greet me. She was wearing that thick coat and those brilliant white stockings.

'Tony! Tony!' She flung her arms round me.

'Let me breathe, Emma Sarah!'

Over her shoulder was slung a little red bag. Letting go of me, she began to fumble in it.

'You've not brought any money, have you, Emma Sarah? We've got no tomatoes, you know. It's the wrong time of year.'

Vigorously, she shook her head, fumbled on and at last produced a piece of paper folded to the size of a postage stamp.

'What's this?' I opened it. Across the creases in large, round writing, was written: 'Dear Tony: I've had to let Emma come and see you. She's been mithering me to death about you. But send her home before it goes dark, please. Mary Swallow.'

I took her into the house. I hung up our coats. I went into the kitchen, filled the new kettle Mother had bought, and switched it on. Then I went with Emma Sarah into the living room. Since Mother and I were out all day the fire was never lit till I came home from school. By the hearth was the shovelful of coal, the handful of kindling, and two sheets of the *Daily Express* which I'd left there the night before. I knelt on the rug to light the fire and Emma Sarah came to stand and watch. Unusually for her, she wasn't saying much this afternoon.

I looked at her. 'I'm sorry about your father.'

For a moment she didn't seem to grasp that. Then her eyes moistened.

'I'm really sorry, Emma Sarah.'

I spread the kindling over the paper and looked up again, expecting to see tears, but other thoughts had jumped into her head. 'We've got no cows.'

'No. I know. You're mother's sold them all.'

'Where've they gone?'

'I don't know. But they'll be all right, Emma Sarah. Don't worry about them.'

She had on little black boots. Above them her plump legs in their white stockings.

I lit the paper.

'Why didn't you come to see me when you promised?' she asked.

'Never mind, Emma Sarah. You've come here again and it's all right now.'

'Is it? When will you come?'

'As soon as I can.'

'My father died.'

'Yes, I'm sorry.'

'Why did he die? Why didn't you come to see me?'

'I've told you. I'll come as soon as I can.'

'I'm knitting you a scarf.'

'Thanks, Emma Sarah.'

The flames were reluctant, so I blew on them. At that moment, the whistling kettle in the kitchen screamed and Emma Sarah's boots jumped up an inch. She gave a little scream, at exactly the same pitch as the kettle.

'Sit down,' I said. 'I'm making myself some tea. You want some?'

She shook her head.

I had something planned this evening and could therefore not wait for Mother to come home to have my meal with her, so I made myself a sandwich. The kitchen was freezing, so I took the sandwich, with my tea and a glass of milk, which I knew she liked, in to Emma Sarah. She accepted the milk and drank half of it at once, spilling only a drop of it on to her skirt.

'Talk away, Emma Sarah,' I said.

But she merely gazed at me, watching every little move I made.

'Are you all right?' I asked.

Another vigorous nod and a big smile. 'Tony, Tony, Tony . . .' she said, still not taking her eyes off me, as if delightedly reminding herself of me.

In recent times her face had changed subtly. Her nose still twitched and her eyes, always squinting very slightly, had not lost their misty look, but I thought her cheeks had filled out. There was a nice smooth curve to them.

I finished my sandwich and tea and she finished her milk.

'I've got to go out, Emma Sarah. And your mother wants you home before dark. So come on, now.'

'Oh,' she said. She wanted to sit there looking at me for ever, but she did at last get up.

It was already dusk outside. 'You'd better leg it, Emma Sarah,' I told her. 'Before you have your mother after me. I'll come down to see you soon.'

'You don't keep your promises.'

'Well I will now. And you can come here as often as you like.'

'Can I?'

'Yes. Just barge in.'

From our gate I watched her until she disappeared around the side of the farmhouse.

I then walked in the other direction to Crompton House. It was quite dark as I pushed open the creaking iron gates. There was thick black silence in the shrubbery on either hand and you could just make out the twisted branches of the trees scratching at the cold sky. But the lights were on behind several windows of the house as though a crowd of visitors had arrived to swarm into all the spaces.

I went in as usual up the steps to the rear door and through the kitchen, which was deserted. Everything had been put away. The central table was bare. Copper pans, hanging by their handles, looked as if they'd been unused, sleeping like bats, for weeks, and tea towels covered humps of something on the side surfaces.

I passed on into the dimly lit lobby. As I did so I heard women's voices coming through the open door of Miss Lovatt's drawing room, quite close. I paused to eavesdrop for a moment and discerned three separate voices – Clara's sharp, quick crackle, Miss Lovatt's gentle hum, and a new sound, a low, smooth, melodious, carefully modulated counterpoint, very pleasant.

I opened the library door to pitch darkness and switched on the light. There, flaked out in one of the chairs, with her head on one side and her legs wide apart, was Alma. A bundle of dusters had fallen from her hand to the carpet.

'Ooops!' She woke startled, staring alarmed at me for a second until she realised who I was. 'Oh, it's only you . . .' She got to her feet, wobbling a little. As was normal with her, her overall dress was not quite aligned across the front and the turban she was wearing on her head had slipped a bit. Flapping, she straightened it. 'I just fell asleep . . . I'm dog tired. What time is it?'

'It must be coming up to six.'

'Good God! He'll be home and no tea ready . . . Where's me things?'

'Dusters on the floor,' I said.

'I had a handbrush.'

'Can't see it, Alma.'

'Oh where the hell've I left it . . .' She gyrated two or three times. 'Oh bugger it!' She stamped a foot. 'I've got to get home . . .'

She made for the door but I stood in her way to ask, 'What's going on here, Alma? Is the place full of people?'

'What d'you mean?'

'All the lights're all on.'

'Oh bugger. I'll have to go and turn 'em off.'

'There's no visitors, then?'

'No. Only her, and she's no visitor. She's here for good.'

'Who?'

'Miss Schofield. Came last week – lovely young woman, paints pictures, lovely. Not like that cow Clara . . . Let me pass, I've got to get off, he'll be hungry and I always like to have everything ready for him . . . What lights have I left on?'

'It looks like all of them, Alma.'

'Oh bugger . . . !' And she scooted.

Her handbrush was lurking behind the other chair, but by the time I found it she'd left the house. As was normally the case, the central heating was not turned on in the library. I looked at one or two books, sat down for a little while to browse, and finally got up to go.

There must have been some mysterious fluence between Clara and me because whenever I went to Cromford House she managed to appear. On this occasion, she was striding in her composed, self-aware way down the lobby. And again, at the sight of me, she paused, stared me up and down, and assumed that irritating smile.

She walked at my side towards the kitchen. 'You've not met Laura Schofield, have you? She's living with us now. But she's just taking a bath. You'll have to meet her when you come again. She might want to paint your picture.' As if she felt she'd made a joke, she laughed.

I made a joke in response. 'That's fine,' I said. 'I'm told I'm smashing. Is she a friend of yours?'

'Very much so.'

'How's Miss Lovatt?'

'She's as usual. Tell me young man, what is the length of your erection?'

I refused to be shocked. 'I don't know,' I said.

'You mean to say you've never measured it?'

'I haven't got a long enough ruler.'

'Well if I were a man I'd certainly want to know my dimensions.'

'But you're not a man, are you?'

'No, but nor are you yet. Go home to your mother.'

'That's just what I'm going to do,' I said.

We parted at the kitchen door and I felt her cool, remote smile following me. What was wrong with the woman?

12

I took up courage and asked Margaret to come out with me. We went to the cinema in Leeds. At the kiosk I was prepared to pay. I had money from Mrs Lovatt for cataloguing her books and Mother was handing cash to me in quantities. But Margaret took hold of my wrist. 'No, Tony. I'll pay for myself.' So I bought some sweets for her and an ice cream at the interval.

We sat on the back row of course, with my arm across her shoulders until it ached. I took a rest and then put it back. She nestled affectionately against me.

When, at the end of the evening, I came to her door with her it was far too cold for anything but another quick kiss. This was frustrating.

'Look,' I said, taking hold of her gloved hand, gazing into her bright eyes, 'Mother's away for two days. Can you come down tomorrow evening after tea?'

'Course I can.'

We embraced, kissed again, and, with surging affection, I watched her open the door of her house. On the threshold, she turned to me for a moment, smiled, and gave me a little wave goodbye.

Next evening, I looked out for her from an upstairs window. It was a black, blustery evening. Dead leaves scuttled down the lane like terrified little animals. Just after half-past seven, with a thrill of excitement, I saw her hurrying through the darkness and I went to the gate to meet her. She walked into my arms and rested her head on my chest. She was quite breathless.

'I'm sorry I'm so late, Tony. Aggie . . .'

'Never mind, never mind,' I said, taking her arm. 'Come on in out of the cold.'

In the lobby I helped her off with her coat. Her face was shining and, when she took off her beret I saw that she had waved her hair nicely.

Out of our fondness for each other and after our moments of physical closeness – the touching of hips, the holding of hands, the little kisses – there was in us both the excited, tense, yearning of young hearts. And so from the start of the evening there were understood expectations. I had banked up the fire and placed the settee square on to it – I had done my bit. I sat her down, brought her tea, and then noticed that she, too, had done her bit. She was wearing an inviolable stiff skirt, but a blue blouse with buttons down the front, a recognised sign of course.

I sat two or three inches from her. For perhaps ten minutes – not longer – we talked about nothing. We put our cups and saucers down on the carpet, looked at each other, and allowed silence to fall. The flames of the fire licked up into the chimney and the wind hissed about the house. She was leaning back against the cushions with her knees close, her hands on her lap, half smiling and looking, I thought, lovely, gentle, waiting.

I put my arm across her shoulders. She nestled into me, sighed and, after a moment looked up for a kiss. As my lips touched hers her arms suddenly embraced me. 'Oh Tony . . .'

I began to undo the buttons of her blouse. But at once she rested her hand on mine to stop me. A potent moment passed. Looking into her eyes I saw a little nervous shadow there. I kissed her again. 'Oh Tony . . .' she said again, and I felt her take her hand away. All she was wearing underneath, covering her ample breasts, was one of those smooth, silky pink brassieres I'd seen so many of. Not used to undoing hooks and eyes, growing more and more excited, trembling, I fumbled, but she helped by leaning forward and doing it for me. But then, as I touched her flesh, I felt a sudden stiffness in her. She put a hand to mine again, holding me firmly.

She had closed her eyes and from under the lids I saw two or three tears escape.

'I'm sorry, Margaret . . .' I said, at once moving my hand.

But she smiled. 'It's all right – it's all right, Tony . . .' And she let my hand go again.

As I stroked her warm firm breasts I was overwhelmed with a tremendous sensation of tenderness for her.

'Ah, Margaret . . .' I heard myself murmuring.

'Oh Tony . . .' she wanted yet another kiss.

We went on canoodling for the rest of the evening. Advancing no further in intimacy but enjoying ourselves immensely.

I walked her home just after ten o'clock.

Longing to be together, we met several times, each meeting within days of the other. It was a constant joy to know that we had someone who was truly fond of us, whom we could see and touch and, in our way, love. Certainly for me, Margaret was a great joy in my life. She was in me, always there to think of, to brighten my day.

Her brother came cycling to the house one Saturday afternoon. As it happens, Emma Sarah had paid another of her visits. I had left her with paper and a thick pencil in the kitchen, drawing, while I watched the six o'clock news on the television.

Beckoning to Gerald, I suggested he might sit quietly for a while, but he preferred not to. He wandered about the room, looking at this, looking at that. He slipped his overcoat off and draped it across one of our new armchairs. He was one who got out of his school blazer whenever he could and he was now wearing a great thick sweater. He seemed to be extending his girth, his weight, every day, and this evening there was a largish bruise on the right hand side of his face, just under the eye. A fist had caught him during a game of rugger on the previous Saturday.

He pointed. 'That's a fancy statue you've got on the sideboard, Bony. I've not seen that before.'

It was a fine porcelain figurine Mother had bought – a woman in flowing robes – pure art deco.

'Everything's new in here,' he said.

'So it is.'

'You're getting too bloody posh.' He strolled over to the sofa. 'Did you need something this big? Or are you planning to do your mother in and hide her in it?' He went to examine the hi-fi and the discs that were on a shelf there.

'Any Brahms?'

'No.'

'Well don't tell Margaret that.'

Finally, he sat down on the sofa. He leant forward, clasped his hands and began. 'Talking of Margaret, Bony . . .'

But he was interrupted. The door opened and Emma Sarah entered. Seeing Gerald, she stopped dead. 'It's Gerald,' I said. 'You know him.'

She nodded.

'Well come in.'

She was carrying the sheet of paper I'd given her. She came and put it under my nose. On it she'd drawn two houses, identical except that one was larger than the other – square, four windows and a door, a path running up to the door, a tall chimney and a lollipop tree in the garden. They were good I thought. I'd tried to teach her the few tricks I knew about perspective but all she could do was remember the drawings I'd done for her myself and reproduce something like them. 'That's great, Emma Sarah,' I said. 'Great, kid.'

She beamed.

'Show it to Gerald.'

She ran across the room, sat down next to Gerald on the sofa, pushed the paper into his hands, and bounced while he looked at it.

'Mmnnn . . .' he went.

'Tell her it's good, man,' I said.

'It's good,' he said, handing it back to her. Clearly, he felt uncomfortable with her. He glanced into her face and again said, 'It's good.' He flapped the paper for her to take. 'Here . . .'

'Go and draw something else, Emma Sarah,' I said. 'A ship.'

'Yes, yes!' she said, excitedly. 'A big ship . . .'

'Don't forget the masts,' I called after her as she closed the door.

Gerald looked at me. 'A bit weird, isn't she?'

'She's what she is,' I said.

'Yes, weird. And I was just wondering . . .'

'What?' I asked.

'What would Margaret think if she knew you were so pally with that one.'

'Don't be stupid, Connolly. I've known her since we were little kids. She lives just down the road. Anyway, Margaret's seen her. She saw her here in this house.'

'Oh. Has she?'

'Yes. And she was a heck of a sight kinder about her than you are. She gave me some beads to give her. I think she's wearing them now.'

'Right – well . . . sorry, Bony. Cut my tongue out. All the same . . .'

'All the same what?'

'Speaking of our Maggie . . .'

'Well?'

'That's what I wanted to see you about.'

'I could tell there was something. Go on.'

'When did you last see her?'

'Last Monday.'

'When will you see her again?'

'Saturday.'

'Well look, Bony, she's my sister . . .'

'Worse luck for her.'

'No, let me speak . . . She's my sister, Bony. She's a bloody nuisance, but she's the only sister I've got, thank God . . . Bony, look, our Maggie's a softee, soft-hearted, daft as a brush. She thinks the sun shines out of your arse and I just want to . . .'

'Oh come off it!' I exclaimed. 'What d'you think I'm doing to her?'

'As I say, Bony . . .'

'Oh shut up! D'you think I'm like you?'

He gazed at me for a moment. 'You're a sanctimonious sod. Did you know that? What d'you mean, like me?'

'Well, all these girls you're supposed to be knicker-legging.'

That managed to bring a grin from him. 'Oh that.'

'It's all talk. Isn't it?' I said. 'It's all theory.'

He grinned again. 'Well at least I'm well up on theory.'

'And the knicker legs?'

'It can be hard going sometimes.' He laughed.

'And as for Margaret and me, Gerald, mind your own business. I think your sister's great. We get on a treat. And anyway it has nothing at all to do with you.'

'All right, all right. Forget it. Sorry I spoke.' He got up and went for his overcoat. 'I'll pedal off. I've got that boring essay to write for Kennedy and I'm going out tonight. You know Henderson's leaving next week? They're emigrating to Australia to join the kangaroos. I think he's going in his mother's pouch.'

Half an hour later I walked Emma Sarah home. I had some work to do myself that evening.

This was the first time I'd been down to the farm since the death of Emma Sarah's father. In the past I'd haunted the place, working for Hector, slogging in the hayfields, snorting with the pigs, mucking out the shippon, saddling old Toby, eating Mary's sandwiches and drinking glasses of the warm cream she pressed into my hands. Mary had liked me, and I certainly liked her – her almost perpetual laughter, her bright eyes, her still youthful energy. But until now there had been feelings in me which had made the thought of confronting her again uncomfortable. At the root of them was the fact that I'd known of my mother's affair with her husband and felt a vicarious but painful sense of guilt. This was irrational in me of course – and even more irrational because Mary knew nothing about their affair. But the feelings had persisted, and even now, as I went with Emma Sarah into the farmhouse, I was uneasy.

But Mary was delighted to see me. She gave me a hug. 'Well, well – if it isn't you! I wondered when you'd condescend to come and see me again.' There was a warm, pleasant smell about her. She'd had her hair permed into an ocean of heaving waves. 'Sit down, sit down, Tony.'

We were in what she called her parlour. In the hearth roared that big fire I'd once envied. 'I was just having a drop of port,' she said, going to the sideboard and pouring one for me. 'Here, have some. It's good stuff.'

I wasn't too keen on port, but I sipped at it.

While I did so, she sat down opposite me and watched me. 'You look as fit as a fiddle,' she said. 'And I like your pullover . . .'

Emma Sarah was standing patiently by, gazing from me to her mother, with her thumb in her mouth and the paper with the drawings in her hand.

'Emma's been drawing,' I said.

'She never stops.' Mary extended a hand to her daughter. 'Come on, love. Let's have a look.' Emma Sarah handed her the paper and she studied it for a moment. Then she looked at me. 'What d'you think?'

'It's good. She's getting very good.'

Mary held her daughter's hand for a moment. 'You hear that? You're getting very good, Emma.' She looked into her face. 'You're tired. Go and lie down for a bit.'

Emma Sarah baulked. 'No.' She was sniffing. She was still cold from outside and her nose was running. 'No,' she said.

'Do as you're told. Tony and me want to talk.'

'No.'

'Get your handkerchief out, wipe your nose and go and lie down. Now. Go, Emma.'

'No,' Emma Sarah said yet again, but, shaking herself, she turned away and, giving me one last glance, left us.

'I can't get her on the school bus of a morning now,' Mary said. 'She's miserable there and why should I let that happen? What's the point? I want her happy. All she ever learns she gets from you. More port?'

'No thanks, Mrs Swallow.'

That annoyed her. 'Oh don't call me that, for God's sake!' she exclaimed. 'You know about that swine.'

'Well – I heard.'

'Don't mention his name, never ever mention it. And I'll tell you something, no male body will ever again cross this threshold. Except you. I've had it with men. Never! Never!' She'd flushed vivid red. 'The bastard.' Fuming on for a few moments, at last she grew calm. She sighed, and then resorted to her loud, shining-eyed laughter. 'But there's always a silver lining, Tony. I've got rid of that sod and I'm loaded. I've sold everything – everything except the house.'

'Yes, I know, Mrs Swallow.'

'What've I just told you! I'm not Mrs Swallow, never have been, never wanted to be. I'm Mary Cartland. That's how I started and that's how I'll finish. Mary! Have you got that?'

'Yes, Mary.'

'Good.' She emptied her glass, held it up for a moment, wondering whether to fill it again, and decided not to. She got up and put the glass on the mantelpiece. In the past she'd worn ordinary frocks or a pinny or something else nondescript. This evening she had on a very attractive mauve dress which revealed that Rembrandt body in a way it had never been revealed before – plumpish, like that of her daughter, and emphatically shapely.

She realised that I was looking at her rather more closely than usual. 'You like my dress?'

'It's very nice.'

'I bought it from your mother's shop.'

For some reason that surprised me. 'Did you?'

'Daisy's doing all right now.'

'Yes.'

'And so am I.' She laughed. 'They told me I'd never sell this land things being as they are, but it went in six weeks. Fat lot they knew.' Another joyful laugh. 'So there. I'm set up, Tony. Every stick, stone, cow, chicken – everything he ever had has gone up the Swanny . . .' She stopped suddenly, came close and touched my shoulder. 'This isn't a home knitted pullover you've got on . . .'

She sat down again, leant back, and crossed her plump knees.

'I hope Emma doesn't get in your way.'

'No. How can she – we're pals?'

'I know that. She can be a pest though. She'd be up at your house every day if I'd let her. I mean, who else has she got? Where else can she find someone who gives a damn about her?' Mary paused and looked into my face. 'She's a grown-up woman now, Tony.'

'Then I'm a grown-up man!' I laughed.

'A few years ago at your age you'd soon be off to fight a war.'

'So I would.'

'You know, don't you, that girls like Emma die very young? I'm going to lose her Tony, I'm going to lose my dear lovely Emma and it breaks my heart. She'll never find someone to marry her, she can't ever have children and she's going to die.'

'No – don't say that.'

'But it's true. She's a woman, with a loving beating heart. She has a woman's feelings, the yearnings, the passion, and she wants to be loved. She needs to be loved, loved Tony, like every other woman. Can you see that?'

'But *I* love her, Mary. I always have.'

Mary smiled and stared at me for several moments. 'You don't know what I'm trying to say, do you, Tony?' She flapped a hand, dismissing all that. 'Never mind, never mind. Yes, I like your pullover.'

'Thanks, Mary. But I'd better be going. I've got some work to do.'

'Let's see more of you from now on.'

'You will,' I said.

'Well don't forget.'

At home, I did my work, watched the television and went to bed. As always, as I undressed, I gabbled through my prayers, mentioning everyone close to me – including my father. I didn't hear Mother come home that night. She'd been out with Sam and must have returned very late.

13

At the end of April Sam moved in with us. He arrived early one windy evening in his polished Mini. I volunteered to help him offload his trappings and was surprised to discover how few there were of them. Into the hall we carried two suitcases and three bulging carrier bags.

'Is this all there is, Sam?' I asked. 'Is there more coming?'

There wasn't apparently. He'd rented the house he'd lived in and, coming to a domicile that contained all – and more – anyone could need, he'd had the house-clearers in and sold his furniture and everything else, except his immediate personal things, he'd ever possessed. He was in his most ebullient mood. Putting down the last two carrier bags in the hall, he beamed at Mother and declared. 'Well here I am!'

'Close the door behind you, love,' Mother said. 'It's blowing a gale through here.'

When, after doing so, he turned to face her again she went to him and smoothed down his wind-ruffled hair.

I picked up one of his suitcases. 'I suppose this lot goes upstairs,' I said. 'Where to?'

'My bedroom,' Mother said. 'Where d'you think?'

I rarely went into Mother's bedroom. It was her sanctum. Its air was tinctured with the subtle scent she wore and, since it faced more or less west a shaft of late sunshine probed through the window and lay across the bed. The one with the iron rails which she'd once shared with my father had long since been sent to the scrapheap, disposed of, along with her unwanted memories of him. This bed, with its carved wooden headboard, had been very neatly made. Its silky green coverlet, shining in the sunlight, had been smoothed out and, folded on its pillow, was Mother's silky nightdress – pink. Her dressing-table mirror had a silky scarf or something draped across a top corner. She'd bought two additional mahogany wardrobes, with more mirrors in their doors, full, no doubt, of her new clothes. In the centre of the carpet was a round fluffy rug, and in the green-upholstered chair under the window sat a large doll, dressed in red, which I'd never set eyes on before.

Sam, with his other suitcase, followed me into the room, put the case down, and gazed about. 'Oh,' he said, involuntarily, suddenly looking, I thought, rather intimidated, embarrassed.

A few days before, Mother had said to me, 'Look, Tony, you know perfectly well I can't marry, Sam. It'll be four years before I can get a divorce, so what am I supposed to do? Don't be upset. Is it my fault . . . ?

'Oh heck, Mother! You don't have to explain anything to me.'

'Thank you, love . . . You always understand me. You're my lovely lad.' A kiss. 'And you like Sam as much as I do . . .'

As we left her bedroom, Sam paused to look into my face. There was a searching look in his eye. He, too, felt it important to see my reaction to his presence here in this sanctum.

'Smells a bit in here,' I said. 'Scent. But I suppose you'll get used to it.'

He beamed again, patted me on the shoulder, and we went back down the stairs.

We had a meal, sat chatting, played some records, listened to the nine o'clock news. At half past ten, I sensed that they wanted me out of the way for some reason, so I went upstairs, made my notes, said my prayers, and got into bed. At about eleven I heard subdued whispers as they came up the stairs. Then I heard Mother's bedroom door – across the landing from me – being very quietly opened and even more quietly closed.

There had been a change in their relationship since Hector had vanished. Those gentle but telling rebuffs that had once touched Sam's cheeks with a little shrinking of flesh, touched his eyes with a little shadow, didn't happen now. 'Thank you, Sam, that's lovely.' And now and then she took his face between her two hands and kissed him warmly – exactly the same thing as she'd always done to me.

But there was something which I found irritating in Sam. He never lost that attitude towards her almost of servility. That he loved her deeply, that in fact he adored her, was obvious. But he also had this overweening admiration for her in another sense. She considered herself nowadays, not without some cause I suppose, to be a woman of substance, a woman with a career, important. As I've said earlier, this had become very clear, and Sam responded to it in a way I thought very silly. He looked up to her as if to someone greatly superior, which I thought was ridiculous. More than once, he actually said, 'I don't know what your mother sees in someone like me.'

138

And she reacted in a way which this behaviour of his actually encouraged. I was ashamed of her. She allowed him to run around after her, fetch and carry, answer the telephone for her, play the servant. 'Oh you twerp, Sam,' I used to think. 'She's only my mother!'

'He thinks the world of you, Mother,' I said.

'Well?'

'Can't you be a bit kinder to him?'

That made her angry. 'What d'you mean! I couldn't be kinder. I'm very fond of him! Mind your own business!'

For the first few weeks Sam worked shifts, coming and going at all hours of the day and night. But then he settled down to regular nights. He drove off some time before ten in the evening and arrived home just after six next morning. He slept till two in the afternoon. This meant that, except on his time off, he and Mother spent very little time in the same bed together. Moreover, he could be away on his long runs twice a week, and of course Mother was often away on her travels.

But, irrespective of my own concerns for them, they seemed happy together, he looking into her face and she laughing into his eyes.

Whenever one of them was away and the other at home, it was understood that there would be a telephone call at eight in the evening. It could go on for a quarter of an hour. But if for some reason the call didn't come Mother would say merely, 'He's not had a chance this evening.' Sam himself would say, 'What's happened? Where is she? What's happened to her?'

We were working together in the greenhouse, Sam and I. In fact, I had to some extent opted out of this occupation. We no longer needed the money from the tomatoes and it was now, to me, nothing more than a chore. But tomato-growing had always been a hobby of Sam's and, to support him, I worked alongside him, side-shooted and sprayed and watered. We'd worked together for about half an hour when he sat down on the trough wall, lit a cigarette and said, 'Tony, d'you know who this bloke Ronald is who's always talking to your mother on the phone?'

'Yes. She buys stuff from him. He rings from Manchester.'

'You know him, then?'

'No. I've never met him at all.'

'Ah. Well it doesn't matter.'

'He's nobody,' I said. 'He's nobody, Sam.'

'Right.' He picked a yellowed leaf from one of the plants, finished his cigarette and we carried on with the job. Ten minutes later, almost sotto voce, he said, squirting the sprayer, 'I don't know what your mother sees in a bloke like me.'

14

In recent time my emotions had undergone a rapid shake-up. I'd been very much a late developer and I can offer no reason for that. But by this time my latent sexual instincts, my libido, had begun to burgeon. My moments with Margaret had seen to that.

It was a warm Sunday morning and I was sitting reading in my hollow under the wall in the field when Emma Sarah turned up with a tennis ball on which she'd drawn a smiling face in felt pen.

I took it, looked at it, and gave it back to her. 'Very nice, Emma Sarah. Very good. But don't talk. I want to read.'

She sat down on the grass two or three feet away, and for several minutes remained so perfectly silent that I forgot she was there. Then she reminded me. A sudden startled spatter of words came from her.

'Ouch! Ouch . . .!'

'Shut up,' I said.

As a rule she accepted that dismissal. But this morning she did not. Insistently, it came again. I was aware of a concerned, questioning, alarmed tone about it. Something was seriously bothering her. 'I've been stung – it hurts, it hurts . . .'

'Oh what is it, Emma Sarah!' I was still reluctant to look up from the page.

'It hurts – it's hurting me . . . Look, Tony, look . . . see!'

I turned to look at her and what I saw was deeply shocking. She was pressing the flesh at the top of her left thigh. Her knees were up, her knickers were round her ankles, and her legs were wide apart.

'See – see!' She lifted her hand. 'What is it . . . ?'

How could I have any idea what it was? Had some insect bitten her? How could I guess? It was Emma Sarah in trouble asking for some kind of help, but that was not how it affected me at that moment. 'Oh God, Emma Sarah . . . !' A surging spasm of confused emotions had taken hold of me. There was a sickened revulsion. The loose flesh, the little folds and flaps of skin, the livid pink of it and the blatant exposure of it all disgusted me. And I was transfixed with embarrassment, profoundly uncomfortable. Yet at the same time there was something else – an acute sexual excitement which, even as it arose in me, turned to rage.

'What're you doing!' I shouted.

She recoiled as if I'd slapped her face.

'Wassermatter Tony, wassermatter . . .'

'You daft sod!' I shouted. 'What d'you think you're doing!'

Tears filled her eyes.

'Pull your knickers up! Get 'em up!'

She didn't move. She sat there limp and tearful, moving her head from side to side, wondering what she'd done wrong.

Utterly furious, I stood up, grabbed her hand, hoisted

her to her feet and pushed at her. But her knickers were still around her ankles and she staggered. 'Tony! Tony!' she said, baffled, crying. 'Don't shout at me . . .'

'Pull your knickers up and go home! Go home!' Again I pushed at her. 'Go home – tell your mother!'

Still hobbled by her knickers, she took two or three strides. Then at last she bent and pulled them up, trapping the hem of her dress. She turned again and appealed to me with her wet bent face and outstretched arms. How pathetic she looked. 'Tony . . .'

'Oh God, Emma Sarah . . . Pull your skirt out of your knickers. Just go home . . . Don't cry. It's all right. Tell your mother . . .'

And away she went, shoulders drooping, wading slowly through the tall grass in her patent leather shoes. She was pressing a hand to herself, obviously still in some sort of pain.

I had loved my dear Emma Sarah. I had always been happy, delighted and somehow comforted to turn my head and see her trailing after me. But now it was all suddenly different. The thought of her had become an embarrassment to me and I felt compelled to avoid the sight of her. It was not at all easy. I had to find a new retreat for myself on the far side of the hill, and I took care not to pass anywhere near the farmhouse. But she was still to be seen. She must have waited for hours at her gate to catch a glimpse of me as I came and went from home. When I appeared, she stepped out on to the lane and there she stood, like a wraith, flimsy and fragile against green distances, motionless, watching me, wanting me. On my way to Cromford House one morning, I turned and saw that she was following me, about a hundred yards off. When I stopped, she stopped. When I walked on again, so did she. So I jumped over the wall and trotted along the river bank out of her sight. It went on like that for some time.

What troubled me now was myself, those new and disturbing sensations which had arisen in me – sorrow and a kind of fear. My dear Emma Sarah had become an object of desire. The thought of her stirred feelings in me that I'd never felt before, painful sexual feelings which brought on unbearable tides of shame. Dear Emma Sarah with her bulging breasts, her little white knickers, her shining thighs, her child's voice, her little girl's babbling chatter, her trusting eyes and her loving little heart. It was a torment of guilt. It followed me about through all the long days and coloured my world.

But then, early one morning, as I was in the greenhouse messing about, Emma Sarah presented herself and there was no way for me to escape.

She stood outside, staring at me through the glass. She was partly obscured by the plants and could have been there for minutes before I actually saw her. She had that loose-lipped, frozen expression on her face and that nervous, plaintive look in her eye. Her hands were clasped across her stomach and I saw that she was holding her little girl's embroidered purse in her hands, so I knew at once why she was here.

She stared at me and I let her do so for a while. Then I motioned her inside.

'You want some tomatoes,' I said.

She nodded.

'A pound?'

She nodded and watched me twist half a dozen or so fruits from the plants.

'Excuse me, Emma Sarah,' I said, and I pushed past her into the shed at the end of the glasshouse. In the shed were the boiler that was used to keep the greenhouse pipes heated, and a high pricking-out bench on which stood a pair of scales and a pile of brown paper bags. Emma Sarah followed me. As I weighed the tomatoes and bagged them, I heard a little mouse sound from her, and when I turned to her I saw that she was crying, peering into my face with saliva shining on her lips.

'Oh God, Emma Sarah, don't cry . . . Have you got the money?'

'Yes.'

'It's a shilling.'

'Yes . . .' She fumbled with her purse. She had short little fingers, each of which at that moment seemed to be at odds with the others. It took her some time even to open the purse. When she did, she gave another agonised mouse squeak. She bent forward, groped inside the purse, found nothing and looked up at me with terror on her face.

'Oh Tony!' she said, bursting into new floods of tears.

'Did your mother give you the money? Have you lost it?'

'I don't know! I don't know . . .'

Oh God . . . that forlorn, baffled look that could so easily come over her almost broke your heart.

'I'm sorry, Tony . . . Don't shout at me.' She held a

trembling hand towards me as tears streamed down her twisted face.

'I'm not shouting at you,' I said. 'Here, take the tomatoes. Take them to your mother. Off home with you . . .'

She stepped back as if afraid that I might grab hold of her and fling her out of the shed. Then, agitatedly rolling from side to side, flustering, obviously searching for words or for some way to appeal to me, she fumbled at her wrist, took off her little Timex watch and, in a hopeless little gesture, offered it to me, blind with tears. 'Tony. Tony . . .' It was abject, pleading, and her wet eyes shone with irresistible affection.

And that did it. All the unworthy and shameful feelings I'd had about her of late evaporated, and here before me stood my dear, innocent, loving, open-hearted little Emma Sarah. I took the watch, held it for a moment, and gave it back.

'It's all right, Emma Sarah,' I said. 'Stop crying. It doesn't matter about the money, you can have the blinking tomatoes on me. Give me a smile.'

At once, the tension oozed out of her. For a second she drooped. And then that magical smile of hers blossomed.

'Put your watch back on.'

But she was still trembling, flustering, and so I put her Timex on for her myself. Having watched me do so, she flung her arms around me and held me tight. She had some strength did Emma Sarah.

'Come on now, kid. Buzz off home.' I loosed myself from her, opened the shed door and held it for her. 'Off you go . . .'

She shook her head. 'I want to . . .'

'No. Off home, Emma Sarah. Your mother wants the tomatoes.'

'All right.' She accepted everything I ever said to her.

As I held open the shed door, I now realised that it had begun to rain out there. I looked at Emma Sarah. She was smiling now, happy, and wiping the last tears from her cheeks with the back of her hand. I thought that I might keep her here until the rain stopped, let her chatter for a while, and enjoy the presence of her as I always did. But her mother would be waiting. I took my jacket off. 'Put this over your head,' I said. 'You don't want your frock to get wet. Come on. I'll come with you.'

When we stepped outside, she put her arm around my waist and, side by side, we trotted to the farm. Mary must have seen us coming.

She was standing in the doorway, laughing as always.

'You didn't pick up the money!' she laughed at her daughter. 'Here, Tony . . .' She put a fifty pence piece into my hand. 'By hell, lad, you're going to get soaked.'

'Who cares?' I said, feeling water trickle down my back under my shirt.

Despite all that, I did my best as time went by to avoid Emma Sarah. My mind was on Margaret. I was seeing her as often as I could. I did not visit the farmhouse and when she came knocking at the door I ignored it, pretending that I was out. On several occasions she was sitting in the greenhouse waiting for me when I came home. I told her that I had too much to do to see her, and sent her off, downcast back along the lane. It hurt me to do that, yet in the presence of her, in her innocent eyes, in her great affection for me, the lingering regret I felt at having had those shameful feelings for her was beyond endurance. I found it too painful to think even of seeing her mother. Presently Emma stopped turning up. Several weeks went by.

15

Our dining room at home had rarely been used, but I found myself in there one evening searching for something in the sideboard drawer. I didn't find what I was looking for but I did discover something else – my father's old camera, a Rolleiflex SLR. I have no idea why he'd bought it – he was never truly interested in photography and nor was I. Its leather case was pristine and the camera itself looked brand new. But as soon as I saw it I was delighted. I could now take some photographs of Margaret.

Over the next few weeks I actually took dozens of her and I still have five in my desk. I'm looking at one of them now.

To please her one Saturday evening I took her to York Minster where the Hallé orchestra were paying one of their visits. I'd seen that some Brahms was on the programme, and some Beethoven and Holst I think. Slyly from the seat next to hers I took this picture of her, in semi-darkness, enrapt, her face touched by pale light. It captures her perfectly, that gentle sense of almost nervous stillness. As I took the picture I wanted to hold her in my arms.

Another photograph of her was taken when we visited a stately home in North Yorkshire. She is sitting on the low wall surrounding the fountain in front of the house. Her head is on one side and she is waddling the fingers of both hands at me. We had set off on a tour of that vast house, moved from room to room being lectured about the priceless paintings, the priceless furniture, the immense richness of everything in sight. After barely a quarter of an hour of it, Margaret touched my arm. 'I think I've had enough, Tony. It's all show, all pride. There's no heart in this place.'

So we bought some pop and a cake, sat for a while on the fountain wall, and walked deep into the grounds. There we lay down and had an hour of innocent love making under trees.

I was surely in love with Margaret, that youthful, excited, madness that renders absence from each other a pain. I took her home and fed her on meals carefully prepared from Mother's cookery books. I sat looking happily at her in the glow of the fire. I bought her bits of jewellery and a little red beret.

One Saturday afternoon, while Sam was asleep in bed after a night driving his locomotive and Mother was at her shop, I walked up to Cromford House. I had almost completed my catalogue of Miss Lovatt's library, a task I'd worked on assiduously for weeks. The lady had supplied me with a large, indexed ledger and I'd so far entered into it about a thousand titles in my best handwriting. It was a labour I'd enjoyed and a work that I was inordinately proud of.

Hoppalong John was in the front garden. His spade was impaled at the edge of one of the flowerbeds and for the moment he was sitting on one of the benches taking a break. I went and sat next to him. One of his gnarled, sinewy hands was resting on the seat between us, tapping

its fingers. His flat cap was tilted backwards and his forehead was moist. The house, with its wide grey face and
its many windows, like glinting eyes, forty yards or so away,
watched us placidly while we talked. Again, a bevy of birds
flew in circles around the tousled crown of the redwood
at the centre of the lawn and away on the far side the trees,
now at their full density of foliage, were like a solid wedge
of green against the pale blue sky. A cat appeared from
around the side of the house and stalked, head down,
across one of the beds.

'Damn things,' John said. 'They pee all over my seeds
and bugger 'em up. I can get some stuff to put down, but
I think it kills 'em, and who wants to do that? That thing
probably belongs to an old woman somewhere who thinks
the world of it. I wonder if a cat would do old Miss Lovatt
any good?'

'She'd have had one, wouldn't she, John, if she wanted
one?'

'I suppose so. She's on her own again now, you know.'

'Is she? What happened?'

'Those two buggered off last Wednesday.'

'Her two pals?'

'Well they couldn't've been all that pally with her, could
they? You could see they were as thick as thieves, those
two. Took the place over completely.'

'Well I know what Clara was like,' I said.

'The other one was all right, really,' John said. 'When
you got her on her own. She was a decent sort – young
and friendly. She was always painting pictures.'

'I know. I saw her at it on the lawn here, painting the
house. She had long red hair.'

'Yes, she was all right on her own. It was when her and that bloody Clara got together . . . Anyway, I'm glad they've gone. They didn't go empty handed though, you know.'

'Didn't they?'

'The old fool gave them the car.'

'What – the Rolls Royce?'

'Aye – and not only that, you can bet your life. They came, leeched off her till they were fed up with her, and then left her, just like that, with the car and a dollop of money, you can bet your life. She's a daft old thing. It makes your blood boil what some people can do. So there she is now on her own again. I don't think she'll realise it, but she's a hell of a sight better off without 'em.'

'I think you're right,' I said.

John straightened. 'I'm planting some fuschia,' he said. 'Should look good in mid-summer. She'll be able to see them from her drawing room window. What're you going to do this afternoon?'

'A bit more work in the library. Not long – an hour . . . I've got exams coming up in July.'

Together we got to our feet.

'Go and have a look at her before you leave,' John said. 'She's a bit in the dumps.'

As it happened, I worked for rather less than an hour. The ink in my fountain pen ran out and Alma, who might have found some for me, didn't work on Saturday afternoons. So I closed the ledger, put it carefully away on its shelf, and, walking down the lobby, knocked on the drawing room door.

I had to wait for a moment. But when Miss Lovatt

answered she knew who it was. She must have seen me earlier in the garden with John.

She'd been dozing. On a low table was a ball of wool or something. Under her hands on her lap was what I first thought was knitting but which I then saw to be crocheting. She was sitting in a high-backed winged chair, upholstered in blue fabric with fringes. Three others chairs, the same, were placed about. There was a high dark oak sideboard surmounted by a large mirror and laden with a collection of silver. The room was panelled to the dado with the same wood. A small but heavy-looking chandelier hung from the ceiling. But the carpet, the heavy curtains, the wallpaper, and even Miss Lovatt herself, were grey. Her grey hair, quite curly when I'd last seen it, was combed smoothly backwards to a little bun. She wore a light, lacy grey dress, long, down to her ankles, and grey velvet shoes. She looked so small, neat, very nice.

For a few moments she remained drowsy. I picked up the ball of thread and put it on to the side table by her chair.

'Thank you, Anthony,' and she put her work down next to it. 'It's good of you to look in on me. You've been to the library again.'

'Yes. I'm well on with the work,' I said.

'I know. Haven't I seen you at it? And I've taken the liberty of looking into the book you're compiling. Very nice.'

'Well at least you'll know where to find things when I've finished.'

'Yes.' She fiddled with a pearl necklace at her neck. It seemed to be irritating her. 'How's your mother, Anthony?'

'Very well. They've made her a manager of some kind.'

'Well isn't that nice? I'm so happy for her . . .' She now touched the lacy fringe of her left sleeve, smiled, and looked closely at me for a second. 'I've told you, haven't I, how like her you are? She wasn't so happy while she was here with me, you know. I could always tell. Your mother is such an open person.'

'Well things had happened.'

'I know. Your father. So sad, so unfair . . . But I hope she's happier now – smiling more.'

'She is, Miss Lovatt. She is.'

'Good.' She looked down rather wanly and said nothing for a moment. But when she looked up she was smiling again. 'Clara and Miss Schofield have left.'

'Yes, John told me.'

'So here I am. With this silly great house to myself again.'

'I don't think it's all that silly,' I said.

'Don't you? Well you don't live in it. My mother never liked it at all, you know. But my father thought it was a kind of heaven. Well never mind. Here I am.'

'Are you a bit lonely, Miss Lovatt?'

She hesitated for a moment, then asked, 'Do you know anything about loneliness, Anthony?'

'Well no. I don't suppose I do.'

'Then I can tell you, it isn't very nice.'

'No. I don't suppose it is . . . But you can always go on those holidays you used to have, can't you?' I suggested. 'Didn't you used to go to Torquay or Bournemouth all the time?'

'Yes. But it's not the same now . . .'

'Isn't it? Why?'

'I can't explain that to you, Anthony. But never mind. Are you taking any books today?'

'No. I'm swotting for A -levels.'

'Then you haven't much spare time. Well never mind.'

'It depends,' I said. 'Why?'

'Well . . . I think I told you I've never read very much myself these days.'

'Yes, you did.'

'I just thought . . . But never mind, Anthony. It doesn't matter.'

'What were you going to say?'

'I thought you might be good enough to come and read to me for half an hour now and then.'

'Would you like me to?'

'Yes, I would. Very much.'

'Then I will. I'd be glad to.'

'Really? Do you mean that?'

'I wouldn't say it if I didn't.'

She smiled. 'No, I don't suppose you would. You're very direct, aren't you?'

'What would you like me to read?'

'Oh I don't know. Anything.'

'What about Jane Austen?'

'I've read some of Jane – but yes, I'd like to hear it again. I'll pay you, of course.'

That offended me and I said so.

She held a hand towards me. 'Oh no – please, I'm sorry. But why should an old woman like me take your time up . . . ?'

'Because I'd like to do it.'

'Really?'

'Yes.'

Again she reached a hand towards me. 'Thank you, Anthony. Thank you . . . When will you come?'

'How about Wednesday evening about seven.'

'Lovely. That'll be lovely.'

As I left, she got up and took hold of my hand. 'Thank you, Anthony. I'll look forward to seeing you.'

16

And then came one of the bitterest moments of my life. I lost Margaret. We met one evening at the stile in the lane and followed the footpath there, which led across country, for about a hundred yards. Then, leaving the track, we walked hand in hand, through the wood, and on until we came to a spot we'd come to know well. Here, at the edge of a patch of tall broom, I put down my jacket for Margaret to sit on, and, hidden from the world on three sides, looking out through an arc of sixty degrees, we sank on to a thick carpet of sheep-shorn grass. We could look away and see in the distance the spire of Sandwell church surrounded by its Scots pine guard of honour, and the wide expanse of the Low Moor. It was early afternoon. The sun was high and under its heat you could hear gentle crackling sounds from the broom and the singing of larks and, at one moment, the rhythmical sound of a train passing three miles away beyond the hill.

Margaret was wearing a white, thin cotton sleeveless summer dress and sandals. Her face, nice arms and strong legs – even her feet – were quite tanned. I had once told her that I liked her pony tail and that was how she'd worn her hair at all our meetings since. But it was now done up in a bright red ribbon and falling loosely. I told her that I liked this style even better.

We sat upright, Margaret with her arms around her knees, silent for a while. Sheep were grazing away over by the wood.

Then she asked, 'Are you still working hard?'

'Not too hard. Are you?'

'Yes. I don't seem to have made much progress of late, though.'

'Why?' I asked.

'My memory seems to've gone dormant.' She gave a little laugh. 'Nothing seems to be staying in my brain.'

'Well you should just read things over three or four times.'

'I do that. But it still slips away.'

'Then write it down three or four times. You'll remember it then. You can always remember what you write. Well, for a while at least.'

'I've tried it all. But never mind. Don't let's talk about that.' She reached out for my hand, held it for a moment, and let it go. 'Dad took Mother and me to a zoo last weekend. I wish I hadn't gone with them.'

'Why?' I asked.

'It made me feel quite sad. There was a lion, a huge, wonderful animal, trapped in a tiny cage, pacing to and fro, to and fro, and looking utterly miserable. In that tiny cage when he should've been roaming free in Africa somewhere. Why do people do it?'

'So that you and your father can see a lion. Have you thought that he was better off in that cage?'

'Don't be silly, Tony.'

'When a lion's roaming Africa all he's ever doing is looking for something to eat, and that isn't always easy to track down, is it? In the cage he just paces about knowing that at any minute somebody's going to throw in half a cow.'

'But how can they confine him like that – when he's known such freedom?'

'But he might not have known freedom, Margaret. He might've been born in captivity. All he might know and want is his cage.'

She slapped my hand. 'You're arguing with me again.'

'Well I'm telling you not to be upset by a pacing lion.'

'But there was a polar bear in a little pit with a little pond in it – doing the same, pacing round in little circles, wrapped up in himself, obviously utterly fed up. It was so sad.'

'Well it's warmer here in England than where he comes from, Margaret.'

'Oh stop it! I'm not going to talk about it any more.' She stretched out her legs and pulled her skirt down over her thighs. As she did so, I put my arm across her shoulders and kissed her cheek.

'You feel hot,' I said.

'Yes. I'm not so cold-hearted as you.' But she smiled.

A bee buzzed by. We watched it zip up, down, back on itself, and off into the sunshine.

Margaret took my hand again. For a while neither of us spoke or moved. But the usual preliminaries were over. Without glancing at me, she stretched out on her back on my jacket, closed her eyes, and waited.

I leant over her and looked down at her face. Margaret

was not pretty in the conventional way. Her forehead was narrow like her brother's and her nose slanted slightly to the left. But I saw beauty in her, in the gentle smile on her face, in the warm, gentle spirit which emanated from her limp, submissive body. As I hovered there, she opened her eyes, wondering at me, and I saw beauty in that gentle brown gaze.

I unbuttoned her dress down to the waist. There was submission in the soft touch of her hands on mine, and willing submission in the fact that she had bought herself a brassiere which untied at the front. Her youthful breasts, quite moist with perspiration, responded as always to my touch with a delightful hardening of the nipples. She put a hand to my face and drew me down to kiss her on the lips.

'I do like you, Tony,' she said. 'Hold me tight for a minute.'

Time passed – half an hour at least. I fondled her, she smiled, touched my hands, touched my face. The sunlight was hot on my back and I could feel trickles of sweat under my shirt.

'You'll get your chest blistered in the sun,' I said.

She raised herself, put her arms around me and, laughing, said, 'No I won't!' Kissing me again, she sank back. She raised her knees, her skirt slipped back a few inches down her thighs, and it was then that I ruined everything for us.

The pleasure of loving Margaret like this, of stroking and kissing her flesh, had always been in that shared excitement, that feeling of great affection, the thrilling intimacy of giving openly to each other. But now, as she kissed me, as she smiled so happily into my face, as my hand cupped her breast, I suddenly felt a passion I'd never before felt in Margaret's presence – a hot, desperate eroticism, a gasping, almost savage sensation, quite uncontrollable. I thrust my hand up her thin skirt and, gripping the elastic of her knickers, began to snatch them down.

I felt the shock go through her. She gave a little cry, reached for my hand and tried to stop me. 'No, Tony . . . No!'

It had no effect on me. I went on pulling.

She tried to wriggle away but I held on. She sat bolt upright. I held on. She slapped my hands. I held on – and an angry little battle began. Her strength surprised me but didn't stop me. I couldn't help myself. It was only when I looked into her stricken face, when she said, 'Oh no, Tony – not you, not you . . .' that I began to realise what I was doing.

Big tears were rolling down her cheeks and she was looking at me with a heart-rending expression of mingled disappointment and pain.

I drew away. She pulled up her knickers, pulled down her skirt, got to her knees and turned her back on me.

Bitterly ashamed, full of regret, I couldn't speak for a moment. And when at last I said, 'Oh God, Margaret. Forgive me – I'm sorry,' I knew already that it was hopeless.

Keeping her back to me, kneeling, head bowed, she put her hands to her face and wiped away tears. Then she stood up.

'I'm sorry, Margaret.'

She turned to me. 'Oh Tony.'

There was nothing more for me to say. My heart had withered.

Side by side, we went around the patch of broom, through the wood, along the footpath and back to the stile without a word being said.

When we stepped down into the lane, she couldn't bring herself to face me. 'I don't want to see you again, Tony.' There were still tears in her voice.

'Very well, Margaret. I'm sorry.' And she walked away from me.

My journey home lasted about fifteen minutes. The shame was still racking me. The regret at having so much upset dear Margaret was acute.

Thereafter, I could not get her out of my mind. She lingered in my heart like an agony. I longed to see her, to have her back in my life, and over weeks, many times, I went to hide from sight and gaze at her home for hours, hoping to see her, hoping for a chance to meet her, talk to her, have her forgive.

Thoughts of her were still tormenting me when I went to read to Miss Lovatt one evening.

As it happened, I arrived a few minutes late this evening. I could expect Miss Lovatt to be in one or other of her fine grey dresses, or in one or other of her fine pale blue ones. Only rarely was she in green. But that's how she was now.

As usual, she was very pleased to see me. She stood up, reached for my hand, and said, as she always said, 'How good it is of you to come, Tony.' (At my insistence she'd ceased to call me Anthony.) She was drinking coffee. 'How's your mother?' She always asked that.

She had thin wrists and pale skin. Today she was wearing her dangling, bright red ruby ear rings. She always wore that pale pink lipstick.

She looked at me, smiling. 'I've got something for you.' Reaching down to her bag at the side of her chair, she went into it and handed me a small parcel wrapped in patterned paper.

'What is it, Dora?' (At her insistence I called her that these days.)

'You'll see if you open it.'

In a smart leather box, on a cushion of white silk, was a Rolex wrist watch.

'Oh now Dora . . . !' I began.

'Don't you dare say anything! Just tell me if you like it.'

'Of course I do.'

'Well wind it up. Set the time.' She looked at her own watch. 'It's just eight minutes past seven. Now put it on your wrist.'

'What you're trying to tell me, Dora, is don't ever be late again.'

She gave her tinkling laugh. 'No, not at all. But I do get anxious when you're late. I always think you're not going to come.'

'Well I'm here now. Let's get back to *Mansfield Park*.'

The light was beginning to fade at that time of day and so I sat to read under a tall standard lamp. I read for almost an hour, had a five-minute break, and read on till shortly after nine.

She always sat with her eyes closed for a minute or two when the reading was over, perhaps absorbing what she'd heard. Then she always said, 'That was lovely, Tony. You do read so very well.'

She took care to look after the book herself. Placing the

red, tasseled silk book mark between the pages, she closed its covers, stroked the binding and said, 'Thursday?'

'Yes.'

'Lovely.'

She reached for my hand. 'I can't tell you how much I enjoy your reading. I so much look forward to it. You're so very kind.'

'I think I've asked you not to say that, Dora. I enjoy it myself.'

'Are you happy with your watch?'

On the third Saturday of June, Mother, Sam and I set off in the Mini for a week's holiday. It was the only week Mother could get off just then, but since it was still term time and examinations were imminent I'd had to plead for permission, which was only granted when I agreed to take work with me. Mother had wanted a hotel holiday. She'd grown used to the luxury of such things. But Sam, used only to lodging houses and railway hostels during his times away, wasn't happy with that, and Mother had quickly relented. They'd taken a two bedroom isolated cottage a few miles south of Towyn in mid-Wales.

On the first evening, we arrived at the cottage shortly after eight, too late for anything but a stroll about the place.

But next morning I got up at about ten and went out to the front lawn just in time to see my mother in a smart red swimming costume tripping across the sand towards the water. Sam was sitting on the lawn. He'd bought a camera.

Resting it on his raised knee to avoid judder, he was

taking her photograph. As I sat down beside him, he wound the spool on and took another. 'Your mother's a lovely woman,' he said.

She reached the edge of the water and began to tip-toe about with her arms outstretched like a ballet dancer.

'The water must be cold,' Sam said.

Mother made a bold effort to wade further in, changed her mind and settled for a paddle.

'I'll get your breakfast,' Sam said to me.

'No you won't. Go and have a swim.'

'I'm not all that good at swimming. I'll get your breakfast . . .'

'Let me get it myself, Sam.'

'Look, lad, I said I'd do the cooking. Your mother's here for a rest.'

'So are you,' I said.

'I don't need a rest. Besides, I'm a damned good cook. You know that. I've lived alone for donkey's years and I've learnt a thing or two.' He made to get up.

'Stay there,' I insisted. 'I'll get my own blinking breakfast. Take another picture of Mother.'

Sam was still ridiculously trying to earn his place in the ménage, chasing after Mother, seeking out her every whim and feeling it necessary to behave like a dogsbody. Just as he'd gone crazy with the vacuum cleaner at home, so here he went crazy with the sweeping brush he'd found in the kitchen. I caught him one morning brushing the carpet in the cottage living room and then having to wipe away the dust he'd created. 'Why're you doing that, Sam?' I asked.

'Well you can see – it's not been done for years. The muck's ingrained,'

'Well it's not our muck.'

'Cleanliness is next to godliness, Tony. Where there's muck there's germs. Shift your feet . . .'

But on the third morning he did go down to the water with Mother.

Sam was only an inch or so taller than my mother and I realised now, as I watched them, that his left leg was slightly bandy. That had never been obvious while he wore trousers. Shorn of his clothes, he seemed quite skeletal, knobbly, fragile. Hand in hand he and Mother entered the sea and paused. Then, loosing herself from him, Mother decided to brave the cold, frothing breakers. She waded forward, swaying from side to side, jabbing her elbows, and began to do the breaststroke. Sam waded out with her, concerned for her, going out until he was up to his waist. He held his arms towards her nervously as if afraid she might either sink and drown or perhaps swim on for ever. It turned out that he couldn't swim at all himself.

Over meals with them, and watching them together, I had recently begun to notice yet another change in their relationship. It had become vaguely awkward again, and again because of Mother. It was not that hint of coolness she had once shown, that hint of fending him off when he appeared to be getting too close – not that smiling, gentle rejection. That had ceased weeks before. No, it was something less easily understood by me. The smiles she'd had for him were still there, the affection, but now and then these days there was a strange kind of – I can only say tolerance in her look. It was as if she was trying to come to terms with something in him, something which only she could see, doing her best to accept it. What was it? What could it be when Sam was clearly so devoted to her, so utterly willing to be a doting slave to her?

I had a poor night on the Wednesday, slept fitfully and, unable to endure it any longer, I threw away the sheets and got up very early. I found Sam in the kitchen.

'By hell, Tony. You're up early. What's come over you?'

He told me he'd seen a place where mushrooms grew. 'I was just going to collect some. You want to come with me?'

'Yes,' I said.

We found a colony of them in the shade of trees.

'I've got a nose for them,' he said. 'I was brought up near Dartford heath and we used to go mushroom hunting all the time.' He'd brought a saucepan. 'Put 'em in here,' he said. 'We'll have these beauties for breakfast.'

We walked back towards the cottage.

'Where's Dartford,' I asked. 'Near London somewhere isn't it?'

'Not all that far. It's in Kent. I was brought up there. My father and my two brothers were clever dicks, you know.'

'So're you,' I said.

He laughed. 'Thanks! But no – they were all fitters, engineers, very skilled people. My father wanted me to take an apprenticeship with him and do the same. But I didn't want to do that. I wanted to drive railway engines.'

'And you got what you wanted.'

'Yes, I did, didn't I?'

We walked on a few paces, then I put a question I'd always wanted to ask of him.

'Did you ever get married, Sam?'

'No.' It was short, final.

'Sorry,' I said. 'I'm just nosey.'

We walked on. But then he looked at me and smiled. 'Well, I once had a girlfriend in Dartford.'

'Did you?'

'Yes. A nice girl. A neighbour. But some other fellow came along.'

'Well how did you come to find yourself in Yorkshire?' I asked.

'It was the job. I changed the firm I worked for. Let's get these mushrooms in the frying pan.'

Since we were leaving on the Saturday morning I had no option but to get up early again. We had breakfast and finished the last of the mushrooms, and then the tedious business of packing began. I bundled everything of mine into my bag and, leaving the others to it, I went outside. There had been that one shower overnight. A miasma of mist hung over the back garden and the plank bench up against the cottage wall was still patchy wet. I wiped a place dry with my handkerchief and sat down to gaze back at the cows by the fence. As always after an early rise, my head was full of cotton wool. I watched a fly crawl about the leg of my trousers, tried to swat it and failed. There at the end of the lane, waiting to rev away on its journey, stood Sam's Mini, a bit dusty at the moment.

Behind me and a yard to my left was the open window of Sam and Mother's bedroom and, suddenly, I heard Mother's voice from in there.

'Where did you say it was?'

Sam answered with words I couldn't make out.

'Well I can't find it,' Mother said.

Then Sam's voice again. 'I left it on the dressing table, didn't I? Hang on, love . . . No. Here it is . . .'

'Good. We don't want to leave that behind. D'you know where Tony is, Sam?'

'He's outside somewhere.'

'Well I hope he's not done one of his vanishing tricks.'

There was some movement, and then I heard, 'Daisy, love, I'm sorry.'

'It doesn't matter.'

'I was just a bit tired.'

'Yes, Sam. You often are. Never mind.'

'Daisy, it doesn't mean . . . Daisy, it's just that . . .'

'Sam, please. How many times do I have to tell you? It doesn't matter.'

'But Daisy . . .'

'Look, Sam, please find Tony. Tell him we're ready to leave . . .'

Anxious not to have them know I'd heard all that, I got up and quickly walked around the side of the house. At the corner, I ran into Sam. 'There you are, Tony,' he smiled. 'Are you ready? We're off now.'

At home on the Sunday, Sam and I converted the bathroom to a temporary dark room and developed the photographs he'd taken. There were more than thirty. There were three or four of me, three or four shots of the landscape around the cottage, a picture I'd taken of Sam with his hand shading his eyes from the sun, and about twenty pictures of Mother.

17

The exams went on over three days. Two Fridays later the school broke up for the summer holidays.

There had been a cooling off between Gerald and me of late. I can understand my part in that. After having, through my own crassness, brought about the end of my friendship with Margaret, and because he had made it clear how concerned he was for her, I felt uneasy with him. As to what might have accounted for Gerald's part in the coolness I had no idea. We'd sat in class as always, talked, walked together, but only briefly, and he hadn't taken the trouble to ride down on his bike to our house. At one time we'd been eager to sit together on the school bus, but lately both of us had been willing to sit with others. However, on our last day, on the way home, we did sit side by side. It was Gerald's final day at school. He reminded me of that.

'I feel as if I've been let out of Armley prison,' he said. 'You're staying on.'

'Yes.' I intended to swot for a quick new A-level.

'You'll go raving mad before you've done at school, you know. I'll bring you flowers in your padded cell.'

'Thanks. Make it deadly nightshade.'

'Margaret's staying on as well,' Gerald went on. 'But

you know that. She wants to go up to teacher training college.'

'Yes.'

'What happened between you and her, Bony?'

I was vastly relieved to hear that from him. Obviously she'd told him nothing. 'She just got fed up with me,' I said.

'Well doesn't everybody? Anyway, it's suit and collar and tie for me from now on. Nine to five. And I tell you, I'm looking forward to it.'

He'd landed a job with his father's employer. But unlike his father he had no wish to drive locomotives. 'I've decided to get cracking, Bony,' he said. 'I've worked out that if I keep my head down I'll get the top job in the firm in about seven years. Then I can retire with a hell of a good pension.'

'What'll you do then?' I asked.

'I think I might decide to play for Leeds United or Harlequins. On the other hand . . .'

'Well?'

'It's just occurred to me. I could open a harem in Guatemala.'

'Why the hell Guatemala?'

'Well it sounds good. Guatemala. The women there've all got big tits.'

'How d'you know that?'

'Well it stands to reason, Bony. Guatemala. Doesn't that mean big tits in Spanish? I might also open a brothel for my mates. I'll let you know. I start on Monday morning. Nine o'clock.'

'Well good luck, Gerald. I hope all goes well for you.'

'Thanks, Bony. I'm going to miss you, you know. But on

second thoughts, no, I won't.' He laughed and slapped my thigh with his big hand.

I felt rather sad. Looking into his large, grinning, so familiar face, I was certain that I myself was going to miss *him*.

'How's Margaret?' I asked.

'Oh still a bloody pest.'

I longed to ask about her, I longed to tell him to tell his sister that I loved her, but what was the point?

I now had to find ways of enduring six weeks' holiday.

18

I awoke one morning with the impulse to walk down the lane and have a look at Mary and Emma. Taking with me some of Sam's tomatoes, last ones, very poor, as an excuse I set off for the farmhouse. Emma Sarah could often be found in the yard there, and I'd hoped that would be the case now, but when I passed round to the back of the house there was no sign of her. Something did catch my eye. I saw a sudden movement close to the now empty barn, but it was such a brief thing that I thought it must be a bird fluttering by.

I knocked at the back door and after a moment or two Mary stood there. She looked rather tired and was wearing the same sort of things she'd always worn in the past as a farmer's wife – a baggy white blouse and a thin white skirt. Her perm had grown out since I'd last seen her and her hair was quite straight. She had on a pair of floppy fabric house shoes.

She was not at all welcoming. 'Well!' she exclaimed. 'You've cropped up again after all this time, have you? You come, you go, and you don't come back.'

'I'm sorry, Mary. It's been nothing but exams for me . . .' I began, but, looking at the bag I had in my hand, she interrupted me.

'You've brought me some tomatoes. I don't think I asked for them.'

'No, but you can always use them can't you?'

'Well all right. I'll get some money . . .' She turned away, obviously not wanting to invite me inside.

'No – I don't want any money. Here . . .' I gave them to her. 'Is Emma about?' I asked.

'Yes, somewhere. But what's that to you, Tony? You kicked her out, didn't you?'

'No, not really. It was as I say – I had my exams . . .'

'Oh rubbish. You sent her away and you nearly broke her heart. That girl loved you. So please, leave her alone now. I'm asking you to do that. Thank you for the tomatoes. Leave her alone, Tony.'

And the door was closed in my face. I couldn't move for a while. But when I did so – as I walked towards the corner of the house – I saw another flicker of movement in the shadows just inside the barn. Realising now that there was actually someone in there, I crossed the yard to it and stepped inside. 'Is that you, Emma Sarah . . . ?'

There she was, hiding in a corner, nervously sucking her thumb. 'Why're you hiding from me?' I asked. I went towards her but she quickly backed away. 'What is it, Emma Sarah?'

'Don't shout at me.'

'I'm not shouting at you.' I stepped closer and again she backed away.

'What's wrong, Emma Sarah?'

She could back away no further. She had come to the wall of the barn.

I hovered over her. 'What is it?'

'Go away, Tony.'

'Don't say that . . . don't say that . . . Look, I'm sorry . . . I told you I was busy . . . But I'm here now . . .' I reached out for her hand but she snatched it away.

'No, no . . . You're not my boyfriend now . . .'

'Course I am.'

'No, no . . . You make me cry.'

'I don't want to make you cry . . . That's the last thing I want . . . Give me your hand . . .'

But now she shocked me. She shook her head, clenched her fists and stamped her foot. 'Go away, Tony! Go away! I've got another boyfriend!'

'What?' It hit me like a pain. 'What? What d'you mean, another boyfriend . . . ?'

'Go away, Tony – please . . .'

'No. I won't go away. Who is it?'

'No – no . . .'

'Who is it!'

'No, no . . . !'

Suddenly angry with her, I grabbed her arms and pushed my face on to hers. 'Tell me!'

'No, no!'

So I shook her. I shook her hard. 'Who is it! Who is it! Who is it!'

Her head rocked backwards and forward. She screamed.

'What's his name!' I shouted. 'Tell me! Tell me!'

'All right, all right. Gerald, Gerald . . .'

It was as if I'd known. There was no surprise with it. 'Has he touched you!'

'You're hurting me!'

'Has he touched you – what's he done to you? Tell me . . .'

'Please don't hurt me, Tony . . .'

'What did he do to you . . . !'

'You're hurting me . . .'

I let go of her and, profoundly regretting having hurt her, I touched her cheek. 'I'm sorry, Emma . . . I'm sorry . . .'

There were tears in her eyes and she was as limp as a sad child. My heart was bursting with sympathy for her and now I could not resist embracing her, holding her to me and stroking her hair. 'I'm sorry . . .'

But there was no response. She stood stiff in my arms and turned her face away.

'Emma . . .'

She refused to look at me. When I stepped back she began to weep in that awful, pathetic way I could never bear to see. 'You hurt me. You don't love me. I love Gerald.'

Turning away from her, deeply concerned, I went back to the door of the farmhouse and knocked.

'Good God!' exclaimed Mary, opening it, looking at my twisted face. 'What's the matter with you!'

'Let me in, Mary, please, I've got to tell you something.'

'Oh what now!' she said, sighing. 'You'd better go on through . . .'

I went into the living room and, closing the outer door, she followed me. She gazed at me for a moment. 'What's that look on your face for?' she asked. 'What's got you now?'

'It's Emma . . .' I began.

'Well?'

'She's having sex, Mary. I'm sure of it.'

Mary simply stared at me. 'Is she?'

'She's having sex with someone I know. I'm sure!'

'What business is it of yours? You kicked her out.'

'Do you know? Do you know, Mary?'

'Of course I know. She's my daughter. I know everything about her.'

'But it's Emma! How can you let that happen! Emma!'

'You have nothing to do with Emma. You threw her out and broke her heart. And you've no damn right to be so bloody outraged.'

'Don't you care!'

'All I care about is that she's happy. Emma's a woman with a woman's emotions and a woman's needs. I've told you all this. You sat in my living room and I told you. But you didn't listen. I'm going to lose her. Who will marry her? She can never be a mother. She is going to die. Let her have some love and happiness while she can for God's sake you awful prig.'

'I know who it is, Mary. I know who it is . . .'

'And so do I. There's nothing wrong with Gerald Connolly. I meet his mother in the shop. They're a decent family.'

'Connolly's a bastard!' I shouted. 'He's taking advantage of her. He's a bastard! Emma — Emma!'

'Well you don't want her.'

'But Emma — with Connolly . . . !'

'Yes, Tony, yes.'

'But Emma . . . !'

'For God's sake stop saying that!' Mary swung away but then turned sharply to face me again. 'Emma's made of flesh and blood. Isn't she entitled to a bit of affection, a bit of happiness! Oh take that bloody silly look off your face and go. Just leave Emma and me alone. Just leave us alone.'

I was speechless, shaking with dismay at Mary and aching with sympathy for Emma. I hovered, paralysed for a moment, and then, turning away, I went out of the house.

As I did so, I saw that Emma Sarah had emerged from the shadows. She was standing looking at me, in her blue summer dress, with her thumb in her mouth. I saw a little smile on her face and she raised a hand in a little wave goodbye. My heart went out to her. There were tears in my eyes.

I knew that Gerald finished work at five. His bus would therefore pass through the village some time after half past. The afternoon dragged. I paced about. But by twenty-five past five I was waiting by the post office in the village. I was there for just over a quarter of an hour. Two people I knew, Mrs Foster and Mr Vickers, stopped to have a few words with me, no doubt wondering why I was hanging about there. But I was hardly aware of what was being said.

At last his bus came grinding into the village. It stopped close to where I was. From it emerged three people, home from work. Gerald was one of them, but, preoccupied, he failed to see me. As he walked away I walked swiftly after him.

'Connolly!' I called.

Now he turned and saw me. He was surprised. 'Hello, Bony. What're you doing here . . . ?'

At the sight of his grinning face anger became unbearable. I grabbed his arm. 'You've been shagging Emma!'

'Shush you fool!' He gazed around. 'Keep your voice down!'

'You shit!'

'Calm down, man. Where've you got that story? It's a lie, Bony. Who told you such a thing?'

'She did.'

'What? *She* did? Christ. What a bloody idiot she is.'

'How could you do it – Emma – a girl like that! You bastard!'

Again he tried to calm me, patting the air with his hands. 'Look, Bony, it wasn't what you think. Believe me . . . I rode past the farm on my bike. She was standing at the gate. She gave me a wave. I'd met her, hadn't I, with you, a couple of times . . .'

'You shit . . . Just your thing isn't it, Connolly! You took advantage of a girl like that . . . ! You shit!'

'Look, I'm trying to tell you if you'll listen! She wanted to go for a walk.'

'With you!'

'Why not? I get 'em that way.'

'It isn't bloody funny!'

'Look, Bony, I'm trying to tell you it wasn't my fault. It was her idea . . .'

'Emma? Never . . . you liar!'

'You obviously don't know what she's like, Bony my friend . . . She loves it. She begs for it . . .'

'Talk like that about her,' I shouted, 'and I'll bash you in the face!'

'You'd have a job on, Bony. I'd break your neck. And if you don't keep your voice down I'll break it anyway.'

'Well I'm telling you, if you don't leave her alone . . .'

'Oh give it up, man! It was only a bit of fun. Who the hell wants to be seen with that moron!'

'She's not a moron!'

'Well what is she?'

'I'm telling you, Connolly – if you ever see her again – and she'll tell me, she'll tell me – I'll tell her mother.'

'What?' That did affect him. 'Don't be a bloody fool. You know that would bugger me up at home – and at work. It'd bugger me up!'

'Well it's no more than you deserve, you bastard!'

He stared into my face with that remote, far-off look of his.

'Christ, you'd do it, wouldn't you . . .'

'I've just told you I'd do it.'

'Well fuck you, you sanctimonious bloody creep. You can have her. Who wants a freak like that anyway! You can have her. And now, Walton . . .' he grabbed my arm and squeezed it with all his great strength . . . 'just fuck off!'

With that, he turned away and marched, head high, towards his house.

Ten or twelve empty holiday days went by. I mooched about. I went for one of my safaris and sat in the middle of nowhere in a trance while it rained on me. I went several times to my hollow on the hill, not to read because I couldn't bring myself to read, but thinking of Margaret, knowing now that after my row with her brother I could never, even if I plucked up the courage to do so, go knocking at her door. I went to Cromford House and read to Miss Lovatt. I went out with Mother and Sam to the cinema in Leeds. I mooched about.

And then, as I sat in the living room, in another trance,

I answered a tap at the door and saw Emma Sarah there
in a thin white sleeveless frock with her thumb in her
mouth. She was offering me a handkerchief, folded neatly
into a small square. In its corner was embroidered a
beaming Persian cat. I took the handkerchief, looked at it
and gave it back to her, as was expected.

'Very nice, Emma,' I said.

Around her thumb was a nervous smile, but in her eyes,
and in her whole body, was an air of tentative, nervous
penitence.

'I love Tony,' she said, appealing to me in that irresistible
way of hers, waiting for my reaction.

'Well we love each other,' I said, and she expanded like
a blossoming flower.

'Come on in.' I took her hand and led her into the house.

We sat together on the settee with some distance between
us. She was bouncing, smiling, gazing intently at me.

'What've you been up to?' I asked. 'What can you tell
me?'

And she began, flapping her hands and bouncing close
to me: 'Well it was that wind and that little dog . . . She
lost that thing in the kitchen and that funny man came
to the door . . . But it was that wind . . .' And on she
went . . .

She was so close to me that I could feel the warmth of
her. When she wriggled, her hip pressed against mine. She
smiled and laughed and swayed about. The presence of
her touched my heart as it always had.

'How are you, Emma?' I asked. 'Are you all right?'

Suddenly becoming silent, looking directly into my eyes,
she took my hand in both of hers; put it to her lips and

kissed it. 'Oh I love Tony! You're my boyfriend. I love him. Shall I take my frock off?' And at once she began to undo the buttons at the front of her dress. 'I know how to do it, Tony . . . Wait, wait . . .'

'Don't!' I said.

'Pardon?'

'Don't Emma.'

'What?'

'Button your dress back up.'

'Why? Why?'

'Please, Emma.'

Now, she sat there staring at me, suddenly limp. As I watched, her eyes filled with tears. 'Why?'

'What shall we do?' I asked.

Her lips were trembling. Tears rolled down her cheeks.

'Oh Emma,' I said. 'My lovely Emma . . . Don't cry.' But I was crying myself. 'Shall we do some drawing. Shall I read something?'

'No.' She got up and turned her back to me. 'I don't want to do any drawing. No!' She looked around the room as if searching for something and then she said, suddenly. 'No. No! I want to go home.'

'Don't you want to do something?'

'No.' She shook her head. 'I want to go home.'

I took her there. Mary opened the door with a tea towel in her hand and a flushed face as if she'd been hovering over a steaming kitchen sink.

'You're soon back,' she said to her daughter.

Emma Sarah said nothing. She slipped past her mother and went into the house.

'You've brought her home, have you, Tony?' Mary asked.

'Yes,' I said. 'I think I might have upset her in some way, and I'm sorry, Mary. I care for her.'

Mary smiled, nodded. 'I know you do, Tony. I know. You always have. You're a decent young man. It showed on you as a little lad, six years of age, when you came knocking at the door. "Is Emma Sarah there?" Would you like a cup of tea or something?'

'No thanks, Mary.'

I was about to turn away when she held up a hand. 'She's all I have, Tony. She's all I've ever had even though I had that rotten sod of a man living here. She's been my life. She means more to me than anything.'

'I know that, Mary.'

'But she's not the same now, is she Tony?' She gazed beyond me for a moment and then turned to me again. She managed to find a smile. 'How's your mother, Tony?'

'She's fine. Away most of the time these days.'

'Well give her my regards.'

She held my hand for a moment, and as I walked away she waved and smiled after me.

19

It was then that the pattern of my life changed abruptly, as if someone had decided to turn a page.

I went into Leeds one day and bought a copy of *Anna Karenina*, which I intended to read to Miss Lovatt. With it wrapped in brown paper under my arm I walked down to Cromford House. It was a cool morning and there was a thin lingering mist. Mists did seem to gather there. I was surprised to see two or three cars in the drive, all parked at odd angles as if they'd arrived there at great pace and braked suddenly. As I walked across the lawn a figure wearing a long flapping overcoat and a cap came out of the mist. At first I didn't recognise him, but then I saw that he was limping. It was Hoppalong waving his arm at me like a policeman stopping traffic.

'Hello, John. What's up?'

'I'm sorry, lad,' he said, coming close. He hadn't shaved that morning and there was a streak of dirt across his cheek. 'She's gone.'

'What? Gone? Who?'

'The old girl. During the night. There's hell on here.'

'Miss Lovatt? Gone? Where? Why?'

'She died, son.'

'Oh don't tell me that, John!'

'I'm sorry. It's a hell of a turn-up. It's a shaker.'

'But how?'

'Heart attack or summat. For the first time in ages she had a party here on Friday and Saturday – all her old mates. They had a great time. On Saturday afternoon she came out to have a word with me and she was as cheerful as I'd ever seen her, wearing one of her fancy frocks. It's hard to take it in.' John put his hand to my shoulder. 'I can see it's knocked you for six. Me too. What's going to happen to this place now – and me?'

'Where is she?' I asked.

'In her bedroom. The place is full of strangers. Never seen 'em before. All after the money I suppose. You'd better just go home, Tony.'

Sad and deflated, with images of the lady filling my mind, I did so. I put *Anna Karenina* on a shelf and there it remained for years.

And then, only a few days later, at about half past two in the afternoon, while I lay half asleep on my bed, I heard Sam come home. Presently, I heard him climb the stairs and go into their bedroom. A minute or two later he came out, went down the stairs and came back up. Up and down he went three times. What was he doing?

But then there came a knock at my door. 'Are you in there, Tony?'

'Yes – come in, Sam.'

He preferred to stand in the doorway. 'I just want to say cheerio, Tony.'

'Right, OK. Where're you going?'

'Well I'm leaving.'

'What? What d'you mean?'

'I'm going, I'm sorry, but it has to be.'

I got off the bed and stood up. 'What . . . ?'

'I'm sorry, lad, but, well, I've got to go.' He turned away.

'Hang about Sam . . .'

'No, it's all right, Tony. I've got my gear downstairs . . .'

'Wait!' I called, but he gave no response. So I followed him down the stairs. His old two suitcases stood in the hall.

'Sam,' I said, gripping his shoulder, 'what's all this about?'

'Don't be upset,' he said. But he was clearly upset himself. His eyes were moist.

'You can't do this, Sam . . . What about Mother . . . ?'

'It's not been right, Tony. We've not had a row or anything, but I've not been right for her.'

'Has she said that?'

'Your mother's a lovely woman and I'm not right for her.'

'Of course you are!' I shouted. 'Does she know you're going?'

'Yes. I understand her.'

'Well I don't!' I said.

'I can't explain, Tony, I can't. So please don't go on. Just let me go. It's been lovely here – the best time of my life. But all good things come to an end. Just let me say goodbye to you.'

'Don't do it, Sam!'

'Look, just let me go,' he said.

Carrying the two suitcases, I followed him to his car and put them on to the back seat.

'Hell, Sam,' I said, 'I'm so sorry.'

'It's all right.' He took my hand and shook it. The tears

were still in his eyes. 'It's all right. Goodbye, Tony, you've been good to me. Goodbye . . .'

And he got into his car and drove away. I never saw him again.

It could hardly have been a month later when a smart new green Volvo motor car arrived at our gate. I saw it from the window.

'Is my hair all right?' Mother asked me.

I didn't trouble to see the man. As Mary had once said, we must get our happiness as best we can. Then and always I prayed that Mother would be happy.

'I'm off, Tony. Is my hair all right?'

And there my recollections come to an end. Have I laid any ghosts . . .? I wonder.

How can I ever forget Emma Sarah? Shortly after my last sight of her, her mother sold the house. She and Emma Sarah left the village. Where they went was a question no-one could answer. I never spoke to Gerald again. He went to America and is no doubt still laughing away there. Margaret married an old school friend of mine and I still envy him.

I went up to Durham University and the years flew by. For three of those years after my return home I sat with Hoppalong John every Wednesday evening in the White Horse doing the pub quiz. John and I became the best of friends.

Kind, gentle Miss Lovatt is with me always. I have worn the watch she gave me every day for all those years. Indeed, the watch is on my wrist at this moment, telling me that it is now twenty-three minutes past eight on this silent autumn evening.

A Morse Code Set

The erosion of innocence is a cruel process,
and especially so, perhaps, if the innocents
are grown up people

I

Half an hour ago, I returned from Philips Park Cemetery, which is just off Briscoe Lane on the northern boundary of Manchester. It was a disturbing afternoon, and the mood it has created will, I know, linger with me for weeks.

The funeral had been arranged for two o'clock, but I was late. There had been fog and ice on the hills and the drive had taken me almost an hour longer than I had estimated. I arrived as the last prayers were being said.

The grave was in a hollow, where the ground sloped away towards the Medlock. I came round the little chapel and, hesitating, looked down across the sooty grass and smears of yellow mud to where the minister and the solitary mourner stood together by the mound of earth.

I don't know why I expected to see more people. If I'd thought about it at all, I would have found it difficult to imagine who else might turn up. But I hadn't thought about it, and the spectacle of those two dim figures, huddled together in the rain, gave me pause. Now, the prospect of meeting Mr Hanson – which, since there were no other people among whom I could lose myself, seemed inevitable – alarmed me, and I stepped back out of sight between the buttresses of the chapel.

It was a cold day. The rain touched my face like

pin-points. Out there in the open, gusts of wind pulled at the minister's robes and flapped Mr Hanson's raincoat limply like a sodden brown duster. Low grey clouds scudded across the maze of factory chimneys in Clayton beyond the river, and the sense of gloom and desolation which overcame me as I stood there was so powerful that my body ached.

I had come to this funeral almost involuntarily – almost as a reflex, not troubling to consider what the act of coming implied or what memories best left dormant the occasion would revive. If I had pondered the point, I would have been better armed against this subtle pain, perhaps. Indeed, I don't think I would have gone at all. Two decades had laid down their strata of forgetfulness, and if I had stayed away this afternoon I should have been able to go on forgetting. But there I was, at her funeral, within a mile of the house, looking away over that well-known view, and those old memories came bursting back irresistibly into my mind. Those long forgotten emotions took hold of me again as though it had all happened yesterday. Despite my thirty-odd years, I was literally trembling again with the fervent misery of a boy.

I like to think that as one grows older one develops techniques for keeping one's feelings more or less under control. This may not be true. It may be, quite simply, that one's emotions are less powerful, more manageable. But whatever the reason, it seems to me that no normal adult ever feels things so keenly as a child – and to be suddenly subjected, as a man, to such an intensity of childish feeling, was an unnerving experience. These remembered sensations of boyhood came back quite unaltered, filling me with infantile bitterness and depression.

The minister, who had been reading from a card which he held close to his chest, suddenly flung out both arms over the grave. For a second, he remained there, poised tensely. Then, with a perfunctory glance towards the sky, he withdrew his arms, tucked the card away under his robes and put his hands into his trouser pockets. Mr Hanson raised his head and looked at him. They spoke briefly. Mr Hanson put his cap on. And then, together, they turned from the grave and came up the hill.

They passed within three yards of me, but neither of them saw me standing there. The minister, his hands still in his pockets, his head to one side, was saying something to Mr Hanson and nodding gently. The sound of his voice, the words confused by the wind, came to me patchily as they walked by. It was over twenty years since I'd seen Mr Hanson, and even now I saw him only indistinctly. But I recognised that face at once. Two decades hadn't changed it much. The long nose, the small chin, that peculiar curve of the forehead . . . But he seemed shorter than I remembered him, slighter. This surprised me, and when they'd passed, I stepped out and looked after them. He was, indeed, an altogether small man, short and thin with sloping narrow shoulders – a figure which contrasted strongly with my memories. At the far corner of the chapel, they parted. The minister hurried inside out of the rain and cold and Mr Hanson walked on towards the cemetery gates.

With a decided effort, I left the shelter of the chapel, crossed the pathway and walked on to the turf. The ground was spongy with contained moisture, but the grass was somehow so brittle that it crackled under my feet like a carpet of twigs. A stray dog appearing from the forest of gravestones farther down, and came trotting to meet me. He circled me twice and went back the way he had come. I found myself contemplating him carefully. I stood still as he sidled round me, and observed his lolling tongue, the dark, matted fur along his spine. I have never cared at all for dogs, and find it difficult to tell one breed from another. They are creatures that mean absolutely nothing to me. And yet, for a full minute, this bedraggled animal occupied all my attention. His arrival seemed significant, and his departure was a distinct disappointment.

The fact was, I realised, that I simply did not want to complete this brief journey to the graveside. The superstitious feeling that the dog's strange behaviour was an omen, a sign to me not to do so, was in itself a reflection of that reluctance. Of course I did not want to go. I watched the dog slink away among the gravestones, and continued to search for it long after it had vanished, holding on to the thought of it in a silly effort to keep those other thoughts at bay.

But there was the grave, a stride or two from me, and a moment later I was at the edge of it, standing in clay and looking down. Even now, my gaze passed only slowly across the smooth, wet side of the pit. Little rivulets of water ran down from the pile of earth on the other bank and cataracted over the brink. On top of that mound, stuck upright in the hump of clay, there stood a spade. My first glance hardly took it in. But almost at once my eyes returned to it, and the fantastic symbolism of it quite paralysed me for a moment. But then, suddenly angry, I strode round the grave, pulled up the spade and threw it away. I was gasping and shaking, and despite the fierce cold, sweating profusely. Standing with my back to the grave, and with deliberately slow movements, as though by forcing my body to behave calmly I would somehow soothe my mind, I took out my cigarette case and matches and lit a cigarette. Then just as slowly, just as deliberately, I turned and looked down. There the coffin lay, at the bottom of that slimy pit, daubed with mud and under a sheet of rain.

For a long time I stared at it, thinking of her. But gradually I sensed something amiss, something wrong. When I realised what it was, I felt myself start. Once again, I had been surprised by smallness. The coffin seemed minute. It could hardly have been five feet long. My amazement was so profound that, for a second, it overwhelmed all other feeling. How could I have been so mistaken?

And yet the answer was obvious. Twenty-one years ago, I was thirteen, and not very tall at that. One's childhood memories are always out of proportion, as I had learnt so disquietingly already this afternoon. One always remembers looking up, and the mind rarely has the ability to make adjustments for one's own growth. But, despite this realisation, the sense of surprise persisted. And as I looked down at that little box, it dawned on me like a revelation that I had not known her at all. Thirteen years in a lifetime is a mere nothing – especially thirteen very immature, introspective years. I had not known her. All those images which had come flooding back into my mind were incomplete – seen through the eyes of a child who understood very little. All those memories were shadows, merely, warped and misshapen by the emotions and inadequate vision of a baby. And all those upsetting sensations, which were so much a part of those memories; they too belonged to another age, another person, almost. I simply did not know her.

For one painful moment, I began bitterly to regret those years of abandonment. If I had stayed there any longer contemplating that coffin, I think I should have gone a little mad with remorse and guilt. But the spell was broken by the arrival of two gravediggers. They came out of the mist like bats, leather capes flapping about their shoulders, and at the sight of them, I turned away and walked back to the path.

Once outside the gates of the cemetery, my mind began to readjust itself. One's defence mechanisms came to one's aid. It was true, I told myself, that I had not known her except as a child knows a person. But what difference did that make? If things had taken another course, if I had come as a man to know her, perhaps I would have understood. But understanding is not always forgiveness – and forgiveness there could never have been, for her, or, I feel in my heart, for me.

As I drove past the gates, I looked back briefly through the darkening vapours to where the gravediggers were piling earth on to my mother's coffin. They worked rhythmically, tossing their heavy spadefuls indifferently into the pit. A light came on in the chapel. It was getting late. Quickly, I drove on, up the hill, under the bridge and away.

2

During the early part of August, 1939, we spent a week's holiday at Anglesey. We had done the same thing every August as far back as I can remember. Reflecting on it now, I realise my parents must have had to struggle to raise the money for this yearly ritual. My father was a clerk in a cotton mill and must have earnt next to nothing. But like most English people of our kind, they regarded holidays as one of the foremost essentials of life. They were convinced that it did us good, that it 'bucked us up' as my father put it, that it strengthened us for the months of winter ahead. My mother often said that my natural immunity from colds during the winter was due to the holiday I'd had in the summer, and at that time I believed her. All this talk about the good air of Anglesey had its effect on me. I used to breathe it with reverence, consuming as much of it as I could while I had the chance. But in those days, I believed everything my parents ever told me.

In point of fact, I doubt whether a week's change of air had any physical effect on us at all. I am suspicious that seven days of unusually exhausting activity could be anything but debilitating. Yet, if my parents were so sure it was a good thing, then, I suppose, psychologically at least, it must have been. They both led undeniably humdrum lives – Father for two-thirds of the time in a musty, shadowy office entering invoices, and Mother for almost all the time in a box of a council house with the railway on one hand and a desert of red brick on the other. The change, if nothing else, must have been a blessing – which could be relished again with memories revived by the dozens of box-camera snapshots we always took. As for myself, those weeks at Anglesey were a delight. But this particular one, in 1939, was to be the last happy holiday we three would ever spend together.

At that time – I don't know whether it is still the same – Anglesey was not popular with holiday-makers. The spot to which we returned every August was a pleasant little bay about five miles south of Amlwch, which itself was only a tiny fishing village, and you could go for days without seeing another soul apart from the farmer who accommodated us, and his wife. Even they were anything but intrusive. This farmer had bought an old railway coach, set it up in one of his fields at the edge of the beach, and used to let it during the summer to visitors such as we.

The fact that my parents chose such a place for their holidays was, I think, significant. The favourite resorts of people living in Manchester were Blackpool and Morecambe, highly organised holiday towns and extremely populous, where it was impossible to escape from one's fellow man. The reason for this, no doubt, was that same herd instinct which, if you park your car irrelevantly at an isolated spot on a country lane, inspires the next half-dozen drivers to park alongside you. Most people feel happier, safer in crowds, of course. A crowd generates mood, and when you are in a crowd its mood takes possession of you. Most

people can manage to enjoy themselves much more, therefore, if they are surrounded by others hell-bent on doing
the same. But my parents, apparently, were different. They
chose to holiday at a place where they could be completely
alone, and this desire to abstract themselves was a potent
sign of the sort of family we were. My parents kept themselves very much to themselves. I never knew either of them
to have any outside friends – up to that time, anyway. They
never went anywhere unless it was together except on those
rare occasions when Father went to what he called 'the
Terriers'. It followed, naturally enough, that this with-
drawing attitude rubbed off on me. I am still the same.
My boyhood friends were very few indeed, and the absence
of other children in no way reduced the pleasure of these
holidays for me. A family which keeps itself to itself is
usually a close-knit family and to me at that time there
was, I'm sure, far more comfort to be drawn from a happy
closeness with my parents than I could ever have drawn
from a large circle of friends.

With the beach to ourselves, the three of us would spend
the mornings bathing and playing games together. In the
afternoons, no matter what the weather, we would go for
walks along the narrow, high-hedged lanes. On one occasion, I remember, we walked as far as Benllech, which must
have been a good twelve miles away. We may have been
stand-offish, but we were certainly energetic.

The fishing was good thereabouts. At the southern edge
of the bay there was the mouth of a little river, over which
passed a narrow footbridge bearing the beach path. At the
ebb of the tide, you could stand on the bridge and see
dozens of fish – rock salmon, flat fish and whiting – trapped

down there in two feet of water. It did not need much of either skill or patience to scoop up your supper with a fishing net. Father and I did it most evenings.

You could catch rabbits just as easily. The fields along the beach must have been unsuitable for cultivation since they always seemed to be lying fallow. They were covered with coarse, stubbly grass and surrounded by low dry-stone walls. These fields were infested with rabbits and over the years Father and I had developed quite a technique for hunting them. You chose a field in which rabbits were feeding, crept quietly into it and clapped your hands. Many of the rabbits, flashing their white alarms, would head for burrows, of course. But some you could be sure would take refuge between the loose stones of the walls. If you ran fast enough after them and noted carefully which part of the wall they entered, you could usually expose one, cowering and twitching, just by removing a few pieces of stone. It was rare that we ate rabbit, though, because Father never seemed eager to kill those we trapped. He would pick up the animal by its ears, hold it aloft for a moment and then put it down into the long grass. It was such things which endeared me to my father. He was just what I thought a man ought to be – strong and brave, I used to think, and good fun, but always kind, never cruel to anyone or anything.

Over the years, we grew to know that district almost as well as we knew our own little corner back home in Manchester, and my memories of the place now fuse one into the other. The pattern of those holidays altered so little that I have difficulty in remembering which of the recollections I have dated from that week in 1939 and which go back to previous years. But one thing I do remember very clearly indeed from 1939 – a snatch of overheard conversation which troubled me.

There were four bunks in the coach, or 'caravan' as we called it, two on either side at one end. I preferred to sleep in one of the topmost, and my parents slept one in each of the two lower bunks. The sleeping compartment was separated from the rest of the coach by a flimsy curtain. As usual, I had gone to bed earlier than they. I had, I think, slept for a while, but something must have wakened me. I remember lying there in that warm and surprisingly comfortable bunk listening to the sound of the sea and watching the gentle movement of the curtain ruffled by the stream of air from an open window, watching the sliver of light from the oil lamp in the other compartment come and go through the gap. My parents were talking in there, quietly, little intermittent murmurs to which, for a while, I paid no attention. But then, just as I was on the point of sleep again, their words began to make sense.

'It terrifies me to think of it,' Mother was saying. 'Can't they do something?'

'All they can do is fight. There is nothing else.'

'But a war! I couldn't stand it!'

Father laughed quietly. 'Don't worry. It won't last long. We've messed about enough. We'll have to get it over – and the quicker the better.'

'But what about us?' The unmistakable anxiety in Mother's voice stirred up uneasiness in me. Not because I had any idea what the war might really mean, but merely because the tone of her voice and the atmosphere of their whole conversation suggested that they themselves were afraid. Their apprehension simply echoed in my own mind.

'Us? We'll be like anyone else, Joyce. We'll be no different.'

'You'll be one of the first to go, won't you?'

'I suppose so. Some of the lads have gone already. In fact I was lucky to miss going last year.'

'I wish you'd never joined the Terriers! Why did you? What made you do it?'

'You know as well as I do. It was another few bob. And there was no talk of war then, was there?'

'If you weren't mixed up with them, you probably wouldn't have to go at all.'

Again that gentle laugh. 'I'm not all that old! In any case, we've got to get it over.'

For a moment, there was silence. And then Mother said something which I remember with absolute clarity. 'I'm scared. You don't know how scared I am. A war would be the end of us, Harry – I feel it in my heart.'

I lay there in my bunk and the sound of her voice lingered on in my mind, as it lingers this very moment. Her words distressed me then, but how much more deeply they would have distressed me had I known how truly prophetic they were.

With the war, everything did change, just as Mother had predicted, and that holiday marked almost the end of a way of life I had loved.

That, I suppose, was the reason why subsequent events progressed so tragically. There was too much happiness, too much love, and too few of us to share it. If I'd had brothers and sisters, if I'd been able to discover faults in my parents, or if there had ever been doubts about their affection for me or for each other, what happened later would have meant much less than it did. In a large family, in a family with a more diffuse spirit, each member develops his own independence: he finds his own sources of solace, either within himself or outside the family circle, and this sustains him in family crises. But in our case, our life together was the entirety of life. When that was threatened it was worrying indeed.

There seems to be a stigma attached to being an only child, and no doubt it is true that most children without brothers or sisters lack a very great deal. But the so-called spoiling of a child depends of course on the parents – on their attitude to him. If they treat him as a troublesome baby who must be kept quiet at all costs, then naturally he goes on being difficult in order to obtain the rewards. Or, on the other hand, if they regard him, since he is all they've got, as an object of worship, and lavish sacrifices on him, he will come to believe that the rest of humanity should sacrifice to him also. I do not believe my parents regarded me in either of these ways. Far from treating me as a baby, they seem, in retrospect, to have dealt with me almost as a contemporary. There was only one level of conversation between us – there was no special tone 'for the child'. Though I realise there were many things which they did not discuss in my presence, though in some matters I was profoundly naive, I think I was in other ways mature for my age. People, indeed, used to speak of me as an 'old man'. I understood something of the financial problems at home and had unchildlike views on lots of subjects. We discussed things together. If I wanted something, we would talk it over and if the decision went against me I understood why and did not pine.

And yet, for some reason, I used to offend people. Once, when I was about eight, I was asked by my schoolteacher, a middle-aged spinster with a nasty temper – whom we nicknamed 'Bloomers' because someone once claimed to have seen that she didn't wear any – to stand up and tell the class, 'Why, just why you so obviously consider yourself to be better than the rest of us!'

I was nonplussed. I stood there with forty faces grinning at me and one bespectacled, angry face, sneering at me, and I couldn't speak. I didn't know what on earth she was talking about.

'You think you're like Lord Almighty, don't you! Nobody's good enough for you, are they! I've been watching you at playtime. No one's good enough – oh no! You want the red carpet, don't you!'

It was an ordeal I never forgot, largely because I never fully understood why she should want to do this to me. The things she said were so ridiculously untrue. Of course, I didn't think myself better than anyone else! How could I?

In some way or other, apparently, I was different. I did not mix easily with other children – but not because of some conscious mental decision not to. It was just part of my nature. If I had an air about me, it was due to nervousness – which people misinterpreted. It seemed to me there was no less viciousness in asking me to stand up and explain why I felt myself better than others than there would have been in asking a boy to explain why he squinted.

Teachers weren't the only people who found it necessary

to humiliate me from time to time. There were also occasional episodes with other boys. Boys are like chickens in
this respect: if one of their community seems a little weak,
a little different, they will peck his eyes out, if they can.
Notwithstanding what one or two might have thought to
the contrary, however, until they learnt otherwise, I was
by no means weak. In my early days at school, I had three
or four progressively fiercer encounters, culminating in a
tussle with the acknowledged 'cock' of the school, a plump
boy called George.

The fight took place during the afternoon break. George
and his friends bore down on me menacingly and, for no
other reason than that it was about time the champion
reasserted himself, I was encircled. George had his jacket
off and I was suddenly at the receiving end of a hail of
blows. I went down once or twice, but the unreasonable
malice I could feel in those heavy, podgy fists infuriated
me. I flung myself at him, picked him up bodily, and hurled
him against the school railings. He fell in a heap, sat up
– and wept. His friends vanished in a twinkling, and I
searched about in vain for other bodies to hurl. I looked
down at the beaten George, prepared in my anger to give
him more. But at the sight of his wet face, his ruffled hair,
his crumpled shirt, and his earth-spattered little fat legs,
my rage evaporated. I helped him to his feet again and
into his jacket, which his departed friends had tossed down
in their retreat.

After that, I rarely had trouble from other boys. For
George was a great champion and the reputation of having
beaten him always went before me.

This burst of temper, however, had disturbed me. It was

as if I hadn't known myself – as if some crazy, uncontrollable spirit had taken possession of me. The same thing was to happen again later, but the terror of that particular moment seems to have suffocated my temper for ever.

Yes, there was something about me that upset certain people. But my encounters with such folk did not bother me over-much. Their disfavour did not unduly colour my naturally happy mood. I enjoyed school. There were things I was good at. Both my parents encouraged me in my schooling, and it was to please them that I tried so hard. It was always a wonderful thing to be able to go home and report some success or other in my lessons. I liked the atmosphere of the school. The regime was enlightened for an elementary school in those days, and in addition to arithmetic and English, as a rule the only two subjects really taught in such schools, we had lessons in history, geography and, I recall, nature study. This latter subject, to children such as we, who spent our lives in a concrete and brick city, was fascinating. During summer, we used to go for trips to various city parks where we had opportunities of spotting birds other than the sparrow, which was all we could otherwise have identified.

It was through the interest of one of the teachers that I became a member of the local church choir. This particular teacher gave us singing lessons. She was an earnest, mouse-like woman. During singing, she would set us off with one or two chords and then creep among us, putting her ear to each mouth in turn. She must have liked the sounds some of us made, for one day, after the lesson, she took two or three of us boys on one side and said, 'Why don't you join St. Joseph's choir? I know the choirmaster there, and they're always short of boys. Practice is on Wednesdays and Fridays. I'll arrange for him to see you.'

We thus had little option. I wasn't very keen on the idea myself. We had never been church-goers at home, and the thought of being a choirboy would never have occurred to me. The other boys were not keen on the prospect, either. But most of them needn't have worried. Only two of us passed the audition. The rest were sent home, highly relieved. My parents were pleased to think of me in the choir. They persuaded me to join and even came to services to watch me now and then. In time, I grew very fond of singing in the choir and attended services and practices regularly for over two years.

There is something fascinating about making music – good music – together with other singers. It is one of the few circumstances in which people will gladly forget themselves, sink their personalities into a community, abandon their individuality in order to create, as a body, something much greater than any of them could ever achieve alone. And in this there is a wonderful sense of satisfaction. Somehow, the singing of sacred music intensifies that feeling. The joy of it, to me, was something quite physical. The magnificent boom of the organ, the perfect blending of voices – that wonderful sound reverberating in the high vastness of the church; there was an emotion in it for me which, I'm sure, had little to do with the thought of God.

Nevertheless, like all children, I believed implicitly if not very avidly in God. One observed the taboos and conformed to the rituals with all awe. One was suitably serious about church. But I could not have been called a religious boy. I sang in the choir because I liked singing. There was nothing more to it than that.

School and the choir were the two things that interested me outside the home. The only real friend I had at that time was Billy. He lived half a mile away across the estate and he was older than me: by the summer of 1939 he had been at senior school for two years. There were boys living much nearer, boys of my own age, but distant and older Billy Hanson was my friend.

Trying to observe with detachment the boy I was two decades ago is really a futile thing. I find it difficult to see myself in that child; since then I have changed fundamentally: in 1940 I became suddenly a different person. Yet I would have thought, because of this, that one could look back at oneself, indeed as a different person, with complete disinterestedness. But that isn't the case at all. For I look back only through the memories of that boy. I can feel only the sensations that boy himself felt. I was wrong about my mother's height, apparently, and by the same token, I must have been wrong about many other things. All I can do is impose an arbitrary set of proportions. In fact, of course, height, weight, colour of eyes – these are only matters of marginal concern. As a child, one was aware much more of the essential personalities of the people close to one. All the same, I feel I must try to see my parents as figures and as they really were.

Mother, I must now believe, was small. She was also slender. I call to mind her hands – long fingers, white skin. Across my mind comes the image of her bandaging my thumb, and I remember looking closely at her hands on that occasion. They were graceful hands, without haste.

That slowness, that carefulness and uncertainty of movement was characteristic of her in those days. It was a
perennial joke with Father and me that we were always
waiting for her. She was always the last to be ready when
we were going anywhere – always tended to lag behind us
as we walked. We would tease her by each gripping one
of her hands and making a show of dragging her along.
Her hair was very fair – a misty yellow colour. Her face
was pale, almost pasty I suppose.

Father, too, must have been quite short – for when I
think of them together, I realise there was not a great
difference in their height. He was as dark as she was fair,
and wore a little moustache. So far as I was concerned, he
had a kind of presence. I could sense whether he was in
the house or not as soon as I stepped through the doorway,
before I either saw him or heard his voice. I used to think
there was something marvellous in this facility. But he
smoked a lot, and I wonder now whether it was simply
that I could smell cigarettes. Just as he was Mother's opposite in colouring, so he was completely unlike her in the
rhythm of his movements. He was quick, mentally as well
as physically. I used to think him extremely bright at mental
arithmetic – a capacity cultivated in him by his job, no
doubt – and he was clever with his hands. This was one
of the aspects of his character which made him so interesting a father. Together, he and I built a model railway in
my bedroom. It took a long time, since we could only buy
parts at infrequent intervals. He was a keen gardener – and
at various times he made me three cycles out of bits and
pieces unearthed from the corporation tip by the nunnery.
He always seemed to be making something or pulling

something to pieces. He couldn't sit still. He and I had such fun together. And he doted on my mother.

A few days after our return from that happy holiday in 1939, the schools were evacuated. My parents had refused to let me go, and I was left behind. Suddenly, all children vanished – even my friend Billy. I don't think there were more than half a dozen children left in the whole estate.

A week later, Father was called up.

3

Those first few weeks of the war were perplexing. Dramatically, everything was transformed. A great stillness descended, a great silence. One looked out from one's bedroom window across the valley of the Medlock and seemed to see a landscape paralysed under the pale September sunlight. Even the hiss and rumble from the factories over there seemed remoter than ever before. The streets, with the disappearance of the children who had brought life and laughter to them, were deadly quiet, crevasses in a desert, and one wandered about them like a lost sheep. After dark, not a light was to be seen; one was suspended in space under the stars. And yet mysterious forces were at work in that lifeless world. The windows of houses and shops suddenly became crisscrossed with paper tape. Large silver balloons hung over the city. Incredibly, factory buildings assumed disguises, and under camouflage tried to pass themselves off as rows of houses. Cinemas closed their doors, schools were locked up and dust filmed over their windows. It was a lonely, confusing time, for Mother no less than for me.

Father's departure devastated us. It was the sadness of his absence, and the consequent sudden change in a routine which had remained invariable ever since I could remember, rather than the awareness that the country was at war, which induced in me a biting sense of uncertainty, of fear. The cadence of one's existence was all at once interrupted – everything one had been used to was either gone completely or else drastically changed. A sense of security is often to a large extent a matter of habit and routine, and such sudden changes, inevitably, left one feeling anxious and empty.

The house itself seemed cavernous and cold. We had an old wireless at home that Father had made himself, and from the morning he went away it was never switched off for days. The noise of it helped a little to detract from the emptiness of the place. Yet even that device was not really very effective, because hours of broadcasting had been severely cut. There were long periods of silence and the programmes that did come over were restricted to organ music and news. Together, Mother and I would spend the first hour or so of the day brushing the carpets and dusting the furniture, often doing everything twice in an effort to keep busy at all costs. Then, sometimes for no reason since we did not always make any purchases, we would go up to the shops and spend half an hour staring into windows. Back home again, I would help her prepare lunch. Meals, though, grew progressively less elaborate. The point of cooking had gone, no doubt, and Mother no longer seemed to have any heart for it. Rations for two were scanty, but in other circumstances rationing would not have prevented her from making interesting meals. As it was, however, we ate baked beans, or chips, or bacon sandwiches. Still, I didn't mind; one's capacity for enjoyment was stunned, even one's capacity to enjoy food. In the afternoons, we would do a little gardening till tea – or sit in the window and watch the trains go past.

But the evenings were the most difficult to endure. News and interminable organ music on the wireless, utter blackness outside and just the two of us, gasping with boredom in the house. Most evenings, straight after tea, we both wrote to Father. It was difficult for me to write about nothing and a letter never took me more than five or ten minutes to finish. Mother seemed to find more to say. I used to watch her. Briefly, while writing to Father, she could abstract herself from the dreadful tedium. But it was a miserable abstraction. She invariably cried over her letters. From time to time she would raise her head and stare blankly across the room, her lips moving, absorbed in sad thoughts. She wrote slowly, with a steel pen, forming each letter with neat curves. When she had finished, she would read the letter over and over again before sealing it in the envelope. The letter, with mine, would go on to the mantelpiece ready for posting when we went to the shops next morning, and then she would take up her knitting. As with everything else she did, she knitted slowly. In six months, all I remember her producing were a balaclava helmet, a pair of mittens and a couple of pairs of socks – and yet she seemed to devote an awful lot of time to it.

For the first week or so, by habit, we maintained our accustomed times for waking and retiring. We had always been down of a morning at eight just as Father left for work. At night, I had gone to bed, normally, at nine and they had followed shortly after. But now it was often gone ten before she called me for breakfast and both of us would be back in bed eight or nine hours later. Mother seemed to have developed a great need for sleep – she found solace in it, I suppose. Sleep was a release. Oblivion was an escape from the sadness and the demoralising boredom.

I watched her grow more and more listless and with-drawn, and concern for her came to overmaster all my private fears and loneliness. My concern, perhaps, was more childish selfishness than anything else, for that strange mood of hers seemed to separate us, and this was distressing. In her dealings with me, now, there was a kind of automatism, an indifference, almost, which hurt me. She didn't talk to me properly any longer – her personality was shut away within her. Nothing I could do seemed to make any difference. In all kinds of ways, I tried to cheer her up. I had some money saved, and one day I went out and bought a Monopoly game which I thought would help. We played for about half an hour on the day I bought it, and it never came out of its box again for months. I used to beg her to let us go bus riding. This had once been a great thing with us. We would buy cheap day tickets and, loaded with sandwiches, spend the day riding about the suburbs. But she no longer seemed interested in leaving the house. Indeed, even shopping became too much for her, and I began to do it all. Now, she rarely even dressed properly but moped about the house in a dressing-gown. Nothing could interest her, nothing could amuse her – and as time passed, it became clear to me that it was futile to go on trying.

It was a bitter realisation, which generated all kinds of bitter reactions. In my own mind, I criticised her and almost, I think, began to hate her. These feelings themselves were loathsome to me – sacrilegious and accompanied by a sense of guilt. They prevailed for days. But I was young enough to have resilience, and gradually I managed to adjust myself to it.

Choir practice had been abandoned, but four or five weeks later it was resumed, one night a week. It was still, however, more academic than practical, since only two choirboys remained after evacuation. One Sunday, a young member of the congregation, a soldier who had once been a member of the choir himself, met my colleague and me outside the vestry with the words, 'Ah – the choir! Both of them!' It seemed a brilliant sally. It was church and the choir, the unchanged ritual and the continuing joy of singing, that gave my life at that time one element of solidity and comfort. From that beginning, the rest slowly followed. Since my mother preferred to be left to herself, I began to spend less time in the house – and, though quite alone, found places to go and things to do. And, moving about the district, I realised that the sense of barrenness which had formerly troubled me had in point of fact been an illusion. The children had gone, and with them the world of the children: on that plane, true, the city was a desert. But on a different plane, in the adult world, life went on at top speed. All sorts of interesting things were happening. Like Alice through the looking-glass, I stepped into a different dimension.

On a patch of wasteland down by the river, a Nissen hut had been built, in which lived several RAF men, guardians of a barrage balloon. There was a noisy winch, driven by a diesel engine which, when in operation, shook the earth yards away. From this winch, a stout hawser passed through a pulley, shackled to a slab in the earth. At the other end of the hawser was the balloon – a gigantic, silver, flabby elephant with three stiff ears. The discovery of this little colony and its bizarre charge was a thrilling development. For a long time I went down there every day and stood by the barbed wire, staring up the rigid rod of hawser at that silver fantasy hundreds of feet above, or else watching with interest while the airmen struggled with the monster on the ground. It was a perverse beast. There was nothing more exciting than to see them haul it down on a windy day. The engine would thud, the winch would scream, and that rod of wire would shaft this way and that across the sky like a huge wand as the balloon rolled in the breeze. As it came down to earth, a dozen men would leap at it, shouting and cavorting, grasping huge handfuls of its floppy flesh. When it was at last securely anchored, they would pat one another on the back, go into the hut, into which I could see from where I stood, and stretch out on their bunks. Those men grew quite used to seeing me there and often winked or smiled at me.

There was also the railway. Living so close to the line as I did, I had never, before the war, really troubled to take any interest in trains. But now I found great pleasure in the railway – an interest largely generated by Mother, who sat at home for hours just watching trains come and go. I found a gap through the railings beyond our back garden hedge, and from there could make my way without being seen from the signal box to a little nook by the bridge. Here I made for myself a comfortable retreat, furnished with a soap box to sit on and an old oil can with holes punched in it in which I could light a camp fire. The railway track was barely six feet away, and to be there when one of the Newcastle expresses went by was a terrific thrill. Those great clanging wheels would seem almost on top of one, and the noise and vibration were awe inspiring. Great clouds of steam would envelop me, and I would sit there holding my breath. There was a lot more traffic on the railway now than ever before. One saw aircraft parts and train loads of all sorts of strange apparatus. Occasionally, even tanks went by on open wagons, held fast by thick chains, and, from time to time, large guns also, their barrels pointing towards the sky.

But even when there were no trains passing, it was pleasant down there by the line. Beyond the railway fence was a separate country – an expansive country of sidings and junctions – full of interesting gadgets, dotted with little brick buildings. It was all the more interesting a country simply because one was an illegal immigrant. Between trains indeed, it was a peaceful country – a quiet plateau. The sounds of shunting at a distant yard came to me like tinkling bells, and you could hear an approaching engine a mile off. Just before it appeared round the bend, the signal wire, which passed down the edge of the track at my feet, would twitch suddenly and the semaphore at the other side of the bridge would lift like a puppet's arm.

To the barrage balloon and the railway, I would retreat every fine afternoon, varying with a visit to the air raid shelters if it rained. These shelters had been constructed – or rather excavated – very rapidly indeed during the first few days of September. They were primarily intended for the workers of the aircraft factory a little way up the railway line, but it was generally agreed that people on the estate should use them, too, until the corporation had finished installing private refuges in back gardens. This situation seemed to me to imply an open invitation to visit the shelters whenever I felt so inclined. They consisted of an intriguing maze of subterranean passages, bottomed by slatted duckboards, off which opened numerous rooms with thick, sloping concrete walls, lined by sandbags. I never succeeded in exploring all those labyrinthine passages, largely because I never felt very happy about venturing beyond the first few rooms. One needed a powerful torch, for it was completely dark in there and the lights were controlled from the factory. It was a distinctly eerie place if one penetrated too deeply. I used to stay by the entrance, where filtered light from above sprinkled the walls and glittered in the pools of water which collected under the duckboards. But even so, I managed to make believe I was really at war – that this was my dug-out, and that the Germans were up there somewhere. I'm afraid my illusions were twenty-five years out of date, based on scraps of things I'd read about the First World War. My platoon of heroes was very old-fashioned as well as imaginary. But the surroundings were authentic enough and I enjoyed myself.

In such ways I began once more to extract some fun from life, to reorientate myself. For my mother, however, there was no such relief. For days on end, she never saw another soul but me. Almost in desperation, she began to visit her mother two or three afternoons a week. This was a significant departure from the normal, for, until 1939, she'd had singularly little contact with the old woman.

Grandmother's cottage was one of a terrace in the very shadow of the wall which surrounded Bradford Road Gas

Works. Mother herself had been brought up in that house, which, to me, was a dismal place. When the appalling stench from the gas works gave one respite to smell other things, the house smelt strongly of age and dampness. The rooms were dark, the furniture was dark and rickety, the carpets were colourless with age. I could never rest in there and, but for one or two occasions when I felt she really wanted me to go with her, I persuaded Mother to go alone.

The house would have appealed to me more, perhaps, if Grandmother had appealed to me. Children are generally intimidated by the aged, unless the signs of age are obscured by familiarity. But Grandmother had never been a familiar person to me. As far back as I can remember, I'd known there was something between her and Father – some antagonism, something which neither of them could overlook. I never discovered what exactly this was, but the older I got the more manifest that estrangement became. It was, of course, the reason why Mother visited her so infrequently, and the reason why, in all my life, I never knew Grandmother to step inside our house.

She was a tall, knobbly, arthritic old woman, who wore ankle-length, heavy dresses and lots of cheap jewellery – like a witch, I always thought. She rarely spoke to me, and when she did she seemed always to speak disapprovingly. I never recollect receiving a single present from her, not even a sweet – and she used to chew sweets herself all day long. While she and Mother talked, I would have to stand by Mother's chair, my legs aching and my head lolling from side to side.

But Mother's spate of visits to Bradford Road did not last long. They came to an abrupt end, and once again she fell back into that impenetrable mood of boredom and listlessness. The only thing which managed to cheer her for an hour or two was the arrival of a letter from Father.

He wrote to us twice, occasionally three times, a week. They were long letters, swift and full of interesting bits and pieces. As a rule, he sent two at a time – a long one for us both and a shorter one for Mother. His address was care of GPO and he wrote from 'Somewhere in England', but we soon gathered he was on the south coast, two hundred and fifty miles away. He had taken our camera with him, and sometimes he would enclose photographs – pictures of him standing, hands on hips, with his back to a wire fence, or sitting on an upturned bucket peeling potatoes, or dressed up smartly and smiling pleasantly from the doorway of a wooden hut. They were all jolly pictures which reflected the happy tone of his letters and which, like them, were calculated to cheer us up. 'It'll all be over soon,' he would sign off, 'so don't worry!'

One morning, when he had been away eight or nine weeks, instead of a letter there came a telegram. He was on his way home for a fortnight's leave. Mother's face lit up. She rushed upstairs, bathed, and put on her best frock.

I went to the station to meet him, arriving half an hour too soon. I sat, tense with impatience, on a parcel trolley and stared down the line towards the city.

He came on the Ashton stopper, pulled by *Conqueror*, an engine I knew well. It seemed fitting that his train should be pulled by an engine which was like an old friend to me. *Conqueror* always did make a lot of steam; the station was filled with it – great billowing clouds that obscured everything like a fog. By the time I saw Father, he was already at the top of the staircase which led down from the station to the street. I called after him. He stopped, turned slowly under the weight of his kitbag and haversack, and peered through the swirling steam. At the sight of me, he dropped his kitbag to the ground and waved both arms over his head.

'Good old Fred! How's things?' he asked, taking both of my hands in his. 'How's your mother? Have you been looking after her like I said?'

'Yes. And she's fine, Dad, now. She's been a bit sad while you were away. But she's fine now. She's making you an extra special feed.'

'Fine. I could do with it, I can tell you. Let's go. Want to carry my rifle for me?'

'Yes, please.'

'Here then. And if we come across any Germans on the way, shoot 'em on sight!'

Happily, we walked home together.

For a fortnight, we were gay again. The house rang with laughter and cheerful conversation. Despite the weather, which was autumnal now, chilly and damp, we went out most days, to Dawson Park, rowing on the pond among the swans, bus riding all over town. I took him down to the barrage balloon, showed him the air raid shelters. He was interested in everything. To my great delight, he fixed up a Morse code set for me – with a tapper and buzzer in my bedroom and another in the kitchen downstairs. He had acquired these instruments while away. They were highly professional-looking and stamped with a crown and the initials 'W.D.'. We spent lots of time tapping messages to one another, reading Morse off bits of paper. Father had brought other things home with him – a handbag for Mother, a pack of snap cards. We played snap and Monopoly and housey-housey and were full of happiness. Mother was herself again, all those weeks of loneliness forgotten. It was a wonderful two weeks.

But, of course, it came to an end.

4

The morning Father was due to go back, just as we were finishing breakfast, he looked at Mother and said, 'There's something I have to tell you, Joyce.'

She raised her head with a start.

'This leave – it was embarkation leave.'

'What do you mean . . .?'

'I'm going to France when I get back.'

'Oh no!'

Getting up, Father went to her. 'I didn't want to tell you before – it would have spoilt things. But, Joyce, don't take it so bad. There's been no fighting to speak of yet – and I still think it'll be over for Christmas . . .'

We both went with him to the station in Manchester. It was a painful scene. Mother was limp with sadness and cried continuously. I helped Father load his gear on to the train, and we stood on the platform by the carriage door, three dejected people holding hands and staring at each other in silence amidst the noisy confusion of the station. Hordes of people, most of them servicemen, buffeted past us, jostling their way down the platform and on to the train.

Suddenly a whistle sounded close by, and we all jumped with alarm. 'That's it,' Father said. Smiling, he looked down at me and squeezed my hand. 'Be a good lad and look after her for me.' He turned again to Mother and, letting go of my hand, embraced her, whispering something I couldn't catch in her ear.

The train began to move and he tried to draw himself away. But Mother clung to him and he hesitated, his face all crumpled.

'Mother!' I cried. 'The train's going!' I took hold of her arm, pulled it away from him, and held her hand in mine.

Hesitating, still, for a fraction of a second longer, Father looked hard at us, his eyes twitching strangely. Then he turned, jumped aboard the train, and was gone.

Mother's stiff hand relaxed. Her whole body sagged again. She sobbed, and as I led her away, she seemed quite blind with tears. She cried all the way home on the bus. We had no sooner got into the house than she was writing to him, sitting there with her coat still on, the tears still wet on her cheeks. But the writing seemed to soothe her a little. She folded up the letter, put it into its envelope, and propped it up, as usual, on the mantelpiece.

Then, taking off her coat, she went and brought some coal for the fire and, sitting in her chair by the hearth, picked up her knitting. Immediately, it seemed to me that awful sense of emptiness invaded the house again. The quiet afternoon ticked away and, almost visibly, her former burden of loneliness and ennui descended upon her again. When Father had come home, two weeks ago, it had seemed, suddenly, as though he had never been away. Now, within two hours of his going, it was as if he'd never been home. During his leave, it had seemed that happiness and gaiety were the norm. Now, I realised how wrong I had been. This was the normal mood of our life these days – this deathly quiet, this wretched vacuum. I sat watching her for a long time.

Next morning it was noon before we got up and she didn't dress all day. Indeed, we were back to normal.

Early in November, a few days after Father had gone back to the Army, we had a heavy fall of snow. I awoke early, my eyes dazzled by the bright reflection of it on the ceiling, and was up by eight. I went down, prepared some breakfast and took some up to Mother. She was fast asleep, her fine hair misting over the pillow. I shook her.

'Mother! Some breakfast for you! Come on – get up. I want to go out!'

She opened her eyes, winced, put a hand to her forehead and closed her eyes again.

'Mother!' I cried again, bending over her. 'Come on!'

Suddenly, shocking me tremendously, the hand that was on her forehead jerked upward and the knuckles hit my nose. I stepped back, quickly, thinking that it had been an accident, that she had simply moved her arm and I had been in the way. But it was no accident.

'Go away!' she said. 'Leave me alone, for God's sake. Let me sleep!'

Dazed by it, I hesitated. Then I put the tray on the chair at the side of the bed and went downstairs. For a long time I sat in that cold room by the empty grate, unable, with the shock of what had happened, to do anything. At the back of my mind, I was afraid that Mother was ill, that there was something serious wrong with her.

At length, still worried about her, I went back up the stairs. I called to her, but she didn't hear. The speckled reflections on the ceiling came down and touched her face with moving lights. She looked all right, I thought. In fact, in sleep, she looked peaceful and almost happy. She seemed to be smiling, and it was that half smile which turned my thoughts, changed my mood. Angry with her now I stamped downstairs and went outside, slamming the door to after me.

I was out most of the day, in the clay pit, where the excavation provided many long, steep, snow-covered slopes. I found an old piece of corrugated iron sheeting, left over from the aircraft factory shelters, and sledged all over the clay pit until four in the afternoon. Even then, it was hunger more than anything else that brought me home.

To my dismay, I found Mother still in bed. The tray was there on the chair at the bedside just as I had left it.

The feelings this created in me were fearful and confused. I did not know what to think, what to do. Had I been right that morning, I wondered? Was there something wrong with her? Tormented with worry, I stood at the foot of the bed looking down at her. She had hardly moved from the position she'd been in all those hours before. In a fit of anxiety, I ran to her and shook wildly. 'Mother! Wake up!'

She awoke with a little tremor, peered at me for a moment and then quickly sat up.

'What time is it?'

'It's half past four, Mother – are you all right? What's wrong? You've left your breakfast. You've slept all day! What's wrong?'

She glanced at the tray and then, resting her hands on the counterpane before her, sighed deeply. 'I don't know. I just want to sleep. I don't know what's wrong with me.

And you brought my breakfast!' She looked up at me, her lips trembled. 'Oh son! I don't know what's happening to me. I feel so lonely!'

I flung my arms about her neck and put my cheek to hers.

'Don't be lonely. There's me, isn't there? And I bet you Dad'll be home again soon!'

She clung to me fiercely and I could feel her heart thudding against my chest.

It was shortly after this that she announced one evening that she was going out the following morning and might be out all day. I asked if I might go with her, but she smiled and wagged a finger. 'No – private. Will you be all right while I'm out?'

'Sure.' I didn't press her to let me go, because the prospect of whatever it was seemed to please her, and that, in turn, pleased me. Besides, I had something I wanted to do myself. I had been corresponding of late with my friend Billy Hanson, who had been evacuated to Edenfield, and I had promised him that I would take a ride over there one day and visit him.

'I'd like to cycle to see Billy,' I said, 'while you're out. It's Saturday and he'll be off school.'

'All that way?'

'It's fifteen miles. But I can do it easy.'

'But what about the weather?'

'The snow's gone – and I've got my cape if it rains.'

So she agreed, and, next day, I set off early on my old bike, heading westwards through Prestwich and Whitefield. It was a cold, clear day, and I rode quickly, relishing a delightful sense of freedom. At Bury, I came upon an enormously long convoy of Army lorries and, dismounting, I stood at the kerb and watched it go by.

Once in Edenfield, I did not find it difficult to track Billy down. There were only about a hundred houses in the whole village, and most of these were in one long terrace. Billy's place was an old, stone-built dwelling with bay windows downstairs and fronted by a small barren garden behind a low wall. My knock was answered by a plump woman with her hair piled on top of her head, who wore, I recall, a bright yellow pinafore. She didn't ask me in, but brought Billy out to me instead.

It was good to see him again, and for the first few seconds we could do nothing but laugh like drains at each other.

'What's it like here?' I asked.

'Not bad. School's all right. We don't do much work.'

'More than me! I don't do any at all!'

'Lucky for you. Leave your bike here and let's walk round. I'm cold.'

Edenfield is in the hills, and a biting wind blew down from the heights. We strolled around the village and Billy bought some mints.

'I've got some sandwiches here,' I said. 'Let's eat these.'

We sat on the wall of a churchyard and ate.

'Father was home a bit back,' I said.

'In the Army, isn't he? Where's his camp?'

'He's in France – fighting the Germans.'

'Wish my dad was.'

'Why? Where is he?'

'He works at Avia. They won't let him join up. Mother's glad, though.'

'I bet she is. Mine's fed up. So am I sometimes.'

'It must be lonely. Why don't you go round and see my people? They'd be glad to have a chat with you. They always thought you were a good kid. Go and see 'em.'

'I will.'

We finished the sandwiches and started on the mints and chatted on. He told me about his billet, which, like many of the homes evacuated children were foisted on, was not too welcoming. Billy was a bright boy – lively and intelligent. To be with him again, if only for an hour, was a great fillip. But that was all it could be – one hour. Almost at the moment the clock in the church above us struck twelve, the figure of Billy's foster-mother appeared at the corner of the street, beckoning furiously.

'Dinner,' Billy said. 'Two chips and a fish bone. It's a good job I had those sandwiches, or I'd've been hungry all afternoon.'

The woman wobbled on ahead of us and waited for Billy in the doorway of the house.

'What's the use me trying to look after you if you run off? D'you want me to chase you all over Lancashire?' She rolled away inside.

'Coming!' Billy called after her, winking slyly at me.

We shook hands solemnly. 'Thanks for coming,' Billy said. 'Don't forget to go and see my mother. Tell her I'm all right. Ask 'em to bring my Meccano next time they come. Write to me!'

He stood on the step and watched me mount my bike.

'Come on!' his foster-mother shouted.

But Billy stood there, waving after me, till I had climbed the hill out of the village and begun to drop away on the far side.

The pleasure of seeing Billy lightened my spirit for days. One was not, after all, completely isolated. Ninety minutes' cycling was all that separated us.

When I got home again, Mother herself had only just returned. She seemed as cheerful as I. 'Sit down,' she said, 'and I'll tell you where I've been.'

'Go on.'

'I suddenly decided last night to go and see an old school pal of mine – Nancy. You don't know her, but we were great friends before I married your father. Nancy's manageress at a factory where they make clothing. I thought she might give me a job.' Mother's smile persisted, but she could not quite look at me. 'I thought I might go to work. What do you think? It would mean being on your own a lot more . . . Would you mind that?'

My first reaction was indeed to mind, and my expression must have made it obvious, for she came and put her hands on my shoulders. 'Don't say yes, son. Please.'

I looked up at her. She wasn't smiling now, but staring intently at me.

'I have to do something, son! It's driving me mad rotting away in this house! Can you understand? Remember that time I stayed in bed all day? I couldn't get up! If I don't find something to do, I'll go mad!'

The memory of that episode revived the anxiety I had felt about her at the time. Quite suddenly, my doubts evaporated. 'OK!' I said. 'When will you be starting?'

She hugged me. 'I knew you'd understand! You're the best son a mother ever had! I'll start on Monday. They're making uniforms for soldiers. I'll be doing my share in the war, and it'll be a bit more money. It'll be good for both of us – just you watch. I'll be starting at eight and finishing at five. You'll only have to get lunch for yourself – and you can do that, can't you?'

'Sure.'

'I'll get everything ready for you before I go of a morning . . .'

The details didn't interest me. 'I saw Billy,' I said, and went on to tell her about it.

So Mother went to work, and it proved to be not nearly so bad as I'd feared. We arose and breakfasted together. When Mother left for work at half past seven, I would light the fire and do a quick dust round. By ten, I had usually finished my chores and was free to do exactly as I wished. I had learnt by now how to entertain myself and was rarely lost for something to do. I spent most of my time outside, returning in the afternoon just before Mother was due home. Life for us was better now – brighter. Even though I did have to fend for myself.

Nowadays, I spent a lot of time in Medlock Vale, periodically attacking the railway bridge. I tried hundreds of times to scale it, just as numerous other boys had tried before me. There it lay, pacing across the valley on its ten tall legs like a shiny red, smoke-streaked dragon. Quite regularly I used to pit my wits and strength against it, and try, by climbing it, to conquer it. But the bridge always beat me, for its sides were almost perpendicular, and even if you scaled them you found the overhanging parapet at the top too much for you.

The vale was an interesting place. There was a privet plantation down there, used by the corporation to provide cuttings for the hedges on the estate. To me, this was

'Sherwood'. I created many new chapters in the history of Robin Hood and King John. The disused clay pit was in the vale, too. You could toboggan there when it was snowy, and when it was dry the ground was covered with puffy clay dust which a pebble from a catapult could spurt up like a genuine bullet. There were craters, too, jagged and lipped like shell holes.

While my mother was out at work, and whatever the weather, I went down to the clay pit almost every day. I built a small shack for myself, a personal den, out of old bricks and cans. I clothed the sides and roof with lumps of turf and rounded the whole thing off neatly so that from a distance it looked like a natural, though perhaps somewhat inexplicable, hummock, a bubble in a brown, undulating sea. I furnished it with soap boxes. When it rained, I could sit, sheltered, and watch the water stream in muddy little rivers by the entrance. I soon found that rats were occupying my den at night, but, though the signs of them frightened me at first, I was never driven out. I even caught two in a homemade trap. When I picked up their broken corpses and felt their soft, damp fur, they seemed so small and weak that I ceased to worry about rats.

But, most frequently of all, I flew kites, kites which I made myself out of tissue paper and bits of cane and which I flew from sewing-cotton procured by Mother from her factory. I became expert both at making and flying these kites. I could judge to a fraction the balance required between the length of the kite and its breadth, between its weight and area of paper surface. I could gauge the wind to the nth degree.

Kite-flying during the war was, I believe, an offence against the realm. But I flew my kites so high and so far that, had any busybody ever noticed one dodging about like a mote among the barrage balloons, he could not possibly have located the flyer. And the vale was always deserted, but for me, sitting there on the ridge with the sounds of the aircraft factory buzzing about me and the whistling of the trains tickling my ears.

As a rule, I made kites to go far, not to last for ever, and continued to run them out, bobbin after bobbin, until I could see them no longer. Then, when it was time to go home, I would cut the kite adrift and let my imagination dance away with the trailing end of cotton.

During those weeks, I learnt how to live by myself and with myself.

5

One evening, I went to meet Mother at her work. I was a bit early and, growing tired of waiting at the gate for her, I drifted off to explore the place. It was a large, single-storey, malodorous factory, in the middle of a scrubby field, approached by a cinder track. As you crossed the field, the smell of rubber came out to meet you. There was a high brick wall and a wide gateway leading to a yard in which several lorries were parked. No one stopped me as, crossing the yard, I went to look in through an open door at the far end of the building.

The smell was powerful there. It surged past one on the draught which, as though the factory breathed, sighed intermittently through the doorway. Before me was a wooden platform, with steps leading down to the factory floor about six or eight feet below, and I looked away over a scene of utter chaos.

This, I think, must have been the first time I had seen industry in operation from close at hand. The surrealist perspective of it, the noise, the confusion; it produced in me the same sort of anxiety as one experiences in a bad dream. At the height of my own head, just beneath the ceiling of the workshop, there was a maze of creaking iron wheels and pulleys and slapping belts, all churning away with the ferocity of madness. At regular intervals, all along the whole length of the factory, belts whirled down and hooked themselves about other wheels, this time attached to black steel boxes. Each box was surrounded by half a dozen women, moving rhythmically and unceasingly, some feeding cloth into the boxes, others taking cloth out. They were like slaves to some tyrannous and insatiable animal. The spaces between these numerous black boxes were crammed with sewing machines, at which sat more women, their hands and arms flashing hither and thither at frantic speed, their bodies swaying.

At the end of each row of sewing machines was a large table, piled high with garments – great haphazard mounds of them. The din of it all was deafening and, notwithstanding the bright lights which hung from out of the overhead machinery, the place seemed full of shadows – ragged, moving areas of darkness.

The sight shocked me. It was oppressive, overwhelming. It was as though those unfortunate women were caught in a kind of treadmill, killing themselves to keep up with the machinery – as though if they stopped for a moment to rest, they would be caught up and ground to powder in those belts and wheels and rods and pulleys. The thought that Mother was down there somewhere quite appalled me and, summoning up courage, I stepped through that veil of noise on to the platform, peering down at the women. In the melee of it, human bodies seemed to merge with the machinery, outlines were indistinct, and for several minutes I failed to locate her. But, eventually, I spotted her. She was standing by one of the tables, taking garments from the pile and putting them into a trolley. I stared at her, willing her to look up and see me, but in vain. Steadily, she went on, picking up the garments, folding them, and piling them into the truck. She was wearing a scarf on her head and a blue overall over her frock, and these clothes seemed as incongruous as her surroundings. How could she survive it? How could she live in this awful turmoil?

A buzzer sounded, and immediately the whine of the machinery faltered and began to die away. The wheels, one by one, ceased to revolve and the belts, becoming still, sagged. The women got up from the machines and stretched their arms. They took off their overalls and, hurrying into the aisles between the machines, pushed their way to the cloakrooms. Within half a minute, the first of them were dashing up the steps on to the platform and crushing past me out into the early darkness. Borne along with them, I went to the outer gateway and waited for Mother there. But the noise of that workshop still rang in my ears.

Mother was breathless and there was a thin film of perspiration on her cheeks which shone in the flickering light over the gateway. She was surprised to see me, and for a moment just stood smiling at me.

'What brings you here?'

'I thought I'd come and meet you. I went to the door over there and saw you working, but you didn't look up.'

'You went there?' She glanced in that direction. 'Did anyone see you?'

'I don't think so. But I saw you with a trolley. It's grim in there!'

'What do you mean?'

I tried to explain – to make her see how wrong it seemed to me that she should submit herself to all that. But she only smiled again.

'Nonsense! All factories are like that. In a year or two you'll be working in one yourself.'

'Not me! You won't catch me in a dump like that! Why don't you leave?'

'Don't be silly!' She seemed so far away from understanding what I felt that it was hopeless to go on. And, because she couldn't understand it, it troubled me all the more. That she should so willingly submit herself to something which I felt was so alien, so degrading, seemed, in a subtle way, disloyal. The factory had offended me. I couldn't see why it hadn't had the same effect on her.

'Come on,' she said, propelling me along at her side, 'and don't be a misery.'

We stepped back into that flood of women, and at once she was in conversation with one of them, laughing merrily at some joke.

'This,' she said to her friend, 'is my lad, Fred.'

A face, greasy with perspiration like her own, poked around her shoulder and smiled at me.

The woman walked with us on to the estate. She and Mother chatted and laughed together – coarsely it seemed to me, while I walked by them, in silence, feeling cut off and abandoned, thinking disgruntled thoughts. She did not only enjoy working in that place – but also, apparently, enjoyed the company of her fellow workers! She had created for herself, in going to work, a realm of happiness in which I had no share whatsoever. While I was at home all day, alone, creating what pleasures I could for myself, she was in that factory, humbling herself and laughing with her workmates. It was lewd laughter, I felt, nasty and unclean.

I never quite got over this irrational sensation throughout all the months she worked. It gnawed at me. It would overcome me suddenly. I would think of her laughing rudely as, like a beast of burden, she hauled that ridiculous trolley behind her. Even now I am intimidated by factories – for that afternoon, it seemed to me, I saw an aspect of my mother's character that had been quite unknown to me, an aspect which, for reasons I could not have explained, frightened me.

I had promised Billy to go and see his parents and, on impulse one day, I did so. I arrived at lunchtime, and Billy's father, who obviously could get home from the aircraft factory for lunch, was at the kitchen table, eating.

Mrs Hanson seemed pleased to see me. She was a very motherly sort of person with, appropriately enough, very large breasts – the only physical feature I can remember about her, apart from her face. It was a somehow misshapen face; bent, as though she were constantly laughing out of the corner of her mouth. But I liked her. I could talk to her.

She sat me down at the table opposite her husband and offered me cake. Though it was only a quarter of an hour since I'd had my own lunch, I forced myself to get it down. Then she gave me a glass of milk, which I also felt obliged to drink.

'So,' said Mr Hanson, nodding at me across the table, 'you've been to see that pest of ours, have you?'

'Poor Billy! We do miss him!' Mrs Hanson leant her back against the kitchen sink and thought sadly of her son. 'I wish we'd never sent him.'

'He's better away,' her husband said, holding his tea cup between his two hands and sipping from it. 'He's safer where he is.'

'But we've had no air raids. There's been nothing. I don't want him away for no reason.'

'There was a reason. And a damn good one. Couldn't call yourself much of a parent to risk a kid's life just because you don't want to part.'

This remark, with its implied criticism of my own parents who had kept me in Manchester, struck hard at me. I felt myself blushing. And at that moment, I began to dislike Mr Hanson – as I disliked him ever afterwards. I felt so uneasy that I had an impulse to get up and go away from that house. But I didn't have the courage. If I had, what a difference it would have made to everything! It was a fatal lack of courage I experienced then. Destiny had presented me with a moment of fateful decision and I didn't know it. I merely squirmed and went red.

Mrs Hanson came to my aid. 'It all depends,' she said. 'If we're to die, we might as well die together. If it had been left to me, Billy definitely would not have gone. I don't know why I let you talk me into it.'

Mr Hanson sipped his tea and stared at me.

'Go on then, Freddy,' Mrs Hanson said, 'tell us what he had to say for himself.'

I passed on Billy's messages.

'Well he can do without his Meccano!' Mr Hanson declared. 'It cost good money, that. It stays here.'

'Billy's dad's a bit strict with him, you see,' Mrs Hanson said. 'But Billy's a good boy. And he's very fond of you, Freddy. I bet he was real glad to see you. I don't think he's very happy with that woman at Edenfield.'

'She's all right,' her husband interrupted. 'Stop groaning! In any case, you can't blame her for being browned off having a kid dumped on her all at once. Who wants the bother without the fun? If he wasn't happy, Billy'd let us know, don't you worry!'

'No he wouldn't. You know what he's like. He wouldn't want to upset us.'

'I saw nothing wrong with her when we went over there. She looked after us all right, didn't she? I don't know what you're on about.'

'We must go again, like he says. We must go and see him again. More milk, Freddy?'

'No thanks.'

'Your father's in the Army, isn't he?' she asked.

'Yes . . .'

Her husband, yawning loudly, drowning my words, got up and put his coat on. 'Got my brew?'

'On the sideboard. What were you saying, Freddy?'

'I said yes, he's in the Army.'

'When was he home last?'

'A few weeks back. He made me a Morse code set.'

'Good.'

'But it's broken.' It was. It had suddenly ceased to function one evening. 'I can't get it working again.'

'I'm off now.' Mr Hanson was fastening his overcoat and had his hand on the door latch. But his wife was still interested in my Morse code set.

'What a shame. Don't you know someone who can fix it for you?'

'I'm off!' Mr Hanson raised his voice.

'*You* fix it for him!' his wife said, turning her bent face towards him.

'Fix what?'

'His Morse code set.'

'I've got no time to be messing about . . .'

'Don't be so unkind, man!' Mrs Hanson was frowning. 'What's wrong with you! Freddy's Billy's friend. Go and fix his Morse code for him!'

'How can I? I'm late already!'

'You can fix it tonight, can't you?'

Mr Hanson sighed. 'Oh all right then.' He turned to me. 'Where do you live?'

I told him.

Nodding once, he went out. 'Tarra!'

Going to the window, Mrs Hanson waved after him. When she turned round again, she was smiling. 'He's not a bad fellow, really. You just have to know how to handle him. Now then, let's go into the parlour, shall we, and have a nice talk.'

I was there all afternoon, and only got back a few minutes before Mother arrived home.

'Oh dear!' she said, when I told her we were to have a visitor. 'And look what a mess the place is in! We must tidy up quick!'

We hurried over eating and hurried over the housework. Mother put on a clean frock and dolled herself up. She even put new covers on the chairs. All this seemed a bit excessive to me. Mr Hanson was only coming to fix my

Morse code set – and in any case, he didn't deserve to be regarded as anyone special. I resented the fuss.

We sat and waited for him. We waited, indeed, most of the evening. He arrived at last at about half past ten, and as he came into the house he brought the smell of beer in with him. His face was red and his eyes were a little watery and he was loudly cheerful.

'Ah! Mrs James! I've come to do a job for your lad. I've come to do a job. I'm a real handyman!'

Despite his laughter, nothing he had said seemed to have struck me as humorous, and yet Mother giggled back at him. 'It's good of you. I remember your Billy. He used to come round often.'

'Billy! A pest he is. Always has been and always will be.' Again that loud laughter. He peeled off his overcoat and did things with his arms like physical jerks. 'Hell, it's cold out there! Mind if I warm my backside before I get cracking?'

'No – no!'

'It's the extremities that freeze first, Mrs James. We can't have that, can we!'

Mother stood smiling, watching him with amused interest as he crossed the room and, planting his feet apart, stood on the hearthrug with his hands on his hips. His behaviour embarrassed me, and I felt embarrassed also for Mother; needlessly, it seemed, for she was quite at ease. There was no-one, I thought, so different from my father as this noisy man, and yet she obviously found nothing objectionable in him.

'Would you like a cup of tea?' she asked.

'I would that!'

'And a bit of supper?'

'Surely. Thanks.'

'Your wife won't be annoyed? She won't have anything ready, I mean?'

'Not Florrie. She knows better than to be annoyed. She'll be in bed, anyway. I always go out Fridays and she always goes to bed. Best place for her, too!'

'I'll go and get something ready, then.' With alacrity, Mother dashed away into the kitchen.

'Now then,' Mr Hanson said, looking at me. 'Where's your blinking Morse code set?' He wasn't laughing now. Indeed, his expression had changed completely. Now that Mother was no longer there, he looked annoyed.

'Part's in the kitchen,' I said, 'and part's upstairs.'

'And what's wrong with it?'

'It just won't go.'

'Checked the wiring?'

'Yes.'

'Battery all right?'

'I think so.'

'Then it'll be something wrong with the buzzers. It would be! I'll have a look at the one in the kitchen. You go upstairs and knock on the floor if it goes.'

I did as he'd said and, putting the tapper and buzzer on to my bed, sat beside it, listening to the murmur of voices from downstairs. I heard the cupboard door open, as Mother found the set for him, and I heard the drawer open, as she found him the screwdriver. After that, there ought to have been silence while he worked. But there was not. That rumbling conversation went on, rising now and then in waves of sound, breaking into peals of laughter. After about five minutes of it, I tried tapping a few times, but there was no response. The talking went on and, gradually, my thoughts drifted away. I lay back on the bed for a while and dreamt. Then, growing cold, I got up and went to the window to look out. There were searchlights over Clayton, fingers of light stroking the woolly bellies of clouds. A train passed, the fierce glare of the fire trapped inside the engine cab by the overhead canopy, but spilling out at the sides and daubing the railings with its liquid orange glow. I grew colder and, in my discomfort, angry with Mr Hanson. I went back and sat on the bed and listened again. They were still talking, but more quietly now, and they were drinking tea. I could hear the occasional rattle of cup against saucer. What was he drinking tea for, I wondered, when he was supposed to be mending my Morse code set? I waited a minute or two longer, but when nothing still seemed to be happening, I went to the head of the stairs, the better to hear what he was up to.

My suspicions that he had abandoned the job in order to have supper were soon confirmed. '. . . Oh yes.' I heard him saying. 'Every Friday . . .' And his mouth was clearly full.

'I never get out at all in the evenings, with Henry being away,' Mother was saying. 'Do you know that, apart from tradesmen, you're the first man I've spoken to for weeks! At work we're practically all women. Three hundred of us!'

'No rest cure for the men who are there, eh?'

Laughter.

'You should get out though. It's not good to stay cooped up all the time, even though you do go out to work. You know what they say about all work and no play. You want some fun. You'll get morbid.'

Mother made a little sound, which suggested that she agreed with him. 'But how can you when your husband's away?'

'That wouldn't stop me!'

Furious that I'd been waiting up there needlessly all this time, I ran down the stairs and into the kitchen.

'Oh!' laughed Mr Hanson. 'I'd forgotten about you!'

Mother laughed too, and I grew even more annoyed.

'I've been waiting up there for ages!' I said. 'Is it fixed yet?'

'Not yet. I'm having a breather. Simmer down, kid. I can see there's discipline lacking here with your dad away.'

'Have some tea,' Mother said. 'And don't be cheeky.'

Sullenly, I drank my tea, staring at the table cloth. But I could sense them exchanging glances over me and smiling to themselves at my obvious annoyance.

'Back you go then,' Mr Hanson said. 'And I'll have this going in two minutes. There's nothing to it.'

I returned to the bedroom. But still, for a good ten minutes, conversation continued down there. And then, suddenly, the buzzer was working. I stamped my foot on the floor, and Mr Hanson's shouting voice sounded clearly up to me. 'Send something from that end!'

I did.

'OK. It's working!'

'Well,' Mother said. 'What do you say to Mr Hanson?' She sounded as though she were talking to a baby.

'Thanks,' I said, with reluctance.

'It's been a pleasure, Mrs James. A real pleasure! Where's my coat?'

We followed him like a retinue into the front room and watched him get into his coat.

Mother opened the door for him. 'It's raining again,' she said. 'You'll have to hurry or you'll get soaked.'

'Drop of rain never hurt anyone.' Mr Hanson, pulling up his coat collar, went out, drawing the inner door to behind him, closing it in my face.

'Good night, Mrs James!' I heard him say as he stood in the hall. 'And don't forget what I said, will you?'

'No. Good night! Good night!'

'You weren't very polite were you?' Mother said when she came in again, looking angrily at me. 'Why were you so rude?'

'I don't like him,' I replied. 'That's why. I just don't like him.'

6

Shortly before Christmas, our Anderson shelter was installed. This job, which was carried out with admirable efficiency, gave me two days' worth of interesting observation. Half a dozen labourers – laughing, brown-skinned men with enormous biceps, great tea-drinkers who had me brewing for them every half-hour – descended on us one morning and proceeded to dig a large square hole at the top of the garden. Next day, they came with great curved sheets of corrugated iron which they put into the hole to form, very cleverly, a half-submerged little shed, on top of which they piled all the earth they'd dug out to form the hole in the first place. This, I thought, was perfect. I had always been one for making dens and dug-outs for myself, and here was one of the finest I had ever seen, built for me by the Government. When the men had finished, I went down and examined my new retreat. It was fabulous: duck-boards over the floor, a little ladder for use in getting in and out, a hook in the ceiling for a lamp – all quite perfect. Tomorrow, I thought, I'll bring some of my stuff down here, some boxes and so on. And perhaps I could even extend my Morse code communication to reach it.

That very night, with astonishing appropriateness, the air raid sirens went. It was not for the first time, of course.

In the past, Mother and I had got up and, taking blankets and pillows with us, gone to lie down under the table in the front room till the all-clear sounded. But tonight, since we had a nice new air raid shelter, we went out into the garden, bearing candles and matches.

'You go down first,' Mother said. 'And strike a light so I can see what I'm doing.'

Backwards down the ladder I went. Between the second and third rungs, however, my foot splashed into water, shocking me and soaking my shoe. I climbed up again, leant back through the entrance, and struck a match. There was a muddy yellow pool of water down there, two feet deep.

Dejectedly, we went back into the house and got down, as in the past, under the table.

The shelter remained flooded for weeks. At last, more men came and put drains in – but by that time, I had lost interest in dug-outs.

It was about this time, too, that Friday night choir practice was resumed. This coincided with the arrival of girls in the choir. My one male colleague and I found ourselves surrounded by girls of ages ranging between thirteen and sixteen. Where they all came from, I could not fathom.

One Friday evening Mother declared that, since I was going out, she intended to do the same. This was an innovation, because she had never gone out of an evening during all the months Father had been away.

'Where are you off to?' I asked.

'Nowhere special. I just feel like a change. I'll walk up to the church with you.'

When we reached the church gates, it suddenly occurred

to me that she might like to come inside and watch us practise. I suggested this to her.

'No,' she said. 'I don't think they'd like me to. I'll be all right. Don't worry.'

I watched her walk off into the darkness towards Oldham Road.

The choir were busy at the time, preparing for the carol service. The girls, however, were a dismal bunch of singers, I thought. Their ridiculous attempts to sound pleasant made me wince, and their thick-chested bumptiousness annoyed me intensely. They all oozed self-confidence. From the very first, these girls were on chatting terms with the choirmaster, the rector and the curate. They used to gather around these gentlemen and talk like old women to them about all kinds of rubbish. I had been in the choir for two years and spoke to the choirmaster only when spoken to, which was infrequently. In all that time, I had exchanged nothing more than nods with the reverends. Until one got used to these girls – a process which took some time – choir practice was something of an ordeal.

That particular Friday in December, the first of the many Friday nights Mother was to go out alone, I was back in the house before nine. It was too early to expect her to be there. In my own mind, I expected to see her about ten. Just before that time, therefore, I got some supper ready for us.

At half past ten, she had still not come, and I began to grow worried. Putting on my coat, I went out, hoping that I would see her on the road. It was an unusually dark night. I reached the church again and stood under the bare branches of the old trees. From time to time people passed, like shapeless black clouds. Twice I called out after women, thinking mistakenly that they were Mother. The clock struck a quarter to, and then eleven o'clock – and still I had not seen her. But there were, I realised, other ways home, and she might well be home now, wondering what had happened to me. She must be, surely. It was eleven o'clock! I set off for home again, and as I went I grew more convinced that I was right. I began to run, as fast as I could, and was home within ten minutes.

But she was not there.

Exhausted with my long run, I sank into a chair. At twenty past, I went and ate my share of the supper. By the time I'd finished it, I was growing very anxious indeed. Switching off the light, so as not to spoil the blackout, I went to the window and looked out. From there, I could see nothing, so I went upstairs and peered out from the bedroom window. There was not a sound nor a movement anywhere. After ten minutes of this, I flopped on to the bed and lay there, worrying keenly.

Despite my anxiety, I fell asleep. I was awakened by the sound of the outer door closing. For a moment, I didn't move, uncertain whether I had really heard it or merely dreamt it. But, hearing the front room door open and close, I got up and crept downstairs.

Mother was sitting by the fire, lolling back, her hands limp on the arms of the chair. She looked ill, somehow – ill and sad and preoccupied. She didn't even lift her eyes when I spoke to her.

'I've been out looking for you,' I said.

Her head nodded vaguely. 'Go to bed, Freddy.'

'Where've you been?'

Now, she did look up at me. Her hair was a little awry, and there was something odd about her eyes. 'Out,' she said.

'But where? It's nearly twelve o'clock.' I went to her and put my arm on her shoulder.

'I'm sorry, son.'

She looked away again – but as she'd spoken, the smell of beer had risen on her breath.

So that was where she'd been! Drinking beer! Involuntarily, I stepped away, staring at her.

She glanced at me again and then, quite suddenly, began to cry. 'I'm sorry, son,' she said again. 'Oh Freddy, I'm sorry!' She put her hands out to me and, standing, pulled me to her. Her body was shaking and her embrace was almost fierce. 'My darling son. I'm sorry! Where's your father? Where is he? I can't live without him, Freddy!'

For several days after that, Mother did not go to work. She was miserable and quiet and wanted me to stay in the house with her.

7

It was one of the few white Christmases I remember. Three inches of snow fell in one night and a hard frost next day crusted it over. On Christmas Eve, a coal lorry got stuck at the bottom of the hill in the vale, and I helped the men to lay old sacks under the wheels till they began to grip again.

Father had promised us so often that the war would be over for Christmas, and yet here was Christmas Eve and the war was still very much with us. The Army was still in France and people, now, were far less cheerful, less confident than they had ever been before. 'We're gonna hang out the washing on the Siegfried Line,' the song had said. But it was a melody you didn't hear any longer. It was going, after all, to be a protracted war, people were beginning to say. Four years, probably, like the last one. The spirit of the war dominated everything. 'Don't you know there's a war on?' had become a national motto. You heard it a score of times every day – in the shops, in the streets, on the wireless. Broadcasting had begun to get back into its stride again, but the programmes all, in one way or another, succeeded in reminding you of the war. There were two-way message programmes, in which soldiers in France talked to the families at home: 'I am well and the grub is good. Look forward to seeing you soon. Love to Jane, John, Walter and little Albert . . .' There were variety programmes from Army barracks, air stations and ships. And, of course, there was the news, regularly, five or six times a day, the special announcements, the speeches by sombre-voiced politicians. Where cinema bills had once been, posters now declared 'Careless talk costs lives!' or else shouted at you to 'Carry your gas mask!' The far half of the clay pit was now being used as a testing ground for tanks they made at a factory on Queens Road. Most afternoons, aircraft flew over the vale – so high that they were like humming midges. Till now there had been little fighting in France, and yet everyone knew that soon the struggle would begin in earnest. People said so. You felt it in the air. It was like those last few seconds before the bell goes, when the boxers adjust their mind to the coming fight, summon up their courage and flex their muscles. They look so calm – yet you know that, with the bell, their smiles will turn to expressions of grim ferocity.

Father's letters arrived a little less frequently now. They were also growing shorter. Often, they were written in pencil and from time to time odd words had been obliterated by someone who stamped himself 'Censor' at the top of the letter. But Father was still cheerful, and the arrival of one of his letters always brightened the day.

Religiously, Mother and I wrote back to him. We sent him magazines and odd packets of cigarettes, and I, at least, tried to be as cheerful as he was himself. I never saw Mother's letters, but I suspected they did not do much to make him feel contented. Even after these months, she still shed copious tears over her writing. Just before Christmas, following that upsetting night she had spent out alone, she wrote every single day for over a week.

The fact that she did write so often at this time, that she'd had a week off work, that, quite suddenly, the peace she had found of late seemed to have abandoned her again, that she was as depressed as she had been immediately after Father's departure – all this puzzled me in a mild way. I couldn't understand it – and yet I didn't feel it particularly necessary to understand. I merely wanted her happy again. When she was depressed, everything was depressing. The house was lifeless and gloomy. There was no talk, no rapport; there was nothing but cold silence which seemed to envelop me wherever I went, in her company or without her.

As Christmas drew imminent, things grew, if anything, even worse. The prospect of Christmas without Father was disappointing even for me. But by this time, I had to some extent grown reconciled to Father's absence. My way of life and attitude had adjusted to it. But for Mother, the prospect seemed demoralising. Her mood was difficult for me to sympathise with, however, for she seemed more concerned about herself than about Father. She seemed more upset by the fact that she would have to spend a lonely Christmas than by the thought of him spending it in some cheerless Army camp hundreds of miles from home. 'What is there for us to do?' she asked. 'Christmas will mean nothing. We'll just have to traipse about on our own!' This self-sorrow on her part rankled a little with me. Once again, I saw a part of her I'd never suspected before. But I somehow felt responsible for her. I felt it was up to me to go on trying to relieve her melancholy, despite rebuffs.

A day or two before Christmas, I took a bus ride to town and spent the few shillings I had saved on a present for her. It was a set of brass ornaments and they cost me eight and six. It had always been our custom at home – it was a discipline in fact – to exchange our presents on Christmas morning, not before. This year, however, even that tradition was broken. Mother came home on Christmas Eve with a train for my set and a couple of games, which she gave me there and then. In view of this, I gave her the present I had bought for her, so that when Christmas Day did arrive there was not even the light relief of an exchange of gifts.

It was a dismal Christmas Day. We were up late. After breakfast, I brought down my train set and persuaded Mother to operate one of the controls. But she wasn't interested. There were several nasty pile-ups, and at one point she sent my new engine round so fast that it jumped the points and crashed to the floor, knocking off one of the buffers. 'Play by yourself,' she said. 'I can't be bothered.' She went and began to knit. Even the pudding and the crackers and other such seasonal trimmings were more saddening than enlivening. They reminded Mother of happier Christmases. She ate little and spoke less. At last, she made up her mind to visit Grandmother. 'Let's get out of this house!' she exclaimed. 'For heaven's sake!'

Grandmother seemed to grow older, to look more wizened and more intimidating, each time I saw her. She had recently been ill, we learnt, and had had to spend some time in bed. For half an hour she complained bitterly that

Mother had not been to see her and help her. 'On me own, all that time,' she grumbled. 'Lying up there with no-one to do a thing for me. Not once did my daughter visit me! Not once did it enter her head to wonder whether I was dead or alive!' On and on she went, chuntering and nattering, sitting hunched in that greasy, high-backed rocking chair, staring sullenly into the fire, the hollows of her cheeks filled with shadows.

Mother and I sat and listened to it, sat in that smelly hovel and clenched our fists to bear it.

'Father,' I said, snatching at a moment's silence, 'says he saw Germans the other day. He says he saw a lot of tanks and things.'

The old woman, without moving her head, glanced at me out of the corner of her eye. 'Children,' she said, 'should be seen and not heard.' It was a favourite phrase of hers. Indeed, I don't think she ever said much else to me.

'It's so miserable without him,' Mother added. 'It's not like Christmas at all.'

Grandmother did not listen. Her lips curved for an instant and, suddenly coughing, she spat into the fire. 'I might have been dead for all you cared. Thinking of him all the time. Not a minute to spare to think of me.'

Mother got up. 'I'll make you some tea. How's that?'

'I don't care.'

'What've you had for dinner?'

'An egg. What difference does Christmas make to me? Who cares about me?' Her lips pouted, and suddenly I saw Mother in her, clearly and amazingly, in that sulky expression; I heard Mother in the self-pitying tone of her voice. When Mother pitied herself, as she had so frequently of late, I found it possible to summon understanding. But Grandmother's self-pity destroyed any sympathy I might otherwise have felt for her. I leapt up, anxious not to be left alone with her, and went to help Mother with the tea.

Grandmother drank noisily, and the sound of it annoyed Mother as intensely as it annoyed me. Over tea, conversation died completely and remained dormant for a long time. Silence grew denser and denser, till it was like a suffocating vapour in the room. Mother and I sat rigid, afraid to move, afraid to breathe, almost, while Grandmother stared and stared into the flames, her nostrils flickering. When Mother rose to collect the crockery, the sound of it was like the clap of hands which breaks a spell. Quickly, we washed up the cups and saucers and, quickly, we put on our things and prepared to go.

'Freddy'll come again in a day or two,' Mother said. 'To see how you are. Won't you, son?'

It was a highly unwelcome suggestion. But, 'Yes,' I said.

'You don't need to bother! You don't need to bother!' Grandmother didn't move from her chair. 'Bang the door after you!'

'He'll come,' Mother insisted, 'all the same.'

I can't imagine that Mother had thought visiting Grandmother would make her feel better. But if she had thought so, she was badly mistaken. Neither of us uttered a word during the walk home. The fire had gone out, and when I began to rake out the grate to light it again, Mother stopped me: 'Leave it,' she said. 'What's the use! I'm going to bed. I can't stand this any longer!'

I was awakened on Boxing Day morning by a loud

knocking at the front door. I got up and went into Mother's room. She had been disturbed by it, too. 'Go and see who it is,' she said. 'Put your pants and jersey on and run down. What time is it?'

It was half past ten. Going to the top of the stairs, I called to whoever it was to wait and then, dressing hurriedly, I went down and opened the door.

Billy, smiling brightly, stood there in the snow. 'Hallo, dopey! Only just getting up?'

I was overjoyed to see him. Just as before, when we'd met at Edenfield, our pleasure at seeing each other again could find no expression but in laughter.

'Who is it?' Mother was shouting.

'It's Billy! Billy's home!'

I brought him into the parlour and set to lighting the fire. 'Why didn't you tell me you were coming home?' I asked.

'Thought I'd surprise you. And I did, didn't I? Caught you in bed.'

'Yes. We do sleep late sometimes. Are you home for good?'

'No. Only for Christmas. Going back tomorrow. Dad wasn't keen on the idea – he said the Germans would bomb us at Christmastime, just for spite. But he was wrong. He usually is.'

'He mended my Morse code set for me.'

'Yes. He told me. Is it all right now?'

'Yes. Would you like to have a go on it?'

'Good idea.'

I took him into the kitchen and set the tapper and buzzer before him. 'You stay here and I go upstairs. That's the code, there.' I pointed to the piece of paper pinned inside the cupboard door. 'I'll send slowly, so you can have a chance to read it off. When I've finished, I send seven dots, and then you send a message.'

Glad to have a chance to have another game on my Morse code set with someone who showed interest, I dashed upstairs. As I passed Mother's room, however, I heard her calling to me.

I looked into her room. She was still in bed, propped up on her elbow. She seemed irritated. 'Have you fetched him in?'

'Yes.'

'What did you do that for?'

The question seemed ridiculous. Of course I'd brought him in. What was wrong with her?

'Send him away!' she said. 'Get rid of him!'

'But Mother . . .' I didn't know what to say. 'It's Billy. He's only home today. He's going back tomorrow. Don't make me send him away.'

Her expression of annoyance prevailed for a moment longer as she stared at me. But then, suddenly, it slipped away. She sighed, sat up, flapped her hands. 'I don't know! I don't know! All right then. He can stay for a few minutes. I'll have to get up now, I suppose.'

'Merry Christmas!' I sent over the wire to Billy.

'And the same to you!'

We communicated for a while, spelling out long sentences. It's a peculiar thing about conversing in Morse code, but, despite one's remoteness from one's contact, one can draw very close to him. In the rhythm of his sending, in his hesitations, one can feel him very strongly.

'Show me what you got for Christmas,' Billy sent at last and, going down, I ran my new engine for him.

Mother appeared, dressed in an old frock and with curling pins in her hair.

'Hallo, Mrs James!' Billy said.

She nodded, 'Hallo, Billy,' and disappeared into the kitchen. Billy, noticing her manner, stared after her.

She called to me. 'Ask him,' she whispered, when I went to her, 'if he's had breakfast.'

I went back and did so. 'Yes,' he said. 'At seven.'

'You don't want anything now, then?'

'No. I told them I wouldn't be long, anyway. We're supposed to be going out to Aunty's this afternoon. Here,' he pulled the sleeve of my jersey, 'your mother looks a bit fed up. Is she ill?'

'It's because Dad's not here. She feels lonely. It's grim sometimes, Billy. You've no idea how glad I am to see you again. Must you go so soon?'

'Yes. But p'r'aps you'll come to Edenfield again when the weather's better. Sorry about your mum. She doesn't look well to me.'

Mother had brought an atmosphere with her. Billy and I talked in whispers. I felt uncomfortable, and all my pleasure at seeing Billy was spoilt. What's wrong with her? I thought. Previously, she had always treated Billy well. She had always liked him. Her attitude at this moment towards him was puzzling and embarrassing. When she called to tell me my breakfast was ready, Billy put on his coat and scarf to go.

'Try to come over again,' he said. 'But let me know next time, so I can tell the old jit. Maybe she'll let us into her front room. Well, I'm off. Cheerio, Fred!' Halfway down the path he stopped and, looking back over his shoulder, said, 'I'm sorry about you and your mum being so lonely. Why don't you get her to go out somewhere?'

'She won't. Anyway, there's nowhere to go.'

Shrugging his shoulders, he walked off, crunching through the frozen snow.

Mother was not in any mood for talking. After washing the pots, we retired to the parlour together, I to read and Mother to resume her endless knitting. The thought of another long and miserable day in the house depressed me. I wanted to be off out. What I had said to Billy had been the truth though – I knew it would have been futile to ask Mother to go anywhere with me. And so I wanted to be off alone, amusing myself in the way I had amused myself in the past four months. But I didn't have the heart to leave her. There she sat, ponderously knitting, her lower lip jutting out, her curling pins like antennae on her head, her chin on her chest, and her eyes staring dully at nothing.

For the second time that morning, the door rattled. It was Billy again.

'We're not to go to Aunty's after all. And Mum's asked me to ask if you and your mother would like to come round to our house for an hour after tea?'

'Wait a minute, Billy, and I'll go and ask her.'

Leaving him at the door, so as to save myself embarrassment if Mother refused, I went and told her what Billy had said. She shook her head, quickly. 'No. No!'

'But what can I tell him? He's waiting for an answer.'

Her eyes flickered from side to side as she searched for

her excuse. 'Tell him I've got a cold – the flu. Anything. No – look . . .' she gripped my arm. 'You can go. On your own. Tell him you'll go – but say I'm ill and I'm going to bed early.'

'But why can't you come? You'll enjoy yourself. Billy's mother's a nice woman.'

She went on shaking her head as if nothing could make her change her mind. 'No. Tell him what I say!'

I told Billy. 'All right,' he grinned. 'But don't you forget to come, Fred. We'll have some fun. Come about seven.'

The afternoon passed with infinite slowness, infinite tedium, the minutes ticked away by the clicking of Mother's knitting needles. Every now and then she sighed, a quick intake of breath and a long drawn-out exhalation. It grew dark, and I put my book down, having read more than my fill. But Mother knitted on, clicking and sighing, clicking and sighing. At about half past five, I got up and drew the curtains, hoping that the movement and the sound of it would bestir her. They didn't.

'I'd better be getting ready, then,' I said. 'Shall I start fixing tea?'

'Go and get washed. I'll do tea.'

Washing and changing into my best clothes took about twenty minutes, but when I got downstairs again Mother was still where I'd left her.

'Shall I do some toast?' I asked her.

Slowly, like an old woman, and wearily, she pushed herself out of the chair. 'So you're going out and leaving me in this miserable place, are you?'

'But . . .' I had been looking forward to it a very great deal indeed. And yet, at the sight of her sad face, I found it quite easy to say, 'If you'd rather I stayed in, it's all right.'

A weak smile passed across her face. 'No, son.' She put a hand to my cheek. 'No. You go. Enjoy yourself.' But then she spoilt it. 'Don't worry about me,' she added, and there was that tone again – echoing perfectly the voice of her mother yesterday. As she walked past me in that floppy old dress, she even looked like her mother. It was like watching two images superimpose and merge into one another. I recoiled from it. Switching on the light, I found my new engine and put it into my pocket, ready to take to Billy's.

Just before seven, I put on my overcoat and prepared to go. She watched me gloomily and so intently that I felt what she was feeling herself. My muscles worked sluggishly, and I could hardly force myself to look at her. In the end, when I was quite ready, with my coat on and the engine in my pocket, I could stand it no longer. I flopped into a chair, feeling very close to tears. 'I'm not going,' I said.

Still she stared at me, her expression a strange, bewildering confusion of feeling for me, sadness, and annoyance. For a moment, we gazed at each other. It was a tense, unreal moment, charged with Mother's powerful but mysterious emotion. Then, shaking her head, she said, 'Yes, you are. And I'm coming with you! The war's not my fault! I'm coming – wait for me!'

I had a most pleasant evening. Billy's house was full of light. There was a Christmas tree and paper decorations and splashes of colour everywhere. It was warm and noisy. There was cake and homemade toffee and ginger beer. Billy and I left the adults to themselves and played games without respite all evening. But from time to time, I looked at

Mother. She seemed to be enjoying herself just as much as I.

It must have been getting on for midnight when the party finally broke up — it might have been even later. In any case it was so late that Mr Hanson apparently felt obliged to walk us home.

'Don't forget to write!' Billy called after me. 'And come over when you can!'

'Right! Right!' I promised. But, as a matter of fact, I don't think I wrote to Billy again after that.

It was not a very long walk. Mother and I held hands, I remember, and, as we walked, she and Mr Hanson talked together. I paid little attention to what they were saying. For one reason, they were talking quietly. Moreover, in the cold air all at once after spending the whole evening in that hot room, I felt suddenly tired, pleasantly lethargic. I simply wanted to get to bed.

But one snatch of conversation struck my consciousness. We were almost at the gate when I heard Mr Hanson say, 'But that's daft, woman!'

I pricked up my ears, despising Mr Hanson's rudeness just as I'd despised his brash noisiness on the previous occasion he'd been with us.

'You're daft! There's no harm in it! How can there be? You talk as if you were a nun!'

Mother laughed, and the realisation that Mother herself was not offended soothed me. I forgot about them again.

'Well?' Mother said, as she closed the door behind us. 'And did you enjoy yourself?'

'Yes. It was fine. Did you?'

'Yes.' She looked away over my head. 'I did, Freddy . . .'

She hesitated. 'Freddy, I'm not the sort who can live alone. I can't help it. I wish I could. I've tried – how I've tried! I want you to realise that, son. Remember it.'

Though I failed to understand what she meant, I did remember it.

8

As if by magic, Mother was as right as rain again. There followed three or four months of something as near contentment as was possible with the war still on and Father still away. Mother was happier and more agreeable than she had ever been since September last year, and this in itself was enough to enliven my own world. Into the bargain, the local cinemas opened two or three times a week for matinee showings, and all through February and March I indulged in an orgy of films. Moreover, as the seasons changed and the sun grew warmer, my stamping grounds in the vale became even more accommodating and interesting. I watched the birds come back to the privet plantation, watched the new leaves shoot forth. Mother talked to me now, as in the old days. We read books together.

Only one thing tended to spoil this new happiness – Mother's insistence on spending at least one night a week out. I never grew accustomed to this, and, though it always angered her, went on trying to dissuade her. My objections were hardly rational or specific, and when she asked me why I didn't want her to go out, I could never give her anything like an explanation. She usually went out on Fridays – choir night for me – and so it wasn't that I expected her to take me with her. All the same, it disturbed me.

Week after week, every Friday she went out. As the year wore on news from France became less optimistic. There was cause now – more than there had ever been before – to worry about Father. And we did worry about him, regularly and seriously. We would often talk about him and, if Mother was anything like me, picture him in all sorts of dangerous situations. This growing uncertainty dampened my own pleasures, and I couldn't understand how Mother could find it in her to go out enjoying herself. She always insisted on my going to bed and would never let me wait up for her, but I used to imagine that the smell of drink lingered in the house all next day.

One evening, I taxed her with it more pointedly than before. I had been visiting Grandmother, as a duty, ever since her illness at Christmas, and I had once mentioned Mother's nights out to her. She had made some very acid comments, which I now passed on. It had begun, as always, with my asking Mother not to go out, or else come with me to the church. As always, she had told me, off-handedly, not to be silly, and, as usual, this had jarred on my nerves, inflamed me, and made me want to be cruel.

'Gran says it's you that's silly!' I declared. 'She says you're like a flapper, that you're weak, that you have no backbone!'

She paled. Her chin dropped. 'What're you talking about!'

'You always say I'm silly. But it's you who's silly – you, not me!'

She gripped my shoulders. 'What've you been telling her?' She shook me. 'What've you been saying?'

'I told her the truth. I told her you were always going out drinking beer!'

She let go of me and, stepping back, glared at me. For a moment, I thought she was going to hit me but she put her hand to her forehead and groaned. 'God Almighty!' She turned away and stood motionless in the doorway. 'So that's what the old devil thinks of me!'

Suddenly, she turned again. Her face was all screwed up and ugly. 'You never go there again! Never! D'you hear? Never! Never! Never!' The door banged and she was gone.

I walked up to the church alone.

Early in May, I went with the choir to a choral festival at Manchester Cathedral. I can't remember what, if anything, the festival signified – perhaps the enthronement of a new bishop – but it proved to be at once a most elevating and a most depressing experience. The choir members had been asked to invite their parents, to swell the congregation, and after much persuasion, Mother agreed to come – at least, for part of the evening. The festival itself was to be followed by a potato pie supper and that was where she drew the line. She would come to the service, she said, and then go home.

It was a memorable service. Choirs from every Anglican church in the diocese filled the vast cathedral. To the congregation, looking down from the galleries, the sight must have been as thrilling as the sound. Being part of that magnificent music, in it, surrounded by it, was an almost stupefying spiritual experience. I have never known anything else quite like it. One's whole personality seemed to be absorbed. One was aware of nothing in the world but that surging flood of music. It overwhelmed one's mind and filled one with trembling elation. The bishop gave a sermon which, since I was a good thirty yards away, I didn't hear. But the mere sound of his voice, echoing through the cathedral, had a kind of hypnotic effect. I sat entranced, understanding nothing of his meaning but quite fascinated with pure sound. The service ended with the hymn 'Onward Christian Soldiers' which at that time had a highly emotional significance. It was almost insupportably moving.

The bustle which followed the service, as the various choirs were mustered and led away, was to me an awful anti-climax. The thought of a potato pie supper was now beyond contemplation. I was spiritually exhausted, and physically, too. I was soaked in sweat and my knees were weak. The wonderful illusion had been shattered; the crystal of sound had disintegrated into laughing, shouting chaos, and I wanted to be away as quickly as possible.

With the rest of the choir, those contemptible girls, I came out into the cathedral porch and saw Mother waiting for me. As I went to her, Mr Wedgewood, the choirmaster, joined us.

'Mrs James – it's a long time since I saw you! Did you like the service?'

'It was lovely,' Mother said, smiling from him to me. 'Lovely.'

'Good. It's rare that we have these festivals, but their grandeur makes up for their scarcity.' He gripped Mother's arm and put his other hand on my shoulder. 'Come along, then. Supper's in the station across the road. Let's hurry or we'll be crushed out.'

Mother allowed herself to be drawn down the cathedral

steps before, stammering and flapping her hands, she managed to find words. 'I'm sorry, Mr Wedgewood,' she said. 'But I hadn't planned to come to the supper.'

We stopped and Mr Wedgewood, lowering one eyebrow in an expression he adopted on occasion with the choir, withdrew his hand from her arm. 'But you're not missing the potato pie! Surely not! It's the crowning touch of the evening!' He smiled.

Mother was still a bit tongue-tied. 'Well, yes, I'm sorry. But . . . well, I've made other arrangements . . .'

In my own mind, I knew she had done no such thing. She was merely creating an excuse. I didn't like to see her telling fibs and floundering like that, so I told them I didn't want to go to the supper either.

'What!' said Mr Wedgewood, throwing up his hands in mock horror. 'You, too!'

'I'm not hungry,' I said. 'I feel tired and a bit sick. I want to go home.'

'No – no!' Mother was suddenly in a flurry. 'You must go! Don't be awkward! You must!' She looked hard at me, trying to communicate her will to me. I misinterpreted, however. I thought she was merely wishing to avoid giving offence to Mr Wedgewood.

'But Mr Wedgewood doesn't mind,' I said. 'Do you?'

'No, Freddy – not really. Not if you prefer to leave it. Go home – but remember tonight. It was the experience of a lifetime. Well,' he backed away, 'I must be going. They won't do me out of it, I assure you!'

'Just a minute . . .!' Mother squeezed my arm. 'Go with him,' she whispered. 'Go with him!'

'Yes?' Mr Wedgewood waited.

'He's coming!' Mother called.

'No – no!' I shook my head. 'I don't want to. I'd be sick. I'd rather go home.'

Mr Wedgewood laughed. 'I'd let him please himself if I were you, Mrs James. He wouldn't enjoy it if he's not feeling well.' He turned, and hurried off into the crowd.

Mother was angry. 'You damned nuisance! Why didn't you go!'

Her anger puzzled me. 'But I didn't want to. I just want to go home with you.'

'What's the matter with you?' she demanded, leaning over me so that I could smell the perfume of her make-up. 'You're a damned awkward little pest. I've a good mind to give you a hiding! I came with you, didn't I? I sat for an hour and watched you, didn't I? What more d'you want?'

'Nothing,' I said. 'I don't want anything. Why are you so angry?'

'Because if you'd arranged to go, you should go. You should go – d'you hear!'

'I did want to go. But not now. Not after that . . .'

'What're you talking about?'

I couldn't have explained the effect the service had had on me, and I didn't try to. 'I feel sick,' I said, simply. 'I feel sick.'

'You're an awkward little swine. But you won't rule me, lad, I'm telling you! You won't rule me!'

I trotted at her side up Market Street to the bus stop. In silence, we waited for the bus, and in silence we boarded a number 25. She was quite stiff with annoyance, and when I sat beside her she prised her elbow spitefully into my side. 'Get up there!'

273

This inexplicable display of bitterness on her part drove away all the exaltation of the festival, and I now felt sick in earnest. Silence prevailed. When Mother got the tickets, I noticed that she asked for a three-halfpenny one for herself, although the fare home was threepence. I seized this as an opportunity to speak to her. 'It's threepence,' I said. 'You only gave him three-halfpence and it's threepence home.'

'I'm not going home,' she said.

'Aren't we? Where are we going, then?'

'*You're* going home – and to bed, straight away. If you're not fast asleep when I come home, you're for it!'

'Where are *you* going?'

'I'm going out – and shut up about it!'

So that was it. Everything was perfectly clear now.

'Why didn't you tell me you were going out?' I asked.

'I'm not answerable to you, am I! I don't have to tell you all my plans!'

'If you'd told me I'd've known what you meant when . . .'

'Oh shut up! Shut up!'

She got off at Butler Street. 'Don't forget,' she said. 'Bed at ten.'

As the bus rolled on, I turned in my seat and watched her till the blackout enveloped her.

Feeling ill and lost, I did as she had told me and went to bed at ten. Sleep, however, was elusive, and I lay awake for a long time, thinking of her, remembering her angry face and trying to imagine where she could be. Often enough in the past when she had gone out and left me alone, I had worried about her just as keenly. But tonight there was a new and deeply disturbing element in my confused thoughts, a tincture of doubt, an edge of suspicion. Something in her manner that evening, something I could not specifically remember, had induced in me the feeling that Mother was doing something she ought not to be doing. What, exactly, I had no idea at all. Yet I felt in my heart that there was shame in it and guilt, that it was something unclean and lewd, an echo of which I had heard in her laughter that day at the factory. To think such things about her, itself, created pain. Yet, try as I could, I found it difficult to dismiss that odious gnawing in my stomach.

If I had been a little less innocent than I was then, if I'd acquired in my twelve years as much as half the worldly knowledge I was to acquire in six months at Bury a year later, I might have been able to give some shape to these vague doubts. I might have been able, for that matter, to see the point of the questions Mrs Hanson put to me when I visited her a week or two later.

It must have been during the last few days of May – on an empty afternoon when nothing interested me – that I took it into my mind to go and see her. It was warm that afternoon, and I found Mrs Hanson sitting in a deckchair in the back garden, her skirts up over her knees, sunning her legs. As usual, she insisted on my eating some cake, and she kindly made tea, after consuming which we went out into the garden again.

We talked about Billy and about the war and about Father, in whom she seemed very interested.

'What's he like, your dad?' she asked.

I went on at some length, and I remember the expression on her face as I told her about him. It was a strange, lop-sided, half-smile, which I didn't think was appropriate to the things I was saying.

'You obviously think the world of him.'

'Yes. I wish he was home.'

'Do you? Why?'

What a funny question, I thought. I really didn't know how to answer it. 'Because I don't like him being away. Things are different without him.'

She nodded slowly. 'How do you mean, different?'

Again I was nonplussed. 'I miss him. It's lonely. He used to do things and let me help him. We used to talk.'

'Don't you talk with your mother, then?'

'Oh yes. But not so much. You can't talk to your mother like you can talk to your dad. And anyway, she's not very interested these days.' As soon as I'd said it, I regretted it, regretted the little twinge of bitterness that had prompted it.

'Isn't she? What *is* she interested in?'

'She works. And when she gets home, she's tired.'

'Does she never take you out anywhere?'

'Sometimes. Not often.'

'And does she go out on her own?'

It was asked casually enough, but there was a kind of intensity in her eyes, a kind of tenseness about the angle at which she held her head.

'Sometimes.'

'Just sometimes. Not often, then?'

As we had got on to this subject, such a sore one with me, I felt momentarily inclined to start complaining, as I had complained to Grandmother. But the recollection of the unpleasant results of that earlier unburdening made me change my mind.

'About once a week. Sometimes twice.'

'Does she have a special night – you know, like people do?'

'Yes. Friday.'

Mrs Hanson's expression changed again, subtly. 'Friday is a popular night.'

'Pardon? Why?'

She smiled. 'It's popular. Naturally, perhaps. People get paid on a Friday. They have a bit of money in their pocket.'

'She sometimes goes out Wednesdays, too.'

'I see. Where does she go? Visiting relations?'

'I don't know. But it's not visiting relations, because there's only Grandmother and they don't get on very well.'

'I don't suppose you care much, anyway, do you?'

'Sometimes.'

'She won't stay out late, though, will she, Freddy?'

'I go to bed. I never hear her come in.'

'Mm. Fridays and Wednesdays.' She nodded the information deeply into her mind. And then, suddenly, she was smiling again. 'Well, Freddy, I'm going to have to ask you to buzz off again now. It's getting up to teatime and I have to cook Mr Hanson's tea for him.'

All this meant nothing to me at the time. It was just talk. When I look back on that conversation, I realise how terribly naive I must have been to have understood so little of what she was trying to get me to say.

9

A day or two later, the post arrived as we sat at the kitchen table having breakfast. There had lately been an unusually long gap between Father's letters; we hadn't heard from him for perhaps a week. At the rattle of the letterbox, I jumped up and ran to the door. Often when there had been a delay in deliveries, two or even three letters had arrived together, and I was now a little surprised, therefore, to see only one lying there on the mat. I picked it up and received another surprise. Previous envelopes had been unstamped and had had 'On Active Service' written across them. This one simply bore our address and – puzzling indeed – an English postage stamp franked at Shrewsbury. I stood turning it over in my hands for so long that Mother, growing impatient, followed me.

'It's Dad's writing,' I said. 'But it's come from Shrewsbury.'

'What?' She snatched the envelope from me and stared at it. 'But he can't be in Shrewsbury!' Hastily, she ripped the envelope open and took out the letter and began to read it, her eyes darting from side to side. I watched her face, trying to see from it what the letter had to say.

Her expression grew more tense, her eyebrows drew together. 'Oh dear!' Sagging, as though all the strength had gone out of her, she flopped into a chair and, letting the note fall into her lap, covered her face with her hands.

Something fearful must have happened. My heart began to beat madly. Fearing the very worst, and fearing even to learn about it, I stood paralysed for a moment. But at length I forced myself to speak. 'What's happened to him?' I asked. 'What's wrong?'

She didn't seem to hear me.

Going to her, I took the letter from her lap and read it. Father was indeed in Shrewsbury, in hospital there. He'd been wounded in the hand and was coming home within a fortnight. The wound wasn't much, he said; just enough to get him out of the war. He seemed as pleased as Punch.

An explosion of uncontrollable joy burst in my chest. 'He's coming home!' I cried. 'For good!' I pranced about, flapping the letter over my head. 'He's coming home!'

But, just as suddenly as it had arrived, my joy vanished again. For Mother still sat there, cowed and stiff, as though we had received news of his death rather than news of his imminent return. I looked at her and tried to understand why she had taken it this way. The suspicious feeling I had had about her of late threatened to crystallise into unwelcome explanations. But such bitterness lasted only a moment. She loved him, just as I did. We both loved him dearly. There must be something else.

I read the letter again. It was one of the brightest he had ever written. Even the two or three sentences about his wound were humorous. But it must be that, I thought. It could only be that. It was the thought of his being hurt that had upset her. I recollected how he had held back the news that he was to go to France until the very last minute of his leave. Perhaps Mother saw, in this passing reference to his wound, cause to fear much more.

I considered the point myself, and the more I thought about it, the more convinced I became that she was wrong. If he was to come home within a fortnight, he would hardly keep in reserve the shock of really bad injuries. He would tell us the truth in his letter, to prepare us for when we met him. And in any case, I felt in my heart that he had told us everything.

I put my arm about Mother's shoulder. 'But it's only a little wound! Listen – I'll read it to you.' I did so. 'See, there's nothing to worry about. It'll soon get better and we'll be like we were before. It's so good I can hardly believe it!'

There was no response. Bending over her, I tried to prise her hands from her face, but her fingers were as stiff as rods of steel. 'Don't worry, Mother. Everything's all right, now.'

Her hands came away. Her face was mottled red and white and, on her cheek, where her ring had pressed against it, there was a little pink depression.

'Go and finish your breakfast,' she said. 'Leave me alone. I want to think.'

I turned away, but a thrilling idea occurred to me. 'If you're worried about him, why not let's go and see him?'

She looked blankly at me.

'We can see how he is for ourselves. Let's go – tomorrow!'

She shook her head. 'No . . .'

'But why not? I can't wait to see him. I bet he expects us to go, too. I bet you any money he's looking out for us!'

'You're probably right,' she said, thoughtfully. 'He will expect it. Shrewsbury's not far away . . . Perhaps we'd better go . . .'

'Let's! Don't worry. He'll be all right. I know it. I'll go to the station and ask about trains.'

I was home again about half an hour later. She was still there.

'Aren't you going to work?' I asked.

'No.'

'I don't blame you. Good.' I produced the scrap of paper on which I'd noted train times and fares. 'If we get to Manchester for half past seven, we can catch an express straight through.'

She nodded and nodded and said nothing.

She was edgy and out of sorts all day. At about ten to five, she left me eating my tea and slipped out the back way. It was an unexpected departure. She set off, hurrying, by the railway railings and disappeared down towards the bridge. She was away about twenty minutes.

'Where've you been?' I asked.

'I needed some matches.'

'But there's no shops down the vale.'

She didn't answer. But instead of sitting at the table she threw her coat over a chair and went into the front room.

'Aren't you having any tea?'

'I don't want any. I'm going out.'

My heart sank. 'What for? We're going to have to get up early in the morning. Don't go out.'

She came rushing back into the kitchen. 'Shut up!' She almost screamed it at me. 'I'm going out, I say! Out! Out!' She raved hysterically. 'And if you say anything about it, ever, to anyone, I'll murder you!' She thrust her face to within an inch of my own and shrieked at me. 'Keep your mouth shut!'

She stamped away upstairs to change, and, gritting my teeth, clenching my fists, I listened to the sounds she made up there. I couldn't bear to hear them, to think of her dressing herself up. In a rage, I ran out of the house, across the garden, down into the vale and to my little hut on the clay pit. For a long time I sat in there, fighting against a flood of resentment which seemed intent on drowning me. I could feel anger pressing against my stomach. I kicked at the hard earth with my heel, viciously and with all my strength, as though venting my wrath on her. And yet, deep in my heart, I longed for her – longed for her to be herself, to be as she had always been in the past. Each one of this swift procession of hateful thoughts was like a knife penetrating my brain.

But gradually the emotion eased and passed. It was growing dusk. The hut was filled with grey gloom, and across the river a haze was gathering, blanketing the factories there. It was growing chilly. Leaving the hut again, I went home, had supper, and went to bed. Tomorrow, I would be seeing Father. Soon, he would be home, and then everything would be all right. I concentrated on that thought, put it into words and repeated it to myself over and over again. Yet sleep did not come. I got up and spent half an hour looking out through the window. I drank some water, and then tried again to sleep. I pressed my eyelids together, and curled up my toes, and willed myself to sleep. But I remained as wide awake as ever.

Sounds from the world outside began to dwindle. I heard

the last bus pass down the lane a good half-mile away. I heard the people next door climb the stairs on their way to bed. And, remotely, I even heard the sound of a clock in someone's parlour striking midnight, a gentle tinsel sound.

Then, from away up the street, I heard Mother's approaching footsteps. I turned on my side, prepared to look like someone sleeping, and listened to her hurrying footsteps draw nearer. I tried to place her in my mind's eye. Now passing Johnson's; now coming up to the lamp post. But she must have been going much faster than I imagined. Long before I expected it, she was walking up the path, and then putting her key into the latch.

The door closed behind her, and I could feel her presence in the house at once. It was relieving, and I snuggled down, suddenly feeling very tired, almost asleep already.

But then I heard the *back* door open – stealthily, it seemed. I stiffened again, raised my head to listen. There was a gentle vibration in the atmosphere, a still little movement of air – the sound of a man trying to talk quietly. I sat bolt upright, my heart bursting, and in a twinkling I was as full of motion as I had been five or six hours before. What did this mean? Who was it? Who was it?

Slipping out of bed, I went to the head of the stairs, kneeling down there and straining to hear what they were saying.

It was the man who was talking, and indistinctly.

'. . . have me on!' I heard. 'By Christ no! What sort of a bloody pickle d'you think I'm in now? I can't stop thinking about you. All day, all night, you're on my mind. I can't change now just because he's bloody well coming home!

Nor can you, unless you've been having me on – and if I thought you were I'd bloody swing for you!'

I ceased to be aware of words, for something about that voice sounded familiar. Words ran one into the other as I listened to that well-known ring and tried to place it. Who was it? Who was it?

But Mother spoke. 'And what about me? You know how I feel! Hasn't it been obvious!' She was crying. 'Haven't I . . .' her voice trailed away, and then became clear again. 'But I can't go on now – I can't! It's impossible. Suddenly, now that he's home, it's different. I still feel the same about you. How can I help myself? But I feel the same about him. You see, you don't understand! I wish I'd never met you. Oh how I wish it! God help me!'

'It may be different for you, but it's not for me. And it's not over. It'll never be over! Bugger him!'

There was a pause. When he spoke again, his voice was gentler, and I sensed that he, too, was near to tears. 'Don't fight me, please, Joyce. I can't stand to think of never seeing you again. Florrie suspects. I know she does. But I don't care. If you thought of me like I think of you, you wouldn't care about him . . .'

Florrie! Now I knew who it was. The shock of it literally staggered me. I almost lost my balance and clutched at the wall. Fearful, lest they'd heard, I got up and tip-toed back to bed. But the conversation downstairs went on.

Mr Hanson! Mr Hanson! Mr Hanson! A great shout built up in my chest and I had to press my knuckles to my lips to stifle it. I wanted to go and kick him in the face over and over . . . I don't know how I managed to prevent myself leaping out of the bed again. But I did so. I buried my head into the pillow so as not to hear anything. I pushed my fingers into my ears. But still I could hear that masculine rumble – or feel it rather, its reverberations, minutely trembling the very bed. It went on and on and on.

Mr Hanson! Mr Hanson! Now I knew whom she was seeing when she went out. Now I understood everything, everything. I set him up in my mind and tortured him. I mutilated his body, tore his face apart – and I was so intent on this that Mother was on the landing on her way to bed before I realised that he had gone.

It would be wonderful to kill Mr Hanson, I thought, wonderful. I could do it in any one of a hundred ways. I had a scout knife in the drawer of my dresser. It would be wonderful to stick it into his face.

I heard Mother's mattress creak, and then the heavy silence of the night closed about the house. With the silence came the reaction. I shuddered violently, appalled at the awful, evil things I had been thinking. Involuntarily, I began to pray – I prayed hard and profoundly that Mother would indeed drive him away, as she had seemed to be doing downstairs just now. Don't let him force her to see him again! Make her drive him away!

A little tinkle broke the silence. It was one o'clock. In six hours' time, I would be off to see Father. Dad'll do it, I thought. Dad'll get rid of Mr Hanson. Just wait. Just wait till Dad comes home! Everything will be fine! Everything will be dandy!

I awoke next morning feeling as weak as a kitten, tormented with anxiety. My stomach ached and I could not face any food at all. Confused thoughts and equally confused emotions so preoccupied me that I dressed and accompanied Mother to the station in a daze. We were on the train, halfway to Shrewsbury, before I really became aware of what I was doing or where I was going. I didn't look at her face once during the whole of this time. I couldn't. I didn't want to see her, hear her, touch her. Nor did I want her to touch me or look into my face, to sense or to observe my resentment, for fear she should suspect what I had discovered.

If she were to learn that I had found out about Mr Hanson, the results, I felt, would be dreadful beyond imagination. Mutual knowledge would, I sensed very strongly, magnify matters a hundredfold, it would be utterly disastrous, it would end everything. When Father came home, when life resumed its normal pattern, I could forget and she could forget separately and quietly. But if each of us had to worry about the other's forgetting, the poison would corrupt for ever. All this I knew instinctively. I had to bear it. I had to purge my mind and body of these noxious thoughts and feelings as quickly as possible. Above all, I had to keep them to myself.

But I needn't have worried that Mother was watching me too carefully. She was as preoccupied as I was myself.

It was at Crewe that I woke up at last. You can worry yourself out of worry, and after a night and a morning of it, my mind began to take in other things. It was not a complete recovery by any means. My stomach continued to flutter from time to time. But mere distance seemed to ring a change. We had been travelling for an hour and a half and were passing through country that was completely strange to me. One might have been in another world, another segment of time, a million miles, a million years away from home and last night. Distance seemed, of itself, to put all that into remoter perspective. I began to think of Father, who now meant more to me than ever. Father was the one sure thing in life – the rock of salvation.

As the train rattled slowly through Crewe, I sat up and took interest in the many engines there, marvelled at that maze of lines and those great gantries of signals. And as the train gathered speed and whistled on westwards, I enjoyed the thrill of it.

The hospital was a vast stone building, like a prison, I thought, a ten-minute bus ride out of Shrewsbury. Our unheralded arrival caused a certain amount of confusion, and we were sent along one echoing corridor after another to and from many glass-walled offices. At last, we were taken by a nurse to a dingy waiting room and left alone. The walls were covered with dark brown, shiny paper, and I remember sitting there, stiffly nervous, staring at the embossed pattern of leaves, and straining my ears for sounds of Father's coming. Mother was nervous, too. She tapped a foot on the floor and her breathing was tremulous. She put an arm on to my shoulder. For a second, I tried to resist it – in vain. All my longing for her rose up from under that weight of despair and, putting my own arm about her waist, I clung to her as hard as I could.

'I love you,' I said.

'I know.' She kissed my temple. 'And you're my own lovely son.'

'Where is he?' I exclaimed. 'Oh Mum, I'm glad he's coming home! Aren't you?'

'Yes. I am.'

I don't know what Father thought when, coming at last,

he saw us. Mother and I clung together as if for dear life, and we were both crying.

As he came into the room, my eye immediately rested on his bandaged left arm. It was a large, bulbous dressing, extending almost to his elbow. Mother must have been staring at it, too, for as he came towards us he lifted his arm up and waved it about. 'Ticket to Newton Heath!' he said.

We literally fell upon him.

He sat between us and for half an hour we talked and laughed together. He smoked, and the smell of it, so evocative, seemed to confirm the reality of this happy reunion. The time of sadness was truly over.

Father was chattering madly, holding Mother's hand, stroking her hair. Every now and then he put a finger under her chin and lifted up her face. Her eyes were still full of tears, and she nodded and smiled, listening to him and saying little.

'How did you get wounded?' I asked. 'Was it a shell?'

'No,' he smiled. 'Just a bullet.' He turned to Mother again, but I was not satisfied.

'Where did it hit you?'

'In the knuckles.'

'Did it hurt?'

'Never mind it,' he said. 'It's nothing.'

'But tell us, Henry,' Mother said. 'Is it bad – honestly?'

'Well,' he looked down at it and jabbed it gingerly with his other hand . . . 'they've taken off the two middle fingers. You could hardly have a simpler and less inconvenient hit. It's not even my right hand! In fact, it's humiliating. They're discharging me because of it. I can't help feeling self-conscious about it when I look at some of the other poor devils in here. Legs shot away, broken backs . . . And look at me with a sore hand!' He slapped my knee. 'Still, I won't deny I'm jolly glad to be heading for home!'

'You look thinner,' Mother said, touching his face.

'Thinner, maybe. But I'm as fit as a fiddle. Up to the last few weeks, we had nothing to do except keep fit. They had us doing PT for six hours a day! No wonder I'm like a rake!'

'When are you coming home?' I asked.

'The doc this morning said I might go next weekend. They'll get me out as quick as they can. They're crowded in here with fellows much worse off than me.'

'That's only . . .' I reckoned it . . . 'nine days!'

'Yes. Nine days!' He pulled my ear. 'Nine short days!'

Our homeward journey was happy. We changed trains twice and hung about on dark stations for what seemed hours. But we paced the platforms together arm in arm, eating sausage rolls and giggling at everything. We didn't get home till eleven – but even then we didn't go to bed, but sat at the kitchen table eating toast and drinking tea and talking about Father.

When, finally, I did go to bed, I felt fine. Just half an hour in Father's company had been enough to transform both Mother and me. There was no doubt about it in my mind now – all that had been bad was already behind us. When Father came home, it would be the easiest thing in the world to forget it for ever.

10

Father came home in style, in a big wheeled ambulance.
That night, droves of neighbours came to pat him on the
back and welcome him home – people with whom, because
we were so withdrawn a family, we had never been very
popular. But their pride in him and their pleasure at seeing
him home again was entirely genuine. They had had a
run-round and brought in with them two bottles of whisky
and lots of bottles of beer which they proceeded to empty
in a long series of toasts, to Father, to England, and to Mr
Churchill. This was the time of Dunkirk. Britain had
suffered a major defeat, but the Army had been saved and
this, it seemed, was cause for great rejoicing. To these
neighbours, Father represented England's indomitable
spirit – he was a hero who epitomised England's heroism.
They feted him in the grand manner.

Father was overwhelmed by it. I hardly got near him all
evening, but caught only glimpses of him now and then
between bodies. They made him drink and drink, glass
after glass, and even poured some whisky down my own
throat. Mother and the other women pooled resources and
made a vast mound of sandwiches and, juggling my way
among the crowd, carrying a large plateful in either hand,
I helped to serve them.

But as the evening wore on, the atmosphere began to change. Father lay on the settee, his legs stretched out across the rug, his eyes shut and a look of smiling contentment on his face. The back-patting and hand-shaking had ceased. Father had subsided and the party went on without him. Talk about the war was over, and what had begun as a kind of national rejoicing had deteriorated into a noisy booze-up. Mrs Webster did a knees-up in the kitchen doorway – and then everyone began to dance, bumping into the furniture, hopping over Father's legs. I felt the anti-climax of it keenly. Mother, tousle-haired and tired, emerged from the kitchen and tried to make her way towards us, but Mr Johnson, a retired bus driver, whirled her away in a capering waltz.

I shook Father's shoulder. He seemed to have fallen asleep. Briefly, he opened his eyes. He tried to lift his head but didn't have the strength. 'Go to bed,' he said. 'Go to bed out of it.'

I protested, but he was adamant. 'Go to bed. That's an order, and let there be no insubordination in the ranks.'

The whole house shook. Sleep was impossible. I lay awake for hours, listening to the din of it.

During the days that followed, Father and we reacquainted ourselves. And it was a reacquaintance, something more than a mere taking up again from where we had left off. For in the past nine months, Father had changed – in little subtle ways. We had all changed, I suppose, for that matter, and Father must have found differences in us just as we did in him. The most noticeable change in him was a tendency to sit by himself, thinking, for half an hour at a stretch. Quite suddenly, he would break off from whatever he was doing, and take himself off somewhere to ponder. It was useless to try to talk to him in these brown studies. You simply had to wait for him to come back to life of his own accord.

It was as if he felt the need to be by himself from time to time – as if there was something in his mind which every now and then rose up and demanded all his attention.

His voice seemed to have changed, too. He spoke faster than he had done and used a great many unusual turns of speech. And on certain occasions, he reacted to certain things differently than he had in the past. This meant that, for a while, I treated him rather warily, sounding him out, as it were, before venturing anything very much.

But these little differences were of the most superficial kind. One quickly ceased to notice them. Within a very few days, all was well again and those long miserable months might never have been. He had been granted four weeks' sick and discharge leave, and he made up his mind to spend it gaily. Everything we had ever done in the past he insisted on our doing again – as though he wished to re-establish a foundation which during his time away had somehow crumbled from under him. We went on our old bus rides, worked like idiots in the garden, visited the zoo, went to the pictures three or four times, played cards – a mad, happy, vigorous round of it. We were as happy as sandboys. Arm in arm and at one again.

One Sunday, they came up to church for matins, and all through service I stared up at them. Ever since that first day at Shrewsbury, the burden of guilt I had borne in knowing about Mr Hanson had been steadily diminishing. With Father's return, it had grown even less troublesome.

And now, seeing them up there in the gallery of the church, standing together singing, kneeling together praying, every last vestige of uncertainty vanished. To me they were enveloped in sanctity. After that there could never be anything guilty or unclean between any of us.

At the end of the first fortnight, Mother returned to work. We had had our usual family discussion about it, but my view that she should now stay at home was in the minority. The money helped a great deal, Mother maintained, and she liked going out to work. It gave her something useful to do towards the war and it broadened her interests. Father supported her. 'If you want to work, Joyce, work. But if we're going to have extra money, let's do something useful with it. We'll buy a house and get out of this blooming estate.'

It was, we all thought, a great idea.

'Freddy won't mind being on his own a bit longer, for such a good cause, will you?'

Put like that, there was nothing I could possibly object to. And yet, though I was as enthusiastic as they about the idea of a new house, though I did not mind in the least being alone if it contributed to such a desirable objective, I was still not happy about Mother's return to the factory. The thought of her working there still troubled me, for the factory had come to symbolise for me a great deal that was unpleasant and depressing. The Monday morning when Father and I watched her hurry off up the road was the first moment of doubt I had experienced since Father's return.

But now, with Mother out all day, Father and I drew together as never before. For the rest of his leave, until he too started work again, we were inseparable. We papered the house, Father hanging the sheets while I pasted, and we painted every bit of exposed woodwork we could find. We repaired the garden fencing, took the wireless to pieces, overhauled everything. No matter what else the war might have done to him, it hadn't by any means reduced his appetite for messing about. Even one-handed he seemed as deft as ever, and my assistance was largely academic. But in doing these jobs together, during this fortnight of intense living, Father and I established a new union. In this more concentrated rapport, I developed a new understanding of him – and the more I understood him, the more I loved and admired him.

Through Mother's absence, paradoxically, I also grew to understand more of their relationship, because during those early weeks of his return Father talked often about her.

'You know, Fred,' I remember him saying, 'without your mother, I'd be nothing. I'm not much as it is – but whatever I am it's because of her. That's life. A man never is anything without a woman. Men are by nature pretty hopeless. I've seen it in the Army. They've no sense of purpose, no objective in life on their own. They need something to focus themselves on. In the Army discipline makes their lives worthwhile. But me – well, it's your mother. Everything I do is done with her in mind. The only real pleasure is in pleasing her. You'll know what I mean when you're older. Get yourself a girl like your mother and you won't go far wrong.'

I remember this little speech well, because it surprised me at the time. A boy thinks of his father as the originator of ideas, the driving force, the stanchion, the regulator and decision-maker of the family. To hear Father confess that in reality it was Mother who was all these things and that he merely reflected her, was somehow disappointing. I didn't believe it.

When we had done everything in the house that needed doing, and a great deal that was unnecessary, we took to going out in the afternoons. I showed him all my secret retreats and taught him how to fly kites in masterly fashion. He became as fanatical a kite-flyer as I was myself, and between us we made some giants which soared to astonishing heights. It was late June now. We would lie on our backs on the grass, watching the kite swoop up there, and talk about all sorts of things. Now and then, but much more rarely than I would have liked, we got on to the Army and his time in France.

It had been, I discovered, a short sharp war as far as he had been concerned. Months of waiting had been followed by a crushing blitzkrieg. The Germans had darted suddenly like a tiger, and the Army, outnumbered and outmanoeuvred, had been mauled almost to death, retreating only in the very nick of time. 'They let us down,' he said. 'They sat us on the Belgian frontier and just bided time till Jerry was ready to come and pounce on us. If we'd had a chance, Fred, we'd have given an account of ourselves that would have gone down in history. This wonderful master race! Pooh! Any English Tommy is a match for four of 'em, any day!' The fighting, it seemed, had been bewildering to Father and his fellow soldiers. 'I can't remember much about it, Fred. Everything was in such a mess. The shells started falling, everyone started shooting, and the next thing I knew I was on my way home. Even now I can't see it all clearly. I try to get it into perspective, but I can't.'

Father had never got to terms with the fighting, apparently. I sensed, also, that he had never got to terms with the Army as such, either. He spoke disparagingly of 'them' – the people who had let the soldiers down, and when I asked whether he had made any friends in the Army, he shook his head. 'There was one chap – but he got posted. I'm the sort of fellow, son, who doesn't make friends easily. I don't do the same things other fellows do – I can't be bothered. I don't go drinking . . . you know the sort of thing. If you're like me, they don't bother with you either. That was the worst part of it, the loneliness. All those months of inactivity and loneliness. That's really what got me down.'

How like me he was, I thought. I understood exactly what he meant, exactly how he had felt. The odd man out. Aware of it and yet not concerned about it because those other people didn't matter. 'I thought of your mother and you all the time. You were all I cared about.'

The Army doctors had passed Father's treatment on to the local hospital. I went down to Ancoats with him twice. On the first occasion, they removed part of the bandage, and on his second visit they took away what remained, leaving him with only a patch of plaster. As he came out of the surgery, and showed it to me, the fact that he had lost two fingers was borne in upon me really for the first time. One had known about it before, of course, but that great bandage had obscured the full horror of it. His arm and wrist were pale, almost white, flecked with protruding blue veins, and the two fingers that remained prodded forth at either side of that ghastly gap like horns, I thought, the horns of some little animal. My stomach turned over, and I averted my head so that he shouldn't see the signs of nausea in my face. In the bus on the way home, he rested the hand on his knee, and those two fingers danced there as though they enjoyed a life of their own. I was deeply ashamed of my squeamishness. 'Fine soldier you'd make!' I told myself. I stared hard at the hand, and then, looking away so that Father would not notice my intentness, peered out of the window, remembering the image of those fingers and concentrating on it, forcing myself to study it.

That evening, when Mother came home, I made a point of watching her reaction to Father's hand. She, too, was obviously shocked and sickened. She blanched and, just as I had done, looked away, pretending that it had had no effect on her at all. I wondered if she felt as ashamed of herself as I had, and came to the conclusion that she had. Over tea, she kept glancing at it and, later, she did something I admired her for greatly. She took hold of that shattered hand and put it to her cheek. But it was surprising how quickly one grew used to Father's wound. After that first day, I don't think either Mother or I noticed it particularly again. Other people did, of course. They would stare at it, frown, and always turn their eyes away. The reaction was invariable. And the odd thing was, when I saw people shocked by it, I despised them for something which I myself had been guilty of.

Father must have noticed people's reaction himself. He could hardly have avoided doing so, and even when the wound was fully healed he rarely went out without a glove over it.

A few days before his leave was due to end, he took me with him on a visit to the mill to see about getting his old job back. Even here, it seemed, Father had been the odd man out. No one looked overjoyed to see him. The office in which he'd worked was large and Dickensian, with high desks and high stools, old-fashioned ink pots and cylindrical rulers. There were four elderly men in there and one woman who, it appeared, had taken over Father's job at the beginning of the war.

'So you're back then,' the chief clerk said, looking at Father over the top of his silver-framed glasses. 'Didn't take you very long, did it?'

The other men nodded at us across their ledgers. 'War's not going too good, is it?' one of them remarked.

The woman, a mouse-faced creature, did not lift her head, but glanced coldly and slyly at us from under her heavy eyebrows.

'We've gone over to blankets,' the chief clerk said. 'For the Navy. You'd better go and see Mr Margetson. He's in his office.' He nodded at a door with a frosted glass window in it which bore the word 'Private' engraved in large baroque letters all hung about with roses and ivy leaves. As the chief clerk spoke, Mr Margetson came out, a rotund Pickwickian figure bearing an armful of papers.

'Ah, James!' he said. 'I got your letter. When do you want to start?'

'Next week, Mr Margetson,' Father replied. 'If that's all right.'

'Mm. It's a bit tricky. I'm on my way to see Mr Marlborough, our new director. Come outside.'

We followed him into the corridor. 'I didn't want to talk

in there,' he said. 'But you know, James, it's a bit tricky. We put Mrs Watson on to your job, and I really can't think how I can find other work for her. I wonder if you'd mind going into the works office for a bit?'

Father and he talked. Why, I wondered, should this pompous, silly man have such power over Father? What made him so superior? He looked, and sounded, I thought, like a fool. I didn't like his big hands, nor the great rings he wore on them, nor that flashy gold watch chain, nor his supercilious, overbearing manner. How could he dare talk to Father as though he were talking to mud!

Mr Margetson walked away, wobbling his big bottom behind him.

'Why,' I asked, 'is he the boss?'

Father laughed. 'Why is anyone the boss! Don't ask me. Anyway, it's settled. I don't fancy the works office though, between you and me. Still, it's a job. Would you like to see the looms working?'

I hesitated. The sight of Mother's factory had satisfied for a long time any curiosity I might have had about industry. But Father mistook my hesitation for nervousness.

'It's all right,' he said, bearing me down the corridor. 'No one'll mind.'

But he was wrong. As we came to the door at the far end, a tall, bony, grey-haired man appeared. Seeing us, he stopped and frowned and asked, 'Where are you going?'

'I'm going to show my lad the looms.'

'Who are you?' the tall man asked, raising his tone.

At this moment, Mr Margetson came through the doorway. 'It's James, Mr Marlborough. One of our men just back from the Army.'

'All the same, I don't think we ought to have people wandering about, Margetson.'

'Sorry!' Promptly, Father swung around, and, grabbing my arm, hurried out with me.

'The skinny old bag of bones!' I exclaimed. 'The rotten old loon!'

Father laughed. 'Don't let it bother you, son. We'll have a game of Monopoly tonight, the three of us. Let's get going home. Come on. We'll get tea and then we'll make believe we own London Town!'

The following Monday, Father resumed work and, once more, I was flung back on my own devices for eight or more hours a day. But now I could concentrate entirely on enjoying myself, for there was nothing to worry about, not a thing. The war never bothered me for a moment, because Father was home and the war for me was therefore over. My self-created pastimes absorbed me, and when I didn't go out during the day, I sat at the kitchen table studying the textbooks Father had got for me. He was concerned about my total lack of schooling. To please him, I made great efforts and progressed well enough. Each evening, as always, I did the table and had things ready for when they came home. This, in the past, had frequently been an onerous chore, but now it was a pleasure. I took pride in having everything just so.

All through July and on into August, this pleasant and reassuring pattern of life persisted. Gradually, as Father settled down at home again, the rhythm grew slower, more normal. He was less interested now in dashing about, and pottered away in the house with his bits and pieces. Mother took up knitting again – still balaclava helmets that she gave away to some organisation which passed them on to wherever they ended up. One day became very much the same as the next, one week differed only slightly from the one before. But that was how I liked it. There was comfort in this kind of stability. Everything, just as I had predicted, was well again – or so I thought.

At the end of August, I was to sustain a serious shock.

One Friday I came home from choir practice to find Father at home by himself.

'Where's Mother?' I asked.

'Gone out.'

It was like a sharp, hard punch in the stomach.

'What's up?' Father asked. 'Why shouldn't she go out if she wants to?'

I couldn't speak.

'You must never try to stop people doing what they want to do, Fred. Remember that. It's good advice. And never try to make them do what they don't want to do. Either way, you just stifle them. She's gone out with one of her pals from work.'

'Why didn't she go with you?'

'Well, this other woman asked her. And in any case, I had to be in for you.'

'No you don't!' I protested eagerly. 'No – it's all right, Dad, honestly. If ever you and Mum want to go out, it's all right!'

'We've not gone out yet without you, and we certainly shan't start now. Look, I've put a new branch line on your train set.'

He had, too. But at that moment, I was not interested in my train set.

The following Friday, she went out again, and the Friday after that, and once again I was flung into an emotional maelstrom. I could not believe that her 'friend' on these occasions was anyone but Mr Hanson, though, in desperate efforts to retain my peace of mind, I *tried* to have faith in her. I was horrified that she could do this to Father – and I dreaded to think what would happen if he found out. There was something mad, crazy, in what she was doing. She couldn't possibly have thought about it – about the fearful sin of it, the disloyalty – or even about the risks of discovery. It was as though she were quite unable to reason about it, as though she were being forced into it, compelled by something in herself. But this seemed in no way to excuse it, to lessen the horror of it. I now began to understand that, fundamentally, she and Father were different. They were not, as I had always fondly thought, the same kind of people; they were as different as they could be. Father had said he was nothing without her, that she regulated his life. But I was now wiser than he about it. This had been only what he himself had believed, and he was wrong. The whole tenor of our existence had been his. It had been Mother who had submitted. When he had gone away, she had found the opportunity of doing the things she wanted to do. She liked other people; she liked going out and meeting other people; she liked working with other people. And she still wanted to do these things now that Father was back. There was a profound sense of foreboding for me in this realisation. Something dreadful would happen, I knew it. Mother's need for other people had led her to Mr Hanson – and Mr Hanson was a fiend.

In my anxiety all sorts of ridiculous notions occurred to me – idiotic solutions suggested themselves. If I were suddenly to be taken ill, perhaps she would come to her senses, I thought, and for days I searched for ways to injure myself or to induce pneumonia. Perhaps if I ran away it would help . . . I even set off one afternoon on my bike and got as far as Disley before my resolution failed. I was home again for seven, and Mother didn't seem to have noticed my absence at all – though Father clouted me for missing tea. But in the end, my bitterness focused on Mr Hanson. I hated the man to a degree that, when I think of it now, hardly seems possible. Several times, I waited on the railway embankment by the aircraft factory and watched him come out of work – staring my hatred into him and willing him to die. Twice, I hung about near his house, waiting for him to come into the street, planning ghastly but vague things. I didn't see him on either occasion, and I can't imagine what would have happened if I had.

One Friday, I missed choir practice deliberately and went upstairs to her as she was getting ready. She was in the bedroom, only half dressed. She had no frock on and was sitting on the edge of the bed fastening her suspenders. There were little frills on her knickers and the sight of those silly bits of lace angered me beyond control. I had intended to cry – something that would have come easily to me at that moment – to cry and arouse her pity and beg her to stay in. But instead I shouted at her, making a lot of inarticulate noise.

'What're you going out for again?' I demanded. 'What're you going out for again!'

Her face contorted. 'Ssh! Shut up!'

But I couldn't be hushed. Stiff with fury, my brain fuddled by it, I searched for words that would frighten her – that would let her see that I knew just why she was going out and where she was going to. But I couldn't. Once again, my courage failed me and I merely stammered and groaned and howled.

She jumped to her feet and came and hit me across the mouth. 'Shut up! Shut up for God's sake!'

The sting of the blow only made me angrier still. I screeched on, seeing nothing, hearing nothing, quite hysterical.

Suddenly, Father was there, gripping my arms and shaking me. 'Fred! Fred!'

At the sound of his voice, my sanity came back immediately. His face hovered over me, his eyes searching mine.

'What's the matter?' he asked. 'Fred, what's wrong?' I shuddered violently and began to cry.

'What's up, son? Tell me . . . What's upset him?' he asked Mother.

'It's because I'm going out,' she said. 'He just doesn't like me to go out. I don't know what gets into him.'

'What a softy!' Father touched my head. 'I didn't know you could be such a big baby. Stop it now, lad! Buck up! Come downstairs and cool off.'

He lectured me for half an hour on the necessity to avoid selfishness, at one point during which Mother popped her head around the door and bade us goodbye.

Shortly after that, while Mother was out one evening, we received a visit from Mrs Hanson. We were playing Chinese patience. Father went to answer the knock and a moment later, recognising the sound of Mrs Hanson's voice, I knew that the thing I had been dreading for so long had happened.

Indistinguishable words bubbled from her in a long, breathless stream. Her voice rang with determination, the sound of it drowning Father's attempted interjections, going on and on. But, just as suddenly as it had begun, that barrage of words stopped. There was a long, trembling pause. Then I heard Father say, 'Come in.' The door swung open.

'Mr James . . .' Mrs Hanson began again, apparently still standing on the door step. 'I can't tell you how I hate having to say this to you. I wish to God you could have found out some other way . . . But I had to. You realise that, don't you? It's my life they're ruining as well. They're out now! It can't go on! We must do something!'

'Come in,' Father said again, softly.

When Mrs Hanson saw me, she stopped dead and stared at me. Her bent face was red and I could see she had been crying. She stood poised, staring at me with a strange, taut expression.

'Freddy,' Father said, 'go upstairs and play with the train.'

I went into my parents' bedroom and closed the door behind me to shut off the sound of Mrs Hanson's voice. But I could still hear it, like the distant buzzing of a wasp, so I opened the window and let in the sounds of the world outside. This wasn't happening, I told myself. There was no one downstairs at all. My parents were out together, arm in arm somewhere. I was in the house alone. Everything was all right. The truth was so terrifying that, for a little while, I succeeded in deluding myself.

It was just going dark out there. The sky was barred across with great blue strips of cloud. A plume of smoke from one of the factory chimneys arose and spread like a giant tree. Night drifted across the valley in a slow tidal wave, lapping over railings and houses and river. Stars came out and sparkled up there. The Newcastle 8.50 flashed past at top speed and rattled away into the distance.

I heard Mrs Hanson go, and I came back, trembling, to reality. Closing the window, I set off towards the stairs. But when I came to the end of the landing, I saw Father in the hall down there, leaning against the outside door and holding on to the jamb for support.

I stopped and looked at him. His eyes were closed and his face was raised up at a curious, unnatural angle. The flesh of his face seemed loose and his cheeks had sunk in great deep hollows. As I watched, he gave a long, awful groan – a grotesque, unnerving sound. He remained like that, perfectly still, for what seemed minutes. When he did move, I became afraid that he would see me and quickly stepped back on to the landing.

He went into the front room and silence fell: an awful deathly silence.

'Dad!' I shouted, tentatively. 'Dad!'

He didn't acknowledge it.

'Dad – can I come down?'

At last, he came and answered me. 'Go to bed, son,' he said. 'Go to bed.'

But it was impossible to think of sleep. I wanted to see him. I longed to go down to him. 'What about supper?' I cried. 'I'm hungry.'

He hesitated.

'I'll get it myself,' I went on. 'Let me come down.'

I heard him sigh. 'All right.'

He was standing by the fire with his back to me, hiding his face. 'Hurry up,' he said. 'And then go to bed.' I was overwhelmed with pity for him and wanted desperately to console him. But I stood there quite helpless.

'Do you want something?' was all I could find to say.

He shook his head.

In continuing silence, I prepared supper and tried in vain to eat it. My mouth was dry. I had no appetite whatsoever, despite what I'd said. I sat at the table, staring into space, and listening intently to nothing.

Getting up, I tipped my supper into the waste bucket. 'There's some tea left, Dad,' I said. 'Do you want some?'

'Go up, Freddy, there's a good lad.' He had not moved from his place by the fire.

Mother returned about eleven. Neither of them came to bed that night, and for hour after hour I listened to them. I had expected a fierce and frightful row. Perhaps that would have been more bearable, less ominous, than those quiet droning words, the long silences, the pleadings and the crying.

I didn't sleep for a moment, and was still awake next morning when Father came up and told me to get dressed. When I went down, he was waiting for me in the hall with his coat on. At his feet was a suitcase.

'Get your mac, Fred,' he said. 'And say goodbye to your mother.'

She was standing just inside the front room, her face streaked with smeared make-up. She looked like an old woman, like a stranger.

'Henry,' she said to Father, 'Henry – don't, please, please . . .'

'Say goodbye,' Father repeated.

Mother flung her arms around me and put her wet face to mine. 'Oh Freddy!'

Father took hold of my arm. 'Come on.' Hurriedly, he led me from the house.

At the corner, I looked back. Mother was standing in the doorway, a sad and forlorn figure.

We'd no sooner got out of sight of the house than Father stopped in his tracks, gave a shudder and put his hand to his face.

'Take the case,' he muttered. 'Go on – go on. I'll catch up. Go on . . .!'

An hour later, we were on the train, heading for Bradford.

12

I've no idea why Father chose to go to Bradford. We knew no one in that city; indeed, neither of us had ever even been there before. For all I know, we might have ended up there simply because it happened to be the destination of the first train we could get on to.

It was a dirty, sooty town, under a pall of smoke from out of which fell a sticky drizzle of rain. Father and I had hardly exchanged a word all morning, and we still didn't speak as, leaving the station, we went and stood by the ugly town hall trying to make up our minds which direction to take. But there was a little café across the road and, noticing it, Father realised that I hadn't eaten since yesterday. 'You'd better have some food,' he said.

The café made the same unpleasant impression on me as the town itself. The large window looking out into the street was misted over with steam, shot with little rivulets of condensation. The table was small and rickety, without a table cloth, like a patch of desert sprouting an oasis of sauce bottles. The cream paint on the walls was peeling away. But one's impressions are always conditioned by one's mood, and I projected my melancholy, my intense apprehension, on to the world at large.

Father ordered chips and fish, but halfway through the

meal he put down his knife and fork. 'I'm going to the police station,' he said. 'Over there in the town hall.'

'Police station!' I repeated, panicking suddenly.

'I want to find some lodgings.'

I watched him as he crossed the road and climbed the town hall steps. Then I looked away up that drab street with its Lowry figures and high black warehouses. Was this to be my home, now? This strange depressing city? As I sat there, the full implication of what had happened came to me. All night and all morning, fear had dominated me, a biting fear that had permitted no rational thinking. But now, here in this dim café, thirty-odd miles from home, I realised the meaning of it all. Father and I had left home – and I would never see Mother again! The thought was physically painful. My mind was suddenly filled with memories of her – memories from happy times of her laughing face, her hands, her hair – and my heart almost broke. This wasn't true, I told myself. It couldn't be true! It was impossible.

Father returned to prove me wrong. He had been given a number of addresses, several of them with telephones and, crushing into a kiosk with him, I read the figures aloud while he dialled them. But he had no luck, and there was nothing for it but to visit the other places on the list.

I remember little of that afternoon. We rode on dozens of buses, it seemed, and knocked on dozens of doors. But no one had any vacancies. The whole afternoon was like a dream – the sort of dream in which you find yourself lost and helpless in a world completely devoid of sympathy. It was early evening before we found someone to take us in – the landlady of a large Victorian house at a place called Frizinghall, a mile or two northwards out of the city. She showed us to a room on the first floor, took some money from Father and left us. I don't recollect seeing that woman again during the whole of the three or four weeks we stayed with her.

There was a gas fire with a shattered element which burnt with a loud roaring splutter. Father draped our coats before it to dry, and, sitting on the iron-framed double bed, we watched the steam rise from them.

'Freddy,' Father began after a long silence, 'I'm sorry for all this. I think I know how you feel. One day I'll explain it to you. But not now. I can't now. I had to do this . . .' His head began to roll, queerly, 'Oh God, what can I tell you!'

'It's all right, Dad,' I said, really not wanting him to try to explain. 'It's all right.'

In twenty-four hours he had literally shrunk. All the buoyancy had gone out of him; his body, his flesh, seemed to droop. And now that we had found somewhere to rest he seemed incapable of moving.

'It's suppertime, almost,' I said.

'I don't want anything, Freddy.' He put a hand to his pocket and gave me some change. 'Slip out and see if you can get something for yourself. Take the ration books. They're in the case.'

'It doesn't matter. I'm not hungry.'

'Yes. Go on – you must eat.'

I found a grocer still open and brought in some cereal and milk. But when I got back I realised there were no plates.

'What a mess we're in!' Father said. 'What an awful mess we're in!'

I grew to loathe that room. It was like limbo for me. Its very air was charged with the distillation of all the misery in the world. Everything about it was alien, invested, it seemed, with a will to resist all my attempts to grow familiar with the place, to draw some solace from it. It was a large room with a wide bay window. The ceiling was extraordinarily high and I used to lie awake at night studying the intricate patterns in its moulded plaster. But even these were disturbing patterns, endless spirals and circles all drawing in upon themselves like the delineations of madness. The furniture was scanty – a double bed, two hard chairs, a chest of drawers, an old, greasy gas stove, and a wash-stand. There was a worn cotton carpet on the floor and dirty ochre distemper on the walls. The only tolerable thing about the place was the view from the window – across a main road to a park, with trees and fine green lawns.

Two days after our arrival at Bradford, Father found a job in a woollen warehouse in the city and yet again I was left to my own devices through those long and introvertive days. Being alone now was different, profoundly so. Everything here was so entirely strange as to defy any attempt at exploration. The sheer scope of unfamiliarity would have outfaced me completely even in a more optimistic frame of mind. As it was, burdened as I was with melancholy, I was beyond the pale, lost, submerged. Because of this, my recollections of this period are vague – as though throughout the whole of those weeks I was never really conscious. I used to sit in the park, on a bench just beyond the wall from the road; sit there, oblivious to everything about me, thinking of Mother, pining for her hour after hour. There was no ambivalence now. Faced with the prospect of never seeing her again, my love for her was boundless. My days were vacant and my evenings hardly less so.

Father was unrecognisable. His personality had undergone a sudden transformation. He, who had never seemed to relax for a moment, who had always managed to find something to absorb his mind and keep him busy, was now almost lifeless. He would come in from work, throw himself on the bed and hardly move or speak all evening. It was all so horribly familiar, for this was precisely what I had had to contend with from Mother during the first few months of Father's service: that same impenetrable withdrawal. And once again, I was powerless to do anything about it or even to regulate myself to it.

I have an image of him in my mind – one particularly clear memory of him at that time. He was sitting in one of those upright chairs before the fire, staring as if mesmerised by the spurting jet of flame. He was in his shirt sleeves. His hands were on his knees, his shoulders drooping and his head nodding gently as if marking his heartbeats. The two fingers of his wounded hand – and how pathetic they seemed to me then – clutched at his trousers like frightened little animals. And as I looked at him, I recollected again what he had said to me: 'Without your mother, I'd be nothing.' Though, in truth, I knew he had been wrong, the tragedy was that he himself had believed it and, believing it, he was now living it out. It was evenings such as that which drained away all my childhood. I grew old at Bradford. In years I was just thirteen. In spirit I became an old man.

His anguish must have been consuming, for it was many days before he could think about my position. When he did, that, too, obviously troubled him deeply. Several times, he tried to explain to me what had happened – needlessly had he only known – but he never quite managed it. Even now he couldn't stand to speak the slightest disparagement of Mother. His gaze would fall away, his voice would fail him, and the words die in his throat. But his concern for me was obvious, and at last, no doubt after prolonged argument with himself, he told me to write to her.

'You want to write, don't you?' he said.

I did indeed.

'Then do so. Tell her how you are. She'll be worried to death about you.'

'You don't mind then, Dad?'

He smiled. 'I'm not so heartless. One day, when you understand, you'll forgive me for all this, Fred. No matter what you think now, you'll see it all differently some day. Write to her.'

When I came to put pen to paper, however, I experienced the utmost difficulty in knowing what to say. I wanted to express my love for her and to tell her how I longed to be home with her again – but these sentiments seemed so much like a betrayal of Father that I could not find it in me to express them. In the end, it was a very brief and impersonal letter, clipped and almost meaningless.

The reply was immediate and its tone induced in me a great surge of hope. Mother wanted us home again just as desperately as I. Her letter was a veritable cry from the heart, and expressed in its incoherent and yet strangely lucid way the same yearnings I felt myself. As I read it, I could see her in my mind's eye, slowly drawing out those large letters, pausing and staring and thinking. It touched me deeply and added poignance to my own tumultuous feelings.

When Father came home, I offered it to him to read. But to my great disappointment, he wafted it away. 'No – no. It's your letter!'

'But she's written it to you as well!' She had indeed. The letter was a confused and uncertain mixture of maternal and wifely attitudes. She had obviously expected him to read it.

'I don't want to see it, Fred.'

I persisted. 'Please, Dad – please!' I felt certain that if he read it he would be as moved as I had been. 'She wants us to go back, Dad. She loves us. She wants us home!'

'Fred – for Christ's sake burn it!' Father seemed to lose all self-control and, snatching the letter from me, threw it against the gas fire. It lodged there momentarily, caught alight, and fluttered to the floor. Stiff and angry he glowered at me. 'I let you write to her and she can write to you if she wants to! Let that be enough! Don't crucify me!'

Hope faded again, and the pain of it lingered on. I didn't have the heart to write again for a week, though I knew she would be waiting anxiously for a reply. Days passed timelessly. That grim room, and those awful, demoralising evenings . . . As if to provide a suitable setting for my wretchedness, it rained steadily for days on end, solid sheets of water, drenching the park, flooding down the window pane, distorting the world and besieging me in my unhappy island. And now, crushed together in that one inescapable room, Father and I began to lose all contact with each other, as each of us spun about himself his own cocoon of misery.

Growing tired of waiting for me, Mother wrote again. What had happened? Why didn't we come home? She would die if she didn't hear from us soon. I couldn't bear it and, putting the letter back into its envelope, hid it away in my pocket. Three days later a letter arrived addressed to Father. I propped it up on the mantelpiece and when he came in stood back and left him to notice it himself.

He spotted it at once and, going to it, he picked it up and stared at it intently. Then, sighing, he went and sat on the bed, with the envelope still in his hand, and wrapped himself up in his cocoon. He still had his overcoat on, but his body seemed to wilt inside it and it hung in great folds about his shoulders. His head was thrust forward. Those two fingers trembled.

'Read it,' I pleaded. 'Why don't you read it?'

He turned slowly to me, as though my words only dimly penetrated his mind. For a second, he stared blankly at me. Then, suddenly springing to life, he threw the letter from him. 'Great Christ!' he exclaimed. 'She's broken my heart – can't she leave me alone!' As he tried to go on, a deep sob strangled his words.

I could not help myself. I ran to him and put my arms about his neck.

'Freddy, Freddy,' he said. 'I love her! I can't help it. It's killing me!'

'Then read the letter, Dad! She wants us to go home!'

'No no!' he eased me away. 'I've had enough. I can't take any more.' He struggled visibly to control himself. Oddly, he went to the sink and washed his face.

It was killing him, he'd said. And I felt that slowly I was dying too. Mother in her letter had said the same. It was all so unnecessary, I thought. Why couldn't Father realise that she really did want us home? Couldn't he see that we meant everything to her? No matter what she had done, it was over now. If she had for a moment realised that through seeing Mr Hanson she would lose Father and me she wouldn't have looked twice at him. It was us she loved. I blamed myself. If I could only have found some way of warning her – if only I could have done something. I had known what she was doing. The fact that I had had this knowledge seemed to me to have endowed me with as much responsibility as Mother for what had happened. She just hadn't known what she was doing – she'd not thought at all. She'd been blind. And now, the result of her actions was as intolerable to her as to us. If only Father could realise this. If only I could explain it to him.

But I never did manage to explain it to him. In the first place, these were feelings rather than thoughts and I could never put them into words. Moreover, I knew Father would not have listened to me anyway. I was a child. I knew nothing of what had happened. I didn't understand. There would be no point in listening to me. We served out our penance together, therefore, each unable to express himself to the other.

Another letter arrived addressed to him, and this, too, he threw away. But that same week, she did something he could not ignore – she came to Bradford herself.

She arrived about four in the afternoon – all red-faced and nervous. To have her turn up there was the last thing I'd expected, and I was so shocked I couldn't speak.

'Freddy!' Taking my face in her hands, she kissed me. 'Freddy – my own lovely son!'

I feasted on her, submerged myself with explosive ecstasy in her presence. We embraced and kissed and cried.

'Take us home!' I begged. 'Make him come home!'

'Where is he?' she asked. 'What has he told you? Will he come home?'

'You've got to make him! I can't stand it here any more.'

'Oh son, it's been a nightmare! I've not stopped thinking of the two of you since the very moment you went away. What have I done! What have I done! Freddy, I can't go on without you and your dad. If he doesn't come back with me, I'll kill myself!'

As the time for Father's return drew near, we waited with mounting nervousness. 'Oh God, let him come home!' Mother kept saying. 'Oh God, let him come home!' We sat on the bed, facing the door, listening and waiting. When at last we heard the sound of his footsteps on the stairs, she gripped my hand fiercely. We both got up and stood tense and rigid watching the door.

It opened and Father stood there. Momentarily, he seemed unable to take in what he saw. He stared, frowning at us. The intensity of our feeling must have been a palpable pressure in the atmosphere. He took a step backwards and gasped. 'You!'

Mother's hand gripped mine so tightly that it hurt. Neither of us moved or spoke.

Quickly, Father came in and pushed the door to behind him, his gaze not leaving Mother's face for a moment. How thin and pale and sick he looked. His face worked and twitched.

Suddenly, Mother ran to him, and, throwing her arms about his neck, sank her head on to his chest. 'Henry – I love you! Henry, come home! It's over – over. On Freddy's life I swear it! Come home!'

Father tried to push her away from him, but she clung tightly. 'Fred,' he said, his voice crackling oddly, 'go on out for a bit. Leave us for a bit.'

I went into the corridor and lingered for a moment there. I listened, but there was no sound and, quite unaware of what I was doing, I left the house, crossed the road and went into the park. I sat on that bench, gritting my teeth with anxiety and staring up at the window, praying that all would be well. Two girls of about my own age came and sat beside me. I felt them staring at me. Traffic on the road thinned out after the five o'clock exodus from the city. Another lodger, an elderly man in special constable's uniform, walked up the path and into the house.

After about half an hour, I half rose to go back, but checked myself in the act. I was afraid of what might be happening in my absence and yet afraid of going to see for myself. Poised between the horns of decision, I stayed where I was.

The girls laughed and walked away. A sudden breath of breeze sprinkled specks of rain into my face. And then Father was at the window, peering down into the road, apparently searching for me. I waved my hand over my head and, catching sight of me, he beckoned. He stayed up there, looking after me, as I went back across the road. His mouth was moving. He must have been talking to Mother. I strained my eyes to see from his face what to expect – and, vague though the sight of him was, I seemed to detect hopeful signs. Breaking into a run, I dashed up the stairs and pushed open the door.

Mother came to me and hugged me. 'You're coming home, Fred!'

'And Dad?' I looked at him. He neither spoke nor smiled, as though in a way he still resisted. And yet the relief he felt shone out of him.

We packed up at once and left Bradford that night.

13

There followed a time of desperate forgetting. All that had happened in recent months had to be obscured. Nothing we did or said must remind us of it. It was a tacit pact between us, and we lived an exaggerated, almost histrionic existence all through the rest of the summer. There was a slightly forced gaiety between us, an emphasised affection, a conscious drawing together. Mother gave up her job, and this, in itself, was a most promising omen. The house was brighter and tidier than it had been for almost a year – and tidiness was a reassurance, for it reflected Mother's renewed interest in her home. There was warmth and comfort again. I could return to the house after a day in the vale and be certain to find her there, with a meal ready, and anxious to hear where I had been and what I had been doing. I no longer had any chores. The days were mine to do with as I wished. And our evenings were pleasanter, too. While Mother had been at work, we had all spent an hour or so every evening doing the housework. With her at home, the routine was more normal, more like those happy years before the war. Mother was trying hard in other ways, too. Not once did she so much as mention going out alone, but, on the contrary, displayed the utmost reluctance to leave the house at all, even with Father or me. She fussed about us both and spent hours cooking elaborate meals for us. It was her idea, indeed, that we should have a holiday that September, devoting to it the money we had earlier saved for a new house – a project that was abandoned without much discussion at all for we all felt that a holiday alone together away from Manchester would reunite us most happily.

And yet it was not to be. We went to the same railway coach we had visited every August, and we did precisely the same things as we had always done: walked and swam and caught rabbits and fished and played card games in the light of the same old oil lamp. But no matter how each of us tried, that old wonderful spirit eluded us. The last three days were empty and silent, full of lethargy and a sense of anti-climax. The night before we were due to come home, the disappointment of it exploded into a row between Mother and Father about whether we ought to take home with us a cheap fishing rod we'd bought. They shouted so much that I left the railway coach and went to sit outside on the grass. All that shouting about a sixpenny toy!

The holiday ended miserably, and miserably we came home. But still we went on trying, no one more hopefully and earnestly than I. I became a model son, a perfect child, a catalyst, I fondly trusted, which would gradually succeed in re-fusing my unhappy parents.

Father was working in the city now, since his sojourn in Bradford had cost him his job at the mill. They had not been particularly interested in taking him back after his service, but they had been obliged to on that occasion. But now that he had left on his own accord for three or four weeks, they were free to refuse him. As it happened, however, he found a much better post in the office of a large merchant in Manchester. He had some sort of supervisory function there and earnt more in wages, which were supplemented by a few shillings he earnt fire watching. Once a week, he returned to the warehouse after tea and spent the night surrounded by stirrup pumps and sandbags, waiting for German incendiary bombs to drop. He never had the opportunity to fight any fires, however, because when the city was bombed, the following December, he was no longer there. But his new job had its effects on him. He'd been given some responsibility and he did not take it lightly. From time to time he brought work home and concentrated on it all evening. Over tea, most days, he talked about his job – a habit that was new to him, for his old post had been nothing but humdrum and there had never been anything to discuss about it. But his new work seemed somehow to trouble him. He had something to do with packing, and so we had packing every day for tea. Mother knew absolutely nothing about the subject. All she could do was smile and nod – but even this seemed to reassure him, and reassurance was, I felt, what he needed. The job, I suspected, more and more as time went on, harassed him.

During September, after almost exactly a year, I went back to school. Gradually, evacuated children had begun to drift back home, and, by the autumn of 1940, there were so many in the district that the authorities found it necessary to re-open selected schools on a part-time basis. For the next three months, I spent two hours at school each day. It was not, however, my old school, but a senior elementary school in Blackley, two miles away. I took up lessons again with enthusiasm. School, even in such token doses, instilled a fresh interest into my life, provided a new focus for my thinking. While Father pored over his papers of an evening, I tried to make up for twelve months of near idleness.

Most of the other children at this school in Blackley were strangers to me – people hailing from all over north Manchester who had returned from evacuation in half a dozen different places. I was even less successful in making friends than I had been at my former school, and even less inclined to try, for that matter. The lessons had a singular lack of variety. For the first hour we did English, and for the second hour we did arithmetic. But I found it engrossing. Having been totally starved of it for so long, education had become idealised in my mind.

The weeks passed, and Bradford and all that had led up to it did indeed grow remoter in my mind. When I studied my parents now, I sometimes fancied that they, too, had succeeded in forgetting it – or almost. The exaggerated pleasantness of those first few days back home, with its hollow and uncertain undertones, had given way to easy familiarity. There were occasions when I could go to bed feeling happy and secure. And yet, at other times, I could not feel so contented. On occasion, without any tangible justification, I felt disturbed about them – as though some nuance in the atmosphere between them, so slight as to transcend the senses, affected me in infinitely subtle ways. They would be talking quite cheerfully and then, all at once, that sickly, depressed feeling would overcome me quite incongruously.

One Monday afternoon, I met Billy at the school gates. 'Late again!' he said. 'I've been waiting for you since half past one. They told me you came here. I was doubting it.'

This was so unexpected that I did not recognise him at first. 'What are you doing here?'

'I've come home. And am I glad! Heck, she was starving me to death. What sort of a dump is this? What do they do?'

I looked at his laughing face and saw his father's round cheeks and glinting eyes. I could neither answer him nor cease staring at him. Did he know?

'What're you gawping at?' he asked. 'Has the surprise turned your brain?'

'Why have you come home?' I asked.

'Mum sent for me. Dad's joined up and she's lonely.'

'Joined up!' I pounced on it.

'Yes. He's in the Army now.'

'But I thought his firm wouldn't let him go?'

'Well they must have done. He's in the Army – joined up in August all at once.'

Relief filled my chest like a suffocating inhalation. So Mr Hanson was no longer in Manchester! I almost jumped for joy. 'When did you come home, then?'

'Saturday. She got fed up on her own. I wanted to come round and see you yesterday, but she didn't want me to go out. Dad went like a flash; didn't even see him before he left. It's upset her.'

'Never mind!' I slapped him on the back. 'Come on, or we'll be late!' Billy knew nothing and his father had gone! I felt like dancing. 'Whereabouts is he?' I asked.

'Don't know. That's the queer bit.'

'Where do you write to him? Care of GPO?'

'We don't write at all. Nor does he write to us. Mother says he's on secret work. Anyway, I don't much care. I never did get on much with him. I'm glad he's gone.'

So was I – so was I indeed! So long as Mr Hanson stayed out of Manchester, I could be happy.

After that day, for weeks, I didn't have a single hour's unease. With Mr Hanson gone, all evil, all uncertainty had vanished from the world.

The news was so indescribably wonderful that I could not contain it. That same evening, I told them about it. 'Billy's home,' I said, 'and his father's joined the Army.'

Very briefly, they glanced at each other. Neither showed any other sign at all – but later, Father said to me, 'So your pal's home, is he?'

'Yes. His mother got lonely.'

'Well, son, I wouldn't have much to do with Billy from now on if I were you.'

He expected me to ask why, and I did so.

'Well – he's a bit old for one thing, and . . . well, various reasons. Promise me you won't go running round to his house . . .'

'All right,' I said. 'If you like.'

I didn't need further explanation, and I didn't want to talk about it any more. All the same, I liked Billy and he liked me. He was the only real friend I had ever had. I would give him up willingly, but I could not help regret it. Billy wasn't responsible for his father. And, obviously he knew nothing about what had happened. But my father, I felt, was clearly right. Billy and I could be friends no longer. It was a problem I had to solve.

14

And yet it proved to be no very great problem after all. Billy was in a different class at school, and I found it easy to avoid him – so easy, in fact, that I suspected he had had similar instructions. If we met in the road or in the school yard, he would wink, wave a hand, and turn away. He took up with another lad in his own class who had been at Edenfield with him, and though we met and talked briefly from time to time I was never invited to join them. 'Howdy, kid!' he'd say. 'OK? Good. *Adios amigo!*' It was an affable falling off, and perhaps all the more affecting for it. I wondered whether he felt the same regrets, and came to the conclusion that he did for, quite unexpectedly, he invited me to join his football team.

'Old Jango has asked me to get a team going,' he said. 'There's a few schools open in the city now, and they're forming a league again. What position do you play?'

It was a long time since I'd played football, but I fancied centre forward. I told him.

'We've got one. What about right half? Do you kick with your right foot?'

'Yes. I'll play right half if you like.'

'We're going to get some school togs. Red and white. Practice after lessons.'

I don't think I was a very splendid player by nature. But Billy persevered with me, despite the fact that there were other boys who claimed to be infinitely better players than I and who couldn't get on the team. With practice, however, I grew proficient, and even today I fancy I know as much about the game as the professionals. After the match, Billy and I would go our separate ways. It was a reasonable compromise.

Very soon, it seemed, we were playing our first competitive match, which I think we won. I do know that during the short time I played for the school we were very successful indeed.

By October, 1940, the Battle of Britain had been won. In the north, we saw little of it, however, and but for the apparatus of war which cluttered up our lives, but for the blackout and rationing and gas masks, we were untouched at this time by the battle that was raging in the skies. By now, in fact, people were becoming more blasé about the war. Most of the air raid warnings had been false alarms – and when German planes did arrive, they often arrived unheralded anyway, passed high above us and dropped one or two irrelevant bombs miles away. Such feeble jabs hardly seemed to merit concern, and it was the done thing now to leave going to the shelters till the very last minute – until you heard the guns. Lots of people ignored shelters completely. It was because of this, perhaps, that so many were caught out in the city when the real holocaust did descend. We at home were as blasé as the rest. We slept on quite unconcerned during night warnings. Only Father's fire-watching affected us – his one night away each week.

Father, as I'd suspected earlier, was certainly not happy

at work. Two or three times, I heard him say that he was going to start looking for another post, and I know he did write one or two letters; but none of this ever came to anything. The job seemed always to preoccupy him, and if he wasn't busy with his papers of an evening, he was reading trade journals or textbooks, swotting up keenly. His job crept into every conversation, as though his mind was so full of it that some aspect of it or other related to every topic under the sun. It burdened him, weighed him down. Yet he struggled on with it, wrapping himself up in it more and more.

And as Father grew more withdrawn, Mother grew more restless. My reactions to their moods were more sensitive than they had ever been. I could feel the growing constraint in her, which would always become suddenly more obvious as soon as Father came into the house. During the day, and when he was out fire-watching, she was almost a different person. I sought reasons for this, but no matter how deeply I thought about it I could find no explanation. We had been back from Bradford about three months. Her routine was monotonous, and Father was so immersed in his work, and perhaps I had been only too right when I had thought that she wanted a more social life than the one we led. If Father could give up his consuming job, if they could get out more, it would be good for us all, I thought.

For a week or two, I took it upon myself to entertain her and persuaded her to go to the cinema with me several times, while Father worked on at home. She enjoyed these occasions, I think. She seemed to be more herself when out alone with me. Though one thing was puzzling: she would never come out on Father's fire-watch nights I assumed that this was due to some unbreakable resolution and never pressed her. On fire-watch nights, she preferred to sit up long after I'd gone to bed, and it was her habit, I learnt, to slip to the telephone kiosk up the road and telephone Father on his warehouse roof. I thought for a while I was succeeding in making her feel a little happier – but apparently it wasn't enough.

In November, I went for a weekend with fifty-odd other boys from school to what was called 'Autumn Camp' at Lyme Park. There were eight camouflaged tents pitched on the side of a hill, and in these tents, swaddled in sleeping bags, we spent two of the most uncomfortable nights I can remember. It was very cold and everyone slept in their clothes, most of us not even taking off our boots. My own sleeping place, to my regret, was close to the flap, through which a fierce draught constantly whistled on to my head. And that wasn't all. Every hour or so, one of the other five occupants of the tent, affected by the cold, would feel the need to visit the lavatory and, half asleep, would trample all over me on his way out. But we had great fun all the same. The camp overlooked Lyme Wood and the grazing grounds of the deer. The place bristled with wild-life, even so late in the year, and our foraging expeditions were always fruitful. On the Sunday morning, the whole party of us went on a five-mile cross-country run and exhausted ourselves for the rest of the day. When the time came to march down to Disley station, we were all limp and groaning with fatigue. I was still weary when, humping my haversack, I arrived home late that afternoon.

As usual, I went around to let myself in at the back. Glancing through the kitchen window, I saw my parents in there – manifestly rowing. Mother was sitting by the table, partly hidden from me by Father who stood leaning over her and gesticulating wildly. Hurrying, I opened the door, stepped into the porch, and listened.

'. . . and so everything's got to be done your way!' Mother was saying. 'You crush me!'

'What a thing to say!' Father shouted. 'I can't understand! You never *used* to be like this . . .! You say I crush you – how do you want to be? What *do* you want?'

'I know, I know. But I mean it! I feel suffocated. I can't help how I am!'

I closed the door behind me and Mother stopped in mid-sentence. Pausing a moment, I opened the inner door and went into the kitchen. They both stared at me, their two faces like pieces of white paper.

'Hello!' I said, trying to smile.

But neither of them spoke. They remained stiff and startled like a tableau in wax. I went into the front room to warm my frozen hands.

That highly charged silence which had followed my entrance prevailed all evening, and I realised that, for all my fervent hopes and efforts, things were far from well with us. Notwithstanding all my attempts to delude myself to the contrary, there was still cause for worry: and so I worried, energetically.

Shortly after that, something happened to give me cause for much greater concern.

One Saturday afternoon, I went with the school football team to watch a match at Oldham between a Services XI and a team of professionals. It was a well-publicised match, and many football stars were included in the teams. The crowds which attended were vast. Thousands of people flooded from the gates when the match was over and filled the streets of Oldham with struggling bodies. And yet, among all those bobbing, bouncing, anonymous faces, I had to spot Mr Hanson's. It was a very brief glance, as he got on to a bus, and yet, beyond any shadow of doubt, it was he. His son was only two yards from me, and I felt certain that he, too, must have seen. I looked quickly at him. But, like the rest of them he was pushing through the crowd and too intent on that to see anything but the body in front of him.

The shock was unnerving, and, unable to resist any longer, I was borne away on the flood in the opposite direction from that in which I ought to have been going.

What did this mean? Mr Hanson was in the Army! What was he doing in Oldham dressed in civilian clothes, attending a football match?

Perhaps he was on leave? That was it! He was on leave!

This thought revived me. Fighting my way through the crowd, I came up to Billy again and tugged his arm.

'Billy! Billy!'

'What's up, kid?'

'Is your father on leave?'

'No. Why?'

'Have you seen him lately?'

'No. I've no idea where he is. Hang on to me and we'll head for that number nine!'

But I couldn't. My strength had drained out of me again, and Billy whirled away out of sight.

What did it mean? What did it mean? The problem obsessed me all weekend, filled my mind constantly. The following Monday, driven by a suspicion that had fermented over the weekend into a firm conviction, I went down to the aircraft factory and waited on the bank, where I had waited in the past, for the five o'clock buzzer. Just as I had expected, Mr Hanson came out with the rest of them, walking jauntily and talking fifty to the dozen to his pals. But now, instead of taking the road through the estate, he went down under the bridge towards Clayton.

Mr Hanson was not in the Army at all. And yet he had left his wife and son. Why? I asked myself. Why?

I sat there on the damp grass of the railway embankment, while the trains roared past and darkness fell over the vale, so absorbed in anxious thought that I could not move. All the tortured bitterness of that dreadful night when I had heard him with Mother six months ago came back to me. And as clearly as though I overheard it at that moment, I recalled the sound of his voice: 'I can't stop thinking about you! . . . I can't change . . . It's not over. It'll never be over!' And I remembered Mother's voice: 'I feel the same about you . . .'

Oh Jesus, it couldn't be true! She couldn't be seeing him! Not after all that had happened!

But the doubts that assailed me were beyond containing. They overwhelmed me utterly. Everything seemed to support them: Mr Hanson still here at the factory; Mother's manner of late, which was so different from her attitude before Father and I went to Bradford; the rows at home . . . Every thought that came into my mind contributed its share of certainty.

I remained there incapable of motion for so long that

when at last I did manage to make my way home, they'd had tea.

But how could she be seeing him? I asked myself. How? When?

I don't know why it took me so long to think about Father's fire-watch nights – nights on which, in recent weeks, she'd refused to come to the pictures with me, nights on which she liked to stay up late and ring Father at the warehouse. When I did think about it, the picture was complete. I was as certain of it as I was of the fact that I lived and breathed. Confirmation was merely academic – and, as it transpired, swift.

Next time Father spent the night away, I forced myself to stay awake and listened to every sound. It was Wednesday, December 12, 1940. Duly at eleven, she went out to do her telephoning. I watched her from my bedroom window till she was out of sight, and remained standing at the window, waiting for her to return. It was raining out there. There was no movement except for the occasional shuddering of the privet leaves, glinting dimly in the intense, blackout darkness.

15

She came back twenty minutes later. But there was no consolation in this, for the telephone was only two minutes away and she was not likely to have talked for a quarter of an hour to Father when it was only an hour or so since she'd seen him. She came upstairs, went into the toilet and then came to my bedroom door and stood there listening for what seemed like minutes.

He's going to come! I thought. She's listening to see if I'm awake – and he's going to come! I'd experienced it all before.

'Freddy!' she whispered, loud enough for me to hear if I was awake, but not loud enough to disturb my sleep. 'Freddy!'

I did not answer.

She went downstairs again and, sure enough, the back door opened gently and closed again, so gently indeed that, had I not been listening out for it, I should never have heard it.

And then those hissing, creaking sounds as they went into the front room and whispered together. It was like going through an old dream, every detail of which one knows beforehand. I lay tortured by the dreadful inevitability of it. Mr Hanson was down there with Mother – again! again! – and the emotion of it seemed to shrivel my whole body.

Hiss – hiss – hiss! Oh God, what could I do? Those frail little sounds seemed to gnaw at my brain like filthy little rats. Hiss – hiss – hiss! Why was she doing this to us? After all we'd been through! My heart pounded and my limbs shook with the steady rhythm of it.

There was a chuckle, Mr Hanson's vulgar laugh, stifled quickly but loud and long enough to conjure in my mind that hateful, hateful face with its detestable grin, its pebble eyes.

And as the image of Mr Hanson rose up before me, the flame of my hatred for him burst in my mind, devouring at once and completely all other emotion. I lay there shaking, absolutely rigid, hating Mr Hanson with every particle of my being.

The idea that I should kill Mr Hanson was not a new one. It had occurred to me before. But on that occasion, it had disappeared in a spasm of guilt. Now, nothing could have purged me of it – nothing. Killing Mr Hanson was all there was left. It was everything. My hands, my arms, my brain – the whole of me was simply one thing: the killing of Mr Hanson. It was what I had been born for. I had to do it. I had to do it.

Suddenly, I was downstairs, running headlong into the room, my scout knife in my hand. I can never see that moment clearly. Only snatches of its ghastly confusion and almost maniacal emotion come back to me.

They were on the settee. They must have heard me running downstairs, for Mr Hanson had got halfway to a sitting position. He stared at me with an expression of profound shock, his mouth wide open, his eyes bulging.

But my gaze went immediately to Mother. She wore only

her underskirt. It was up about her waist and her white legs seemed to prod upwards fantastically. Her breasts dangled out between her shoulder straps and as I ran into the room, she put her arm across them to hide them from me.

It was this gesture which stopped me in my tracks. For an instant, I hovered there, staring at her, appalled and weak with shame at the sight of her. Then I lifted my knife and plunged it, with a ferocity that makes me cringe when I think of it, deep into her thigh just below the stomach.

She screamed. Mr Hanson leapt up and hit me with his fist. I fell back against a chair.

'You little bastard!' Mr Hanson screamed at me. 'You little bastard!'

I remember watching the trickle of blood from Mother's leg drip down the side of the settee to the carpet. But nothing else. Whether I fainted, or whether Mr Hanson hit me again, I can't say.

But merciful darkness descended.

16

And so those brief and confused flashes of awareness flickered on through the night, punctuated – it seems, when I look back on it – by periods of apparent unconsciousness.

I locked myself in my bedroom and for a long time no-one appeared to notice my absence. An ambulance arrived, screeching to a stop outside the gate. Two men bustled down the path and into the house. A police car pulled up behind the ambulance and the whole car-load followed the ambulance men through the door. Curtains in neighbouring bedrooms trembled. Darkness again. And then a policeman in a flat cap was talking to me. He had two gold teeth, and his nose was bent upward like a pig's.

'Your mother's gone to hospital,' he was saying. 'What happened?' He asked the same question, it seemed, a hundred times, a thousand times, a hundred thousand times. 'What happened? And then what happened? And what happened next?'

I don't know what I told him. All I was aware of was his pig's nose, his gold teeth, his flat cap and his questions.

'Go back to bed,' he said at last, putting a vast heavy hand on my shoulder. 'There's no-one in the house but you, so I'm leaving a constable downstairs. We're going to see your father.'

Darkness. And then, grotesquely, the buzzer of my Morse code set sounding garbled dots and dashes. Rain against the window. The sound of a car outside and, a moment later, Father, standing there over the bed looking down at me, his face dark with shadows but for a faint glint of light in his eyes.

'Fred.'

'Yes, Dad.'

'I've been to see your mother.' A long, long pause. 'She's all right. She'll be home again in a day or two. You're going to your gran's for the night. The car's waiting for you.'

Darkness.

Father's face, still clothed in shadows, poised over the lowered window of the car, nodding, nodding goodbye. His figure, standing on the curb, watching after us as we sped away. Two thick black arms, one of them bearing three stripes, crushing either side of me. The head of the driver, upright and unmoving – the head of a statue. And Grandmother.

They must have visited her earlier, for she was downstairs waiting for us, her grey hair standing out from her head. The sergeant came in with me, into that gloomy, smelly, oppressive house. Ignoring me completely, averting her face as though the sight of me was intolerable to her, she stood before the sergeant and shouted up at him.

'I knew it! I knew that man'd bring disaster on her head. I knew it. I told her never to marry him!'

Letting go of my arm, the sergeant backed out of the house.

'Are you going to leave me alone with him?' she screamed.

But the sergeant didn't come back. He ran off through the rain back to the car.

'They are!' Grandmother exclaimed. 'They're leaving me alone with him!' Locking the door, she sidled away from me, feeling behind her with her bent old hands.

'Sod!' she said at me, grating the word in phlegm in her throat. 'Little murdering sod!' Going to the other door, leading to the stairs, she opened it and stood in the gap, bending towards me. Drawing her lips back, she spat at me. 'You evil, evil swine of a sod!' Stepping back, she disappeared, locking that door, too, behind her, and creaked her way upstairs.

Darkness. And then, suddenly, light, morning, pressing against the blackout curtains, seeping between the threads in millions of bright pin-points. Someone was rattling the door.

It was another policeman. 'Is your grandmother up?'

There were thuds upstairs in answer as she got out of bed.

'Tell her I would like a word with her.'

'The door's locked.'

'Is the key in this door?'

'Yes.'

'Open it then. Let me in.'

I did so.

Crossing the room, he went to the stairs door and shouted. 'Are you there?'

'Coming! Coming!'

The policeman looked down at me, remotely and impassively. 'Sit down,' he said. 'Go over there.'

'What is it now?' Grandmother, all loose and amorphously black, oozed into the room.

'Bad news, I'm afraid.' He began to whisper, and as he whispered, they both turned towards me, frowning hard.

'Well what do you want me to do?' Grandmother asked.

'Couldn't you . . . couldn't you break it?'

'Tell him yourself. And get him out of here with you. I don't want him. I never wanted his father and I certainly don't want him. Take him away!'

The policeman turned from her and, coming over to where I sat, got down on his haunches. His head rolled. He smiled, then frowned, then leered stupidly.

'What's your name, sonny?'

'Freddy James.'

'Well, Freddy, I'm sorry, but I've got bad news for you. I want you to be brave . . .'

'It's Mother . . .' I started.

'No – no. She's all right. But your father . . .'

'Father!' My breathing stopped.

'I'm sorry, sonny, but . . .'

'What's the matter with him?'

'He's had an accident. You've got to be brave . . .'

'What's the matter with him?'

'He's dead, sonny. He was knocked down by a train an hour ago, near your house . . .'

And the memory of him, shrouded in *Conqueror*'s steam, on some happy morning long ago.

17

I never saw my mother again – nor Mr Hanson, till that day at Dawson Park Cemetery four weeks ago.

I spent the next five years in an institution in Bury. They were kindly to us and as interested in us as it is possible to be in irrelevant waifs who will probably grow up into equally irrelevant adults. But I was a rather special case. I was a bit of a risk – someone to be watched a little more carefully than the rest. I might grow up into a full-blown murderer.

When I was eighteen, I left the institution for the Navy, in which I served for three years. At last, I had a taste of independence. At last, I began to slough off my past. Since leaving the Navy, I have made my living as a signwriter, first as an assistant and latterly on my own. The rewards are adequate if not very great and the work suits my temperament perfectly.

As the years went by, I managed to develop a facility for living for the present, for the moment, a state of mind in which one looked neither backwards nor forward. It was, I thought, better that way. But how wrong I was!

Having recalled all these painful memories which for years have lain locked in my mind, having given way to the pressure and re-lived it all again, I now feel, all at once, happier than I have ever felt since I was a very young child. It is as though some nagging and constant ache has suddenly disappeared. I feel ridiculously care-free.

For, after all, life is wonderful. The mere act of living is a declaration of hope. And I am sure it can never be too late to realise this.